Critical Praise for

ROSANNE BITTNER

"Bittner's characters spring to life...extraordinary for the depth of emotion with which they are portrayed."
—*Publishers Weekly*

"Rosanne Bittner retains her title as a premier romance writer... Poignant and startling."
—*Romantic Times*

"True-to-life characters who stay with you long after you've turned the last page!"
—*Los Angeles Daily News*

And for WHERE HEAVEN BEGINS

"Bittner brings to life the dangerous and beautiful Alaskan wilderness of the gold rush days. Clint is a hero who'll pull at your heartstrings."
—*Romantic Times*

"Rosanne has written a truly inspiring high adventure that will invigorate your senses and reaffirm your faith in God's wisdom."
—*Affaire de Coeur*

ROSANNE BITTNER

WALK BY *Faith*

Steeple
Hill®

Published by Steeple Hill Books™

STEEPLE HILL BOOKS

ISBN 0-373-78532-1

WALK BY FAITH

Copyright © 2005 by Rosanne Bittner

This edition published by arrangement with Steeple Hill Books.

www.SteepleHill.com

Printed in U.S.A.

Dedicated to my mother-in-law,

Florence Irene Umphrey Bittner, better known to the whole family as "Grandma Bittner," who turned 101 years old in November 2004. Until she had to go into a nursing home in her late nineties, Florence attended Midway Baptist Church in Watervliet, Michigan, faithfully every Sunday morning, as well as often attending Sunday evening services, Wednesday evening services and most other church functions, in spite of bouts with breast cancer, colon cancer, two broken hips and arthritis that finally put her in a wheelchair. Even when using walkers and a wheelchair, she still attended church.

As of the writing of this book, though totally wheelchair-bound, Florence is still of sound mind and still attends church services at Countryside Nursing Home in South Haven, Michigan.

Though a host encamp against me,
My heart shall not fear;
Though war arise against me,
Even then, in this will I be confident.
For in the day of trouble
He will hide me in His shelter;
In the secret place of His tent will He hide me;
He will set me high upon a rock.

—*Psalms 27:3, 5*

Chapter One

❧

March 16, 1862, St. Louis, Missouri

Clarissa was not sure where she'd found the strength to get dressed and open Seaforth's Dry Goods this morning. She felt numb with worry, not for her husband's safety, but for where he might be...and what he might be doing. She set items on the counter to fill the last of a customer's order.

"There you are, Mrs. Shelby. I think that's everything. That's two dollars."

"Oh, my!" The older woman put a wrinkled hand to her chin. "Put it on my bill, Clare dear, will you? My husband will be by to pay it. And can you wrap it for me?"

"Certainly." Clarissa wrote the woman's name on the tab and added "Owed." Like her father had always done, she extended credit to most hometown customers. Until his sudden death three years ago, Henry Seaforth ran this store most of his life. Then Clarissa married Chad Graham, who took over the store and had run it ever since so that she could stay home with their precious little girl, Sophie.

She pulled a length of brown paper from its roll and tore it off to wrap Mrs. Shelby's items, resentment toward Chad growing as she silently packed the order. It was because Chad was her baby's father that Clarissa had struggled to ignore rumors of her husband's infidelity over the past two years. Now, this morning, the reality of those rumors was burrowing deeply into her mind and heart. Apparently she could no longer avoid the awful truth, though she still did not want to believe it.

Chad was gone. So were all his clothes. Where was the man to whom she'd given all her love, her faith, her trust, her virginity, her heart? Where was the man who was now the legal owner of Seaforth's? That's how much she'd trusted him. This business that was her father's life now belonged to the man her father warned her before he died not to marry. Now that man was missing.

She'd even given up a nursing career for Chad. Getting into Washington University here in St. Louis had not been an easy task for a woman. She'd had to settle for nursing rather than becoming a doctor, but at least she'd made it that far. Then she gave up her nursing job at St. Louis City Hospital when she learned she was expecting Sophie.

The terrible unrest and sometimes-violent street fighting that occurred almost daily now over the war between North and South was enough to worry about. How could Chad disappear at such a dangerous time, with Federal troops swarming the streets and guarding the St. Louis Arsenal, and with Missouri Confederate militia still hiding in the southern part of the state and attacking northern sympathizers at every opportunity? St. Louis was filling up with families who'd fled battlegrounds or who'd been routed out by rebel raiders. And the hospital was becoming crowded with wounded men, from both North and South. She wished sometimes that she could help them out with her nursing experience, but Chad wanted her to stay home with Sophie.

A lot that helps now, she thought. She tied string around Mrs. Shelby's wrapped items, yanking on them with secret anger. With Chad gone and this store their only means of income, she had to handle things alone until she found out what had happened to her husband.

She handed her customer the package. "Thank you, Mrs. Shelby."

"And where is that precious little girl of yours?" the woman asked. "Chad is usually the one who waits on me, you know." She put a hand to her chest. "My, what a handsome man you married! It's a good thing you are so exceptionally beautiful, young lady, or half the women in this town would be trying to steal that man from you," she teased. The aging woman chuckled. "If I'd been younger, I certainly would have tried for him myself before he up and married you."

Her heart aching inside, Clarissa managed a smile. "Thank you. Chad is on a business trip," she lied.

"Well, you shouldn't have to watch this store. That young man should have found someone else to do it. You're a mother now. Little Sophie needs you more than this store does. And with those Home Guardsmen prancing around out there, threatening any person who dares to talk of secession, who knows what will happen next in this city. It's no longer safe for woman or child."

"We're fine, Mrs. Shelby. Sophie is with the Harveys. Carolyn Harvey agreed to watch her so I could work today. Sophie likes to play with their little girl, Lena. And I'm not about to let this senseless war force me to close down and lose business, especially now that it belongs to me and my husband."

"Oh, of course, dear, but it just doesn't seem right for a mother to work. I hope Chad will be home soon."

Clarissa turned away. "So do I."

"What's that, Clare?"

"Oh." Clarissa turned. "I just meant Chad wasn't sure how long he'd be. He took a train to Chicago to see about getting more stock for cheaper prices."

"Well, wouldn't you know? I was in here just two days ago, and that man never said a word about taking a trip."

He never said a word to me either, Clarissa thought.

Mrs. Shelby smiled. "I'll see you in church tomorrow?"

Clarissa nodded. "Yes, ma'am."

Mrs. Shelby left, and Clarissa breathed a sigh of relief, glad she wouldn't have to come up with any more explanations. The ominous sight of Chad's empty wardrobe hit her again like a knife in her heart. For months he'd not shown as great an interest in her as when they'd first married. She'd blamed it on the time she needed for Sophie after she was born, and the weight she'd gained. Still, she'd soon lost all that weight. When she looked in the mirror she saw the same slender woman Chad Graham had married. There was no premature gray in her deep red hair. Nothing about her had changed, and she'd given Chad such a beautiful, charming, red-haired little girl of whom he could be so proud.

But something was wrong...something she'd refused to face in spite of the warning a few months ago from old Rachael Grimes, a founding member of the Light of Christ Church, where Clarissa had attended since she'd been a young girl. She'd even met Chad there, when he was new in town and began attending in order to meet people.

Rachael Grimes was also one of the town's biggest gossips. *Your husband has been unfaithful, dear. You must be doing something wrong that has driven him from you. Don't you let that man get away and don't let him wrong you. You talk to him and find out what you need to do to keep him in your own bed.*

The words still stung. She'd loved Chad with her whole being, falling head over heels when he began teaching the young-adult Sunday school class. Chad was strikingly handsome, with his sandy hair and green eyes, solid build and sparkling smile. He was smart, had a good job at the bank, dressed impeccably and was a social hit with everyone. Half the young women in church had vied for his attention, but it was Clarissa who'd won it.

Chad had been so attentive and sympathetic when her father suddenly died of a heart attack. It was a dark time for her. Her mother died years earlier, and Henry Seaforth had been Clarissa's whole world. Chad stepped in and comforted her, reading scripture to her, consoling her—attention that led to something much more. He'd sworn his love for her, asked her to marry him. She'd barely had time to recover from her father's death before she was walking down the aisle of the Light of Christ Church as Chad Graham's bride, in spite of her father's distrust of the man.

Her wedding night with Chad, and many nights thereafter, had been blushingly passionate, and her whole world became Chad Graham. Within just ten months she'd added little Sophie to that world. Chad had taken over running the store, and because of his friendly, social nature and his knowledge of accounting, he ran it well.

Everyone liked Chad, but her father had thought Chad's background was too obscure. So did her good friend Carolyn Harvey. But Carolyn and her husband, Michael, were wonderful Christian people who were willing to give Chad the benefit of the doubt, since Clarissa was so much in love and Chad had become so active in the church. Chad claimed to be an orphan from Chicago, who'd struggled and worked to make something of himself and whose faith in Christ had helped him through the bad times. He'd seemed so sincere and dedicated.

Now her father's and Carolyn's warnings haunted Clarissa, as did old Mrs. Grimes's hurtful words. If the woman was right, why did she think that whatever Chad might have done was Clarissa's fault? The thought of somehow being responsible hurt deeply and made her feel painfully inadequate as a woman. She'd married Chad blindly, her heart so full of love and passion that nothing else mattered. In her mind she'd been the best wife and mother she could be. Why on earth would Chad ever want to leave her?

The bell above the front door jingled as someone came inside then, and Clarissa turned to see Margaret Baker, one of the founders of the Light of Christ Church. The woman's dark eyes drilled into Clarissa as though she'd done something terrible.

"Hello, Margaret." Clarissa greeted the woman with a smile. She and Margaret's daughter, Susan, had attended school together and were often involved in the same activities at school and church. "What can I help you with today?"

Margaret came closer, looking so angry that it changed her whole countenance into a stern, stiff, almost witchy air. She raised her chin as she spoke.

"You can bring back my Susan!"

Clarissa frowned. "What do you mean?"

"I mean that you can straighten up and be a proper wife so that you don't drive your husband into another woman's arms and drive my daughter to sin in the eyes of God!"

A horrible picture began to take form in Clarissa's thoughts. She felt as though her blood was draining from her brain down and out through her feet. "I have no idea what you're talking about," she answered.

"Don't you? Where is Chad, Clare? Do you know where he's gone?"

"He's…on a business trip."

Margaret sniffed back tears and handed her a folded piece of paper. "Wake up!" she seethed. "This is from Susan."

With now-shaking hands Clarissa took the paper and opened it.

Dear Mother,

Please forgive me, but I am totally in love with Chad Graham. Chad loves me, too, and now I am carrying his child. We have left St. Louis to share our lives together. As soon as Chad can get a divorce, we will be married. I have loved Chad since before he married Clare. Chad will sell the store, and with that money we will start a wonderful new life together.

I know this is right, Mother. I feel it in my heart. Chad has never been happy with Clare, but I make him happy. After we are married and the baby is born, I will let you know where we are. I hope you will come and visit.

All my love, Susan

Stunned, Clarissa felt faint. She handed back the letter. "Why on earth are you angry with *me?*" she asked Margaret. "Your daughter and my husband have committed adultery! Susan is pregnant by a married man who is currently still married to a woman who used to call Susan her friend!"

"Surely you knew my Susan loved Chad when you turned around and married him yourself!"

"No, I *didn't* know!"

"I don't believe you! And it serves you right to learn that Chad only married you because he needed this store! You threw yourself at him and used this store as a way to catch him, and now he will profit from it!"

A lump began to form in Clarissa's throat and she turned away. The reality of the kind of man Chad really was hit her like a club slammed into her stomach.

Divorce! Susan said Chad was going to get a divorce! Had he already sold the store out from under her? How could she face anyone in town or at church if she was a divorced woman? What would people think of her?

Such shame! Such utter betrayal! Such deep, deep hurt she'd never known.

"Get out," she told Margaret.

"Gladly! And I hope you're proud of yourself, hurting my poor Susan by marrying the love of her life!"

The woman stormed out. Clarissa realized Margaret was defending Susan as a mother would, not wanting to face the sin of what her daughter had done. Still, Clarissa could hardly believe the woman could stand there and spout her daughter's innocence in the ugly affair. And ugly it was. The realization of what Chad had done even made *him* seem ugly now! Behind that handsome face and those fetching green eyes lay pure evil, an evil that had cost her her trust, her pride, her means of living and maybe even her faith. Right now she felt God had abandoned her.

She managed to walk to the front door, close and lock it. She turned the Closed sign toward the street and pulled down the shade. She could not face one more customer today. How could she face *anyone* ever again?

Chapter Two

❧

April 7, 1862, Tennessee

"If there's a hell on earth, Lieutenant, this is it."

First Lieutenant Dawson Clements nodded in agreement. He sat huddled behind a mobile cannon with Sergeant Jared Bridger listening to the hideous screams and groans of the thousands of wounded who lay sprawled among thousands more dead soldiers.

"They say Shiloh is a biblical name meaning 'place of peace,'" Dawson told the sergeant. He shivered, pulling his rubber poncho up over his head against the cold rain. "Pretty ironic, isn't it?"

Both men were painfully hungry, and neither had slept all night, mostly because of the haunting cries of the unattended wounded and the stench of blood that ran past them in rivulets along with the rainwater. Behind them, thousands more Union soldiers made temporary camp at Pittsburgh Landing, waiting for the arrival of relief troops.

"Grant says Buell will be here soon with a good seventy-five-hundred relief troops," Dawson told his sergeant. "Come sunup we'll push those Rebels clear back past that little church and get this over with." He watched Sergeant Bridger pull his ragged wool blanket over his head and felt bad that rubber ponchos were given only to the higher officers. The fact that he and the sergeant sat here talking alone was not particularly proper army protocol, but nothing about the past twenty-four hours had been normal or proper. They were simply taking advantage of this chance to rest and gear up for what looked to be another bloody onslaught a couple of hours from now, when the sun would rise on the horror in the fields around Shiloh, and General Grant would lead a new march to take back what the Confederates had claimed earlier today.

"I've never seen anything like this, sir. In all our battles out west against the Apache, the Comanche, the Cheyenne—none of it can compare to this slaughter. I've seen men walking around still alive with their guts hanging out, bodies on the ground with no heads, an arm with no body nearby. It will be a long time before I can go to sleep without the cries of those boys ringing in my ears. I'd rather be back out west."

Dawson rubbed his eyes. "Well, we've got to go where they send us, Sergeant Bridger. That's what happens when you're dumb enough to join the army in the first place."

Bridger chuckled. "I do wonder sometimes why I got myself into this mess."

Dawson shifted to relieve a sore hip caused from a horse falling on him earlier in the day. "I know why I did. It was because I had nothing else to do with my life—no home, no family, no goals—"

And because I'd left a man behind me to die. For one quick moment a flash of memory from the day he'd run away actually made him wince.

"I was thirteen when I joined," he continued. "I was big for my age so they believed me when I said I was sixteen. I fought in the Mexican War at fourteen years old, saved a major's life and that major's family had money. He sent me to Philadelphia to get a decent education and then made sure I was gradually promoted to where I am now. He was killed by Indians, and I still think about him. He did a lot for me, probably the only person in my life who ever cared if I succeeded at anything."

Bridger frowned. "Sir, why are you telling me all this?"

Dawson shrugged. "Maybe because I know I might be dead in a couple of hours. Such thoughts make a man do and say things he never would normally."

The sergeant grinned. "Maybe so." He reached inside his Union blue jacket and pulled out a piece of paper. "Which prompts me to give this to you."

Curious, Dawson took the paper. "What's this?"

"It's my will."

"Your *will?*"

The sergeant nodded. "For what it's worth."

"Why are you giving this to me?"

Bridger moved closer to the dwindling fire, the hot coals having a hard time keeping up with the rain. "Because earlier today you bayoneted a Graycoat who was about to shoot my head off. We were so busy fighting I never had a chance to thank you, sir, but I am grateful. I want you to know that. I have some money in a bank in St. Louis, and I've got no family left, so in case I'm the one who ends up with his face in the mud later today, I want somebody worthy to have my money. It's not a whole lot, but enough for a man to get a pretty good start in life. I hope you can put it to good use."

Dawson put the note into his own pocket without reading it.

"Don't you want to know how much I've got?"

"No, because it won't matter," Dawson said. "You're going to be just fine, Sergeant Bridger. You'll end up back out west with me once this war ends." He leaned against a wheel of the cannon cart. "Tell me, how did a man on sergeant's pay manage to save up any money at all?"

A patient inside a nearby hospital tent let out a gut-wrenching scream that quieted both of them and sent shivers to Dawson's very bone marrow. He closed his eyes and shook his head. "Another man has lost a limb, most likely."

More screams came from the tent, and in the distance the continued groans and sobbing of other wounded men pierced the dark night. Dawson's face burned from black powder that seemed to eat into his skin, and his eyes stung from it washing into them because of the rain, which the wind drove into his face in spite of the brimmed hat and the poncho he wore.

"Well, sir, to take your mind off that poor fellow in there, I'll tell you how I came to have that money. It came from my grandma."

"I thought you said you had no family."

Bridger chuckled. "I didn't know I did. My ma was good to me, but she was…well, let's just say she never knew who my pa even was. Funny how we've fought together out west and now here, but we never knew all this about each other. Anyway, I grew up helping out in a saloon where Ma worked, and when she died I joined the army—kind of like the reason you joined, I guess. Anyways, low and behold I got this letter about six months back from a woman who claims to have been my grandmother. I don't know how she found me, but she did.

Come to find out, she lived in the same town where I grew up, St. Louis, Missouri. She wrote that her and my ma never got along, so I was never told about who she was or where she lived. The letter said she was soon to die of cancer and she wanted me to have some money she'd saved from working two jobs in her old age. Said it helped her passing to know somebody carrying her blood would go on in this life and maybe be a better person than she or my ma ever were."

Dawson nodded in understanding, thinking how young Bridger was for being a sergeant; but then this war seemed to spur promotions that would never normally be given. Men were badly needed, and those with the slightest bit of army knowledge and any kind of schooling rapidly became in charge of the others. He was himself just twenty-nine, but before this war ended he could end up a general. He'd seen other colonels and generals who were barely any older.

"Anyway," Bridger went on, "I couldn't think of one other person than you who ought to have the money in case I die. It's in the Federal Bank of St. Louis. So, if something does happen to me, it's yours. Just make sure there's a grave site someplace in St. Louis with my name on it, even if my body isn't there. Just something that shows I once existed. My name and birth date are on that piece of paper."

Dawson reached out and touched his arm. "I'll do that, Sergeant, but like I said, you're going to be just fine."

Bridger sighed. "I sure hope so, sir. I just—do you believe in God, sir?"

The question caught Dawson off guard, and it brought back painful memories. He could still see Preacher Carter's face plain as day, his scowl, his piercing dark eyes and sharp nose, his face red from giving Dawson another beating with his wide, black belt, screaming that he needed to "beat the devil" out of him again.

"Sure I do," he answered Bridger, only because he knew that was what the man wanted to hear. "Why?"

"Well, I mean, do you really think a man goes to heaven when he dies, where everything is beautiful and peaceful and all that?"

Dawson decided this was not the time to tell a man there was also a hell, where some men, including himself, were bound to go no matter what. The worst part was that Preacher Carter would probably be there, too.

"Of course there's a heaven," he answered, forcing himself to sound positive, "but you'll be an old man before you get there."

"Lieutenant Clements!" A young private ran up to salute Dawson, interrupting the conversation. "I was told by a Major Coldwell to tell you to prepare the men and artillery for attack. We're going to sweep this whole area clean of Rebels forthwith! General Grant is mustering all troops as well as the new arrivals, sir."

"They're here then?"

The private grinned broadly. "Yes, sir! All seventy-five hundred of them! They're coming off the steamboat right now at the landing!"

Dawson saluted in return. "Thank you, Private. Tell the major we'll have our cannon and rifles ready."

"Yes, sir!" The private hurried away, excited now that it looked like enough help had come to turn this battle around. Dawson heard a man crying bitterly inside the hospital tent, and he supposed it was the same man who minutes ago had screamed in agony. For all he knew, after the next few hours of fighting he'd be missing a limb himself, or worse.

He stood and nodded to Sergeant Bridger. "Thank you for thinking of me, Sergeant. Go and prepare your men."

The young man stood up with a tired groan, and the two men saluted one another. "Yes, sir."

Their gazes held a moment. "God be with you, Sergeant," Dawson told him, sure he detected a trace of tears in Bridger's eyes.

"And with you, sir. Once this is over we'll—"

A shot rang out before Bridger finished the sentence. His body lurched forward and fell, just missing landing in the campfire. In his back was a bloody, gaping hole.

Startled, Dawson watched a wounded and badly bleeding young Confederate soldier crawl toward him, a smoking pistol in his hand. It took Dawson a moment to realize what had just occurred.

While the wounded soldier fumbled with his pistol, Dawson quickly grabbed his musket, bayonet attached, from where it rested against a nearby log. Swiftly he jammed the tip of the bayonet against the Confederate man's forehead. "Don't bother reloading, mister!" he warned.

The young Rebel looked up at Dawson and grinned. "At least I got one more of you yellow-bellied Yanks before I meet my Maker."

"And meet your Maker you *will!*" an enraged Dawson answered. He pulled the trigger of his loaded musket, wiping away not just the man's grin, but nearly his entire face. Never in his life had he considered committing such a heinous act, but in this moment of pain and disbelief, he didn't care.

Grief washed over him with the cold rain when he managed to turn his gaze to the young man who'd just willed him what little money he had in the whole world, and all because he'd saved his life earlier today. This time he'd failed him.

He'd promised that boy that he'd be all right, but then such promises were only for God to make.

He knelt and gently he turned Bridger's body over, hoping beyond hope that he might still be alive.

"Sergeant," he spoke, a sob engulfing him at the same time. He felt at the man's neck for a pulse, but there was none. He struggled to keep from breaking into all-out tears over the man's shockingly sudden death, as several men gathered to see what had happened.

"Sir, are you all right?" someone asked.

Dawson nodded. "Go away—all of you," he told them gruffly. "Get ready for the advance."

"Yes, sir. What about Sergeant Bridger? We can't bury him right now, sir. Grant is ordering—"

"I know what we have to do!" Dawson barked. "I'll be along!"

"Yes, sir."

Dawson sensed the men leaving. Dawn was barely breaking, and men who'd lain wounded all night still cried and groaned throughout the surrounding woods and orchards. How strange that he should feel so sad over the death of a young man he'd known only as a fellow soldier for the past year and a half. Preacher Carter had been right. Maybe he was evil and deserved this constant punishment.

He removed his rubber cape and laid it over the sergeant to keep his body dry and respectfully covered until he could return and bury the man. Feeling numb and strangely removed from reality, he headed for duty. There was a little church situated somewhere south of them, and their goal was to reach it before the sun set again.

The cold rain began soaking his blue greatcoat and running down his neck under his shirt. He thought it only fitting and proper that he should suffer from its chilling wetness. The discomfort would help shroud his inner pain for the next few hours.

When I was in trouble, I called to the Lord,
And He answered me.
Save me, Lord, from liars and deceivers.

—*Psalms* 120:1-2

Chapter Three

❧

April 20, 1863

Breathing deeply to calm her nerves, Clarissa glanced around the land agent's office, studying the marble floors, the mahogany furniture and glass bookcases, the high windows with fancy drapery. As she appreciated the beauty of St. Louis's grand courthouse and its magnificently painted central rotunda in the main hall, she had to wonder how long it would be before she saw such civilized grandeur again after leaving this city where she'd grown up.

It was almost impossible to calm the butterflies in her stomach at the thought of what she was doing. If not for Carolyn and Michael Harvey she would never have had this chance to finally leave St. Louis and start a new life.

After her embarrassing divorce, a kind and understanding Carolyn continued watching Sophie so that Clarissa could go back to her nursing job at City Hospital to support herself and Sophie. Chad had indeed sold the store and all the inventory without her knowledge. Thank goodness the house they'd shared had been her father's and willed to her. When she married Chad the house was never put into his name.

Apparently Chad had only cared about the store because it was paid for free and clear but the house wasn't. Clarissa was left with that debt, but she'd worked hard to keep up the payments on the two-bedroom frame home she'd now miss dearly. She'd sold the house and most of the furniture in order to have the necessary money to leave St. Louis.

Michael Harvey planned to settle in Montana under the new Homestead Act. The cotton wholesaler for whom Michael worked had gone out of business because of the war, and being deeply religious, Michael refused to join the fighting for either side. St. Louis was in chaos, and danger lurked everywhere. For the sake of their little girl, Michael intended to head west with his family, and Clarissa and Sophie would go with them. Clarissa's latest embarrassing ordeal made her more determined, because she'd been fired from her nursing job just for being divorced! Ordered to take care of only the female patients, she was let go when she dared to help a poor, wounded soldier that no one else seemed to have time for. The firing was partly because that soldier was a Confederate, and Confederate soldiers always got helped last; but it seemed obvious to her that helping the man was also the hospital's excuse to get rid of a woman about whom other nurses, and even some patients' wives, had complained should not be around any of the "lonely, vulnerable male patients."

Her embarrassment had turned to anger at such foolishness. One thing the hospital needed now more than ever was doctors and nurses, with so many hundreds of wounded soldiers coming in almost daily. It seemed incredible that her divorced status should cause so much havoc in her life.

Even Carolyn and Michael had suffered. Michael, a deacon at the Light of Christ Church, where Clarissa had attended so faithfully until Chad left her, had grown disgusted over the insinuations from other men in the church, even the deacons and the minister, that he should not be known to associate so closely with a divorced woman, or he could be asked to leave the church. Michael refused to let such ugliness destroy his and Carolyn's happiness. And because he wanted a place where Clarissa could also feel free to worship, he left the church and started his own ministry at his house. Now he hoped to take that ministry to Montana and start his own church there for the hundreds, perhaps thousands of people who would settle there under the Homestead Act. Thousands more had gone before because of a fabulous silver strike at what some said was now the thriving town of Virginia City, Montana.

It was time to move on and start over. Surely a place like Montana needed nurses, and the more she thought about leaving behind all the bad memories here in St. Louis, the more excited Clarissa became over her decision.

"Mommy, I want to go home," Sophie complained, turning from a big window where she'd been watching the street traffic outside.

"We'll leave soon, honey," Clarissa answered. She picked the girl up and set her on her lap, pushing some of the child's red curls behind one ear. "You've been very good."

Thank goodness she'd received enough money for the house after paying off the bank to be able to pay for her own supplies and even her own wagon. Michael would buy all the oxen, and Clarissa could hardly bear the wait. The sooner she got out of St. Louis, the better.

"Here you are!" The land agent, Eric Fastow, interrupted her thoughts when he finally returned to his desk. "Your official Homestead Certificate. I made sure your section would be located adjacent to Mr. and Mrs. Harvey so you could all be together. Everything is signed. Mr. and Mrs. Harvey each signed up for one-hundred-sixty acres, so between all three of you, you'll have four-hundred-eighty acres to build a fine ranch! And it's all located just five miles south of Virginia City! You'll be close enough to go there for supplies whenever necessary, as long as mountain snows don't hold you up."

Clarissa took the paper, studying it a moment. There was her name as owner: Clarissa Lynn Seaforth Graham. "Oh, my!" she exclaimed, showing it to Sophie. "See, Sophie? We'll have land that's all our own! We're going on a long trip to live there."

"Can Lena go?"

"Oh, yes. Lena and Carolyn and Michael are all going!" Sophie clapped her hands and smiled. This child was another reason to leave St. Louis. Away from here Sophie never had to suffer from gossip and teasing. Clarissa folded the deed and placed it into an envelope Fastow handed her.

"Thank you so much, Mr. Fastow."

"My pleasure!" The thin, bespectacled man put out his hand, and Clarissa set Sophie on her feet and got up from her chair, shaking the man's hand. "I wish you good luck, Mrs. Graham. I'd be worried about you if you were doing this alone, but as long as you are traveling with the Harveys, you should make it just fine."

Clarissa squeezed his hand and then let go, appreciating the few people who treated her like a respectable person in spite of her being divorced. She put the deed into her handbag. "Thank you again, Mr. Fastow," she said before taking Sophie's hand and leading her back out into the lobby.

Immediately Sophie again pointed to the spectacular rotunda and stared upward. "Look, Mommy, it's high!" The child spoke loudly, obviously enjoying the way her voice echoed in the large hall. "Can we go up there?"

"No, we certainly cannot. I'm not climbing all those steps just so you can get up there and fall and hurt yourself. Besides, I have to get you home. We have to meet Carolyn and Michael there to get some shopping done. We have so many preparations to make for our long trip. It takes a lot of planning."

They walked across the marble floor toward the courthouse entrance, literally having to stop and dodge people who swarmed inside the busy lobby. The Homestead Act had created quite a commotion this year and last. People were excited about free land, theirs to keep as long as they farmed or ranched it and made it worth something. The government was aiming to settle and build the West, Indians or not, and there were plenty of people ready to help, especially since the war was escalating.

Already many had lost their farms and large plantations. Men were dying by the thousands, and homeless people filled St. Louis, many of whom were the ones most willing to head west to start over.

Clarissa kept hold of Sophie's hand so she wouldn't lose her among the throngs. She thought about the note from Chad that accompanied the divorce papers, saying he hoped she would sign them quickly and not prolong the matter. Such a cold, unfeeling letter. He'd not even asked about Sophie, but he made sure to tell her that the store had already been sold and the new owner would be showing up soon to get the keys from her.

She was almost glad Chad had been so coldhearted. That made it easier for her to stop caring about him. She knelt down to help Sophie put on her little woolen coat. Early April had brought a damp cold that seemed to go to the bone, and Clarissa was anxious for the warmer weather that should come very soon now. She buttoned up Sophie's coat and tied a wool scarf around her head, then stood up and retied her own wool cape, pulling up the hood.

She took Sophie's hand, and they slowly walked down the courthouse steps, Sophie insisting on jumping down one step at a time. The girl's sweet nature made it easy for Clarissa to be patient with her. Always all smiles, Sophie found excitement in the smallest of things. She seldom asked about her missing father anymore, which made Clarissa both sad and relieved.

Once they reached the bottom of the steps, Sophie suddenly tore away from Clarissa, squealing something about a kitten.

"Sophie!" Before Clarissa could react in any way, she watched a man wearing a dark blue duster and black, wide-brimmed hat scoop up Sophie with one arm just in time to keep her from being hit by a team of horses pulling a wagon. However, he didn't get out of the way in time to keep a wagon wheel from catching one leg and knocking him down. He cried out as he rolled out of the way, still clinging to Sophie and keeping her wrapped safely in his arms.

The wagon driver shouted "Whoa!" and looked back with terrified eyes as the stranger holding Sophie got to his knees. "You all right, mister? Is the little girl okay?"

"She's fine." The stranger waved the man off. "Go on. I'll be all right."

The wagon driver shook his head and drove off.

"Sophie!" Clarissa ran to the site, kneeling down to take Sophie from the stranger's arms. "Look what you've done because you let go of Mommy's hand! This poor man is hurt now!"

Sophie began crying, and the man who'd saved her got to a sitting position. "Don't do that!" he told Clarissa rather gruffly. "Don't blame the child. An accident is an accident."

"I'm so sorry!" Clarissa told him. "And it *is* Sophie's fault!"

A man passing by stopped to help the stranger up, and the man limped to a street lamp where he grabbed hold for support.

"You *are* hurt!" Clarissa said, setting Sophie on her feet and ordering the still-crying girl to stay put.

"It's just a war wound that's not quite healed," he said.

"Let me get a cab and take you to the hospital."

"Never mind. My horse isn't far. Besides, I just got out of the hospital a few days ago."

Clarissa could see the pain in his eyes. "Please."

He shook his head. "No. No more hospitals."

"Then tell me where your horse is. I'll go get it for you and call a cab to take you to the house where I stay. Sophie can ride with you and I'll follow on your horse. It isn't far. I'm a nurse. My name is Clarissa Graham. I can take a look at your leg and rebandage it, or whatever else it needs."

Clarissa could tell by the way the man closed his eyes and sighed that he was embarrassed at his condition. He stood a good six feet tall and had a rugged look that told her he preferred to fend for himself. Under his Union blue great-coat she saw scarlet trim on a short jacket, which she knew meant he was part of an artillery unit and probably an officer, although because he wore a plain black hat rather than the common small kepi with an insignia on it, she couldn't be sure what his station might be.

"Please let me help you," she urged again. "It's the least I can do after what's happened."

He met her gaze, and a quick surge of something unexplainable swept through Clarissa, something she hadn't felt since the first time she looked into Chad Graham's unnerving green eyes. This man's were a striking blue, almost too dark, as though some kind of cloud hung somewhere behind them. She'd not realized until just now how handsome he was, in spite of several days growth of beard.

"I'll let you help me if you promise to tell that little girl what happened was not her fault," he told her. "I can't tolerate a child being blamed for an accident."

Clarissa thought what a strange request that was. "All right." She knelt down to Sophie and wiped tears from her pudgy cheeks. "It's all right, darling. You just scared Mommy, that's all. Sometimes when we're scared we yell and say the wrong things." She kissed her cheek. "Just tell this man you're sorry you ran into the street without looking."

Sniffing, Sophie craned her neck to look up at the tall stranger. "I'm sowwy, Mistoo," she told him, still having trouble with her r's.

He managed a smile. "It's okay, honey. What's your name?"

"Sophie. What's yours?"

The man looked from her to Clarissa. "Dawson Clements—*Lieutenant* Dawson Clements—of the Second Illinois Light Artillery Battery, now retired from the army. I, uh, I really don't want to put you out—"

"Nonsense. It's the least I can do—"

"Well, ma'am, I'm afraid I'll take you up on the offer. The leg is hurting pretty good."

"Wait right here then." Clarissa looked at Sophie. "And you stay right here by Mr. Clements." She stepped off the curb and waved down a one-horse cab coming toward them from farther up the street, hoping Carolyn and Michael wouldn't mind her bringing home a stranger.

Chapter Four

❧

Carolyn and Michael appeared almost comical as they scurried around the house following Clarissa's orders after she arrived with a limping Dawson Clements. Because the fair-haired, brown-eyed Carolyn was actually taller and more robust than Michael, a short, slender, quiet man with black hair and deep brown eyes, they seemed mismatched physically, but Clarissa could think of no other couple more devoted to each other than these friends who'd been so good to her, especially since her divorce. If only her own marriage could have been so happy and perfect.

Little Lena, one year older than Sophie, had her father's dark hair and eyes, quite the contrast to Sophie's orange-red hair and pale blue eyes. The current excitement in the house kept the girls glued nearby, staring at the tall stranger who'd come unexpectedly into their midst.

Carolyn gave Michael orders for towels and whiskey and hot water while Dawson sat down in a kitchen chair. He winced with pain as he obeyed Clarissa's order and let her help put his wounded right leg up on an opposite chair. She pushed up his pant leg to see the entire calf of his leg was wrapped in bandages showing stains from both old and fresh blood.

"Oh, my!" She looked at Dawson with a frown. "How long has it been since this was changed?"

He shrugged. "Five, six days, something like that."

"Didn't they tell you how important it was to keep the wound clean? If it gets infected, you could lose your leg."

He sighed. "I am well aware of that. I've seen piles of legs and arms lying outside of hospital tents at a friendly battle-ground called Shiloh."

They all gasped. "We've heard about Shiloh," Carolyn said with an air of sad respect.

"Nevertheless, why haven't you kept treating this wound?" Clarissa asked.

"Look, Mrs.—Graham, did you say?"

"Yes."

"You're the one who insisted I come here. Don't be scold-ing me for not changing this thing. I don't have a friend or relative to my name, so there's no one to care whether I lose a leg or not. I was told at the hospital that they'd done all they could do and that it should be all right, so what more could I do? I've been traveling through the camps outside of town talking to families who've lost their homes because of this senseless war and I haven't had time to tend to the leg. I haven't even had a bath or a shave for days. Just clean it up if you must and I'll be on my way."

His abruptness made Clarissa bristle. "I don't know of one person, man or woman, who wouldn't do everything they possibly could to keep from losing a limb, so don't try to tell me you don't care. Whatever you're angry about, you needn't take it out on me." She began cutting off the bandages with scissors Michael handed her.

"Here's some hot water," Carolyn said, bringing over a pan of water. "Michael, did you get those towels?"

"Right now, dear." Michael hurried into a back room and emerged seconds later with several towels and washrags.

"I'll get some clean bandages," Carolyn told Clarissa.

Clarissa glanced at Sophie and Lena. "You girls had better go and play."

Sophie's eyes were teared. "Did I make it bleed?" she asked. Clarissa glanced at Dawson, remembering his deal—she was not to blame Sophie for any of this. He gave her a warning look, and Clarissa turned to Sophie. "No, Sophie. His leg was already wounded from the war. This is not your fault. Now run and play."

"Can I give him a hug?"

Clarissa had to smile, then. "After I fix his leg, okay?"

"Okay." Sophie grabbed Lena's hand and the two girls ran up the narrow, enclosed stairway to Lena's room upstairs, closing the stairwell door behind them.

For the next few moments no one spoke as Clarissa peeled off the bandages. She could see Dawson's calf muscle tighten and knew the leg was hurting him, but he made no sound.

"Set a bucket under his leg, Michael, will you? I have to wash this off and water and blood will drip."

"Sure thing," Michael answered, hurrying to the kitchen.

Clarissa looked up at Dawson. "Bullet wound?" she asked.

"Shrapnel."

Michael returned with a bucket, and Clarissa began washing the blood off Dawson's leg. "You said you're retired from the army?"

"My time was up just a few days after I was wounded, during Grant's campaign to free up the Mississippi to Union control. After sixteen years of fighting Indians and then seeing the horrific things I've seen in this war, I decided not to re-up. I'm doubting that decision, since the army is all I've ever known since I was thirteen years old."

"Thirteen!" Michael had drawn up a chair beside Clarissa to see if there was anything he could do to help. Carolyn sat down across the table from them. "You've been in the army since you were thirteen years old?"

Dawson grinned, then suddenly winced and grunted when Clarissa got close to the still-festered wound. "They thought I was sixteen."

Michael chuckled. "Well, considering your size, I can understand that."

"I'm going to have to douse this with whiskey, Mr. Clements," Clarissa told him.

"So be it."

Clarissa uncorked the small bottle Carolyn handed to her and took a deep breath before splashing some into the wound. Dawson grunted and jerked his leg, then cursed.

"I'll not have such language in my house, Mr. Clements, although I can understand why you want to use it," Michael told him. "This is a Christian home."

"I'm sorry, Mr. Harvey." He grunted again with another douse of whiskey. "But maybe if I'd been allowed to drink some of that liquor before Mrs. Graham here poured it on my wound, I wouldn't have felt it quite so much."

"We don't allow drinking in our home, either," Carolyn told him.

"Well, then, by the time this nice lady is through cleaning up this wound, I'll have to be leaving," Dawson answered. "Right now a good, stiff drink sounds pretty good."

Clarissa inspected the wound. "You're lucky, Mr. Clements. It's slightly festered, but if you keep whiskey on it and keep the bandages changed, I don't think it will be that bad. We have caught this in time to keep it from getting worse." She looked up at him. "I'll wrap it for you and give you clean bandages to take with you. Please promise me that you will change them at least every other day, and that you'll pour whiskey on the wound as often. Just buy extra when you're sitting in a saloon drinking," she added in a tone of chastisement.

Dawson actually chuckled. "Yes, ma'am."

Their gazes held, and again Clarissa was struck by the handsome man she could see behind the scrubby beard and long hair. For one quick moment she thought he might have read her thoughts, and she quickly looked away and began wrapping fresh bandages around his leg. "So, what will you do now, Mr. Clements?" she asked, anxious to get a conversation going again. "You said something about visiting the camps of the homeless."

"I was thinking about heading back out west," he answered. "I served in the west most of my army years. It's beautiful country. Figured maybe I could make a little money by guiding some of those displaced folks who've decided to also head west under the Homestead Act. The West and Indians are things I'm familiar with, so I figure I could do a pretty good job of it. Once I get there, I'll probably look for gold. Or maybe I can work for one of the mines as a guard or something."

"We're headed west, too!" Michael told him. "Me and the wife and Clarissa here."

"That so? You've no husband, Mrs. Graham?"

Clarissa glanced at Carolyn before answering. "No," she said, adding no explanation.

"Killed in the war?"

Clarissa wrapped his leg quietly for a few seconds. "No," she said again. "Nothing quite that honorable, Mr. Clements. And I don't wish to talk further about it with a stranger."

The room hung silent for several awkward seconds. "Fine with me," Dawson finally answered. "Mind if I ask if you work at City Hospital? I don't remember seeing you there."

"I did work there, but I...I quit in order to get ready for our trip west," she lied. How could she tell him she was fired because she was a divorced woman? "We'll be leaving in a month or less. In fact, I just today received my very own deed to one-hundred-sixty acres in Montana." She tied off the gauze and looked up at him, putting on a brighter look. "That's why I was coming from the courthouse when this accident happened."

"I see." Dawson leaned over and checked out the dressing. "Nice job. I'm sure your services would be needed more than once on a trip west. All kinds of things can happen. Men who seldom use guns end up buying them and then shooting themselves in the foot. People get sick, a lot of them die. There's snakebites, bad food, sometimes bad water, Indian attacks, women having babies, kids getting hurt, toothaches, blistered feet, sunburn, you name it—it will happen on a trip west, mark my word. I hope you folks are truly prepared for what you're about to do."

"We're ready," Carolyn answered. "This is a dream for us. My husband has lost his job and we're about to lose this house, too. Thank goodness we had a fine piano and some good horses to sell, as well as some genuine silverware my grandmother gave me and a real fine buggy. And all our furniture was paid for, so we're selling that, too. And the parishioners from my husband's church actually collected some money and gave it to us. That was so kind of them."

Clarissa was surprised at the sudden scowl on Dawson Clements's face at the mention of church. He looked at Michael.

"You're a *preacher?*"

"Yes, I am. Started my own church a few months ago. We meet right here at the house. I intend to start another parish when we reach Montana."

Dawson looked him over with an odd air of mistrust. He straightened then and put his leg down, pulling down his pant leg.

"Do you have something against preachers, Mr. Clements?" Clarissa asked.

"You might say so," he answered, still looking down. He finally looked at Michael. "Just those who don't really practice what they preach. I suspect you do, so take no offense, Mr. Harvey. I just don't have much use for preachers or God or any of those things. Neither one ever did me any good."

Carolyn actually gasped. "Mr. Clements! You're coming close to blasphemy!"

He waved her off. "Sorry I mentioned it. And I don't know any of you well enough to go into all the reasons, nor do we have the time. I will take myself off your hands now, and I do thank you for your hospitality." Dawson picked up his hat from the kitchen table and put it back on, nodding to all of them. "Good luck on your trip. Maybe we'll meet along the way, or you can ask around about me if you're wanting a good guide for your journey. I'll be at Independence in about two weeks. I won't be able to leave for another couple of weeks after that. The ground would be too soft and the rivers too high. At any rate, look me up if you've a mind to." He turned to Michael. "Unless you don't want a heathen leading you west," he finished with a wink and a hint of a smile.

Michael put out his hand, and Clarissa noticed he held on to Dawson Clements's hand extra long as he replied. "Something tells me you're no heathen at all, Mr. Clements. In the meantime, I will pray for your safe journey, and for your soul. Christ will find his way back into your life somehow."

Dawson pulled his hand away, looking very uncomfortable at the remark. "Save your prayers for those who deserve them, Mr. Harvey." He turned to Clarissa, looking her over in a way that told her he appreciated her figure. "Thank you for your good nursing skills, ma'am. I have business to tend to, so I'll be going."

Clarissa folded her arms. "You should stay and rest a while, Mr. Clements."

"You know what they say—no rest for the wicked, or something like that."

Clarissa grabbed a roll of bandages. "At least take this with you, and keep your promise to put clean bandages on that leg, or I won't sleep at night for worrying about it. I gather that wherever you go you'll have plenty of whiskey on hand."

This time he laughed out loud, taking the bandages. It was a nice, deep laugh, and his teeth were white and straight. He had a nice mouth. "Yes, ma'am, you're right about that."

In spite of his smile, Clarissa still saw a deep sadness somewhere behind those blue eyes. "You promised Sophie a hug before you left, Mr. Clements."

"Oh, yeah, I guess I did. Well, tell her to come down here."

He limped toward the door as Clarissa called for Sophie. The little girl came down the stairs as fast as a three-year-old could make the steps. She ran up to him with her arms open, and Dawson leaned over. "Honey, I can't kneel down to you. My leg hurts too much."

Sophie reached up, and Dawson lifted her, giving her a hug. She kissed his cheek. "Will you come back?"

"No, little lady. Your mother fixed me all up."

"She's a noose!"

"I know. And I think she's a very good nurse." Dawson set her down.

"Bye!" she said, giving him a smile that would melt any heart.

"Goodbye, Sophie. And you remember that what happened was just an accident and wasn't your fault."

"Okay." Sophie turned to Lena and the two girls giggled.

Dawson tipped his hat to Clarissa. "Thanks again, ma'am." He eyed Michael and Carolyn. "And to both of you for opening your home to me. I'm sorry if I offended you with my remarks about preachers and all that."

"God be with you, Mr. Clements," Michael answered.

"You *will* be in our prayers, whether you like it or not."

Dawson sobered. "If you want to waste your time on me, that's your decision." He turned and left, and Clarissa walked to the door to watch him gingerly mount his black gelding. He hesitated a moment, probably waiting for the pain in his leg to subside, then rode off.

"What a strange man," Clarissa commented.

"Indeed," Michael added.

"And quite handsome, too, don't you think?" Carolyn teased.

Michael chuckled. "Not exactly the God-fearing kind," he said, shaking his head.

"No." Clarissa still watched him as he disappeared around a corner. "Why do I feel like what happened today is some kind of—I don't know—like it was meant to happen?"

"God works in strange ways, His miracles to perform," Carolyn answered. "Maybe Michael planted a seed today that will grow in that man's heart."

And maybe it's more than that, Clarissa mused. She quickly chastised herself for the silly thought and turned away from the door. "I have my deed!" she said then with a smile. "And we have a lot of shopping and packing to do, so let's get at it!" She called the girls from the kitchen, fighting the secret thought that if they could get to Independence within ten days, perhaps they could travel with Dawson Clements after all.

The Lord will protect you from all danger;
He will keep you safe.
He will protect you as you come and go,
Now and forever.

—Psalms 121:7-8

Chapter Five

❦

April 30, 1863

The congregation of people from all walks of life at Independence was far bigger than Clarissa expected. Ages ranged from the very old to the very young and everything in between. The combination of free land and wanting to get away from the war was all these people needed to spur them on.

The atmosphere was both exciting and intimidating. Children, chickens and dogs ran everywhere, and in the distance livestock grazed. As she and Carolyn and Michael walked among the host of wagons, oxen, horses and people, they noticed with great relief that most travelers were families. Still, a few men were camped here without families, some in groups, some by themselves. Several looked questionable in nature, and last night an ugly fistfight had taken place, spawned by an argument over the war and who was right or wrong. One man actually pulled a gun, but another had knocked it out of his hand.

Clarissa had not given thought to danger from the travelers themselves. Indians and the elements were enough to worry about. Because of the confusion that abounded, and the mix of people gathered here, she kept Sophie close, afraid she'd never find her if the child ran off. "I'm so glad I'm going with you and Michael," she told Carolyn. The three of them, and their daughters, walked among those gathered here, learning all they could about who was leaving when and who would guide them. "I don't think I'd have the courage to do this alone."

"Yes, you would. You're a brave woman for even going with us," Michael assured her, "with no husband and no guarantee of what you will do when you reach Montana."

"I'll help you build a ranch. That will keep me plenty busy for quite some time," Clarissa answered with a smile. She noticed that some wagons carried pianos, grandfather clocks, fine furniture and the like, and she had to wonder if they would make it through the mountains with such huge loads. Word was, it was foolish to cart such things along.

"I didn't think we'd find all this chaos," Carolyn commented. "Most of these people don't seem to know quite what they're doing."

"Maybe we should look up Dawson Clements," Michael suggested. "He seems like a man who'd know what he was about when it comes to traveling west, since he's done so before and served out there with the army."

"He's terribly rough around the edges," Clarissa commented. "And I'm not so sure he'd want a preacher along."

"That's not his decision," Michael answered. "I am sure the families headed west would appreciate having a preacher along, and most likely find need of one, with all the calamities that can take place. That was quite a list of possible troubles Mr. Clements rattled off to us a couple of weeks ago."

"I have a feeling he's a man who looks for the worst side of everything," Clarissa answered.

"You've been thinking about him, haven't you?" Carolyn said with a sly grin.

Clarissa shrugged. "Some, mostly because he seemed like such a lonely, troubled man."

"That he did," Michael added. "I've been praying for him."

Their conversation was interrupted when they heard someone crying loudly, as though in pain. Clarissa gasped with horror when to her left she saw a man beating a young boy of perhaps ten years old with a belt at the rear of a wagon.

"I'll teach you to obey what I tell you!" the man roared. The boy cringed and wept, covering his head with his hands and begging the man to stop.

Clarissa picked up Sophie and turned away so the child could not see the brutality. People stood around staring, all hesitant to interfere with a family matter; and the man doing the beating looked big and strong and furious.

"I'll stop him!" Michael declared, taking off his hat. Before he could make a move, a large man wearing a blue greatcoat and riding a black horse charged past them so fast that he raised a cloud of dust. His dangerous speed caused Clarissa to turn and look as the man dismounted before his horse even came to a stop. He landed into the father and ripped the belt out of his hand.

"Try picking on someone your own size," the man fumed. Women screamed, and more people gathered and cheered him on as the stranger began using the belt on the father, whacking him several times while the boy moved away to cringe beside his mother, who'd been wringing her hands and watching the beating, obviously afraid to try to stop it.

"How does that feel?" the man who'd interrupted the beating raged.

"It's Dawson Clements!" Clarissa exclaimed, recognizing the horse and the greatcoat first, then managing to get a look at his face.

The father cowered, putting up his hands. "What I do with my son is my own business!"

Dawson tossed the belt aside. "It's *my* business now!" He landed a fist into the father, and the man flew backward against his wagon. Then the father charged Dawson, managing to punch him in the face. Dawson returned the blow with several of his own, appearing to become almost out of control. Finally the mother screamed for someone to stop him.

"He's killing my husband!" she wailed.

Michael and several other men moved in and grabbed Dawson away while the man he'd beaten slumped to the ground beside a wagon wheel. It took five men to gain control of Dawson, who finally shook them off and told them to leave him alone. The man's wife ran to her husband, and the young boy stood there crying and looking at Dawson.

"Now he'll beat me worse because of what you did," he sobbed.

"No, he won't," Dawson vowed. "Because if he does, I'll be back! I'll lay welts on him that will *never* heal!" He brushed himself off and bent down to pick up his hat, which had been knocked off in the skirmish. He plunked it on his head and turned. It was then he recognized Michael. He looked at the man strangely, then scanned the crowd to see Clarissa standing there with Sophie in her arms. Still breathing heavily, he limped toward them. Clarissa noticed his knuckles were bloody, and there was a cut on his left cheek. A bruise was quickly forming around it.

"I'm sorry you had to see that," he told Clarissa. "And you, ma'am," he added, looking at Carolyn.

Clarissa could still see the rage in his blue eyes, lurking there behind those dark clouds. "You did what you felt you had to do," Carolyn told him.

Clarissa looked away, not sure what to say or what to think of him now that she'd seen the violent side of the man.

"Hi, Mistoo Clement," Sophie spoke up. She seemed not at all intimidated by Dawson's bloody, disheveled look. "You got a owie," she added, pointing to his cheek.

Dawson's whole countenance changed when he addressed the little girl. "Hello, Sophie," he told her.

"Do you still got a owie on you leg?" she asked.

Dawson removed his hat and smoothed back his hair, which was still extremely thick and wavy even though he'd obviously had it trimmed. His face was clean shaven, and even more handsome, with a square jaw and deep-set eyes. He replaced the hat, glancing at Carolyn. "The leg is much better. It still pains me now and then, but I never got an infection, and the wound has closed. I expect I have you to thank for that, Mrs. Graham."

Why did this man have a way of somehow moving her deeply? "I'm glad I was able to help."

"You nearly killed that man, you know," Michael told him.

"Maybe I should have. The boy and his mother would probably be better off."

"'Vengeance is mine, sayeth the Lord.'"

Dawson rolled his eyes. "Yeah, well, maybe the Lord uses some of us to wreak that vengeance," he answered. "I happen to have a short fuse when it comes to treating a helpless child like that."

"Quite obvious," Michael answered with raised eyebrows. Dawson nodded to the women, then brushed past them to get his horse. He mounted up and rode closer, pointing to a huge oak tree on a hill in the distance. "See that tree?"

Clarissa shaded her eyes. "Yes."

"That's where I'm camped," he told them. "I have rounded up about eight families heading for Montana. I wasn't going to take on any more than that, since it might be too much to handle, but you three and the little girls are welcome to join us if you're still looking for a guide. We're hoping to head out in five or six days, unless we get a lot of rain. Come on over tonight and camp with us if you like. That will give you a chance to get to know some of the others and make up your mind if you want to travel with us."

"Is there a preacher among your group?" Michael asked.

Dawson scowled. "No. I suppose you think they need one?"

"Of course they do," Michael answered, giving Dawson a smile and a wink. "I imagine they'd appreciate having one along. They *are* Christian people, aren't they?"

"I suppose. I didn't bother asking," Dawson answered, obviously irritated by the question.

"Well, then we'll come by and get acquainted," Michael told him.

"Suit yourself. Just don't expect me to be part of any praying or preaching."

"I wouldn't dream of asking you," Michael answered with a teasing note to the words.

Dawson nodded. "Good." He glanced at Clarissa. "See you later then." He turned his horse and rode away, and some of those who'd watched the fight stared after him.

"Did you see what he did?" someone commented.

"A very violent man," said another.

Michael turned to Carolyn and Clarissa. "What do you two think? Should we join his group?"

"I think we should do whatever you feel is right, Michael," Clarissa answered. "After all, I'm more or less the tagalong on this venture. You're the one who should make the major decisions." She was not about to admit that the thought of traveling with Dawson Clements filled her with a strange, pleasant excitement, mixed with apprehension. She realized that ever since the day she'd nursed his leg, she'd been hoping they might run into him again. Still, after what they'd just witnessed...

"Well, I say we give it a try," Michael said. "I'm thinking the Lord wants us to go just because Dawson Clements is the guide. I have a feeling God means for me to do something to help that man, much as he'd resent it. There is something about him that strikes the heart."

Yes, there is, Clarissa thought. She liked the fact that there was nothing fake or pretentious about the man. Clements didn't try to pour on the charm like Chad would do. He had an air of honesty and no nonsense about him. Dawson seemed to be a man who meant what he said and very likely a man who did not break promises or lie to get what he wanted. He was *nothing* like Chad, and perhaps that was what she liked most about him.

Chapter Six

❧

May 1, 1863

Clarissa switched her lead oxen and shouted, "Giddap!" She'd practiced driving the four-oxen team for the past two weeks and felt confident she could handle them. The man who'd sold the animals to Michael told him that by the time they reached their destination, they would be very attached to the poor beasts that would haul them and their belongings all the way to Montana.

Already Clarissa could tell the man was right about getting attached. She'd already named the four that pulled her wagon, Moo, Bee, Sadie and Jack. Buck and Betsy were tied to the back of her wagon for spares, so the animals could be rotated to avoid too much work for any one of them. She already knew each ox by its distinctive markings. Michael thought she was silly to name them, but for some reason that made it easier for her to handle them. She just hoped she had the strength to keep up with them and to help hitch and unhitch them every day.

She hated the fact that Michael usually had to help, especially yoking them whenever the oxen would not properly hold still. She had no doubt that by the time she reached Montana, she might be built like a man for all her hard work.

They headed toward Dawson's camp at the big oak tree in the distance. Michael and Carolyn took two wagons— Michael's pulled by six oxen because of an extraheavy load of farm tools and books, including a supply of Bibles and hymnals, donated by others for his new church.

Carolyn's wagon carried lighter household necessities, and Lena and Sophie rode together in it, bouncing around atop a pile of quilts and having a joyous time. Clarissa thought how oblivious the girls were to the difficulties that surely lay ahead. She prayed things would remain that way— that nothing would happen to either child and they wouldn't end up stranded and starving to death.

The latter seemed unlikely, as they had packed plenty of food. Distributed among all three wagons was dried beef, rice, tea, spices, dried fruit, beans, baking soda, flour, sugar, baking powder, canned pickles, bacon, potatoes, sweet potatoes, large tubs filled with plenty of lard for packing fresh meat to preserve it, salt, coffee, wheat, oats, cornmeal. She kept reviewing the list in her mind, worried they'd missed something.

They also carried a tin washtub, two washboards, lye soap, three coffee kettles, tinware, several fry pans, cooking utensils, trunks of clothes, plenty of blankets, quilts, pillows, heavy boots and warm coats. Michael had even thought to buy each of them capes made of India rubber, something new that worked well against rain.

A milk cow, which Lena and Sophie had named Trudy, was tied to one side of Carolyn's wagon, and it balked at leaving. The rope grew taut and stretched the cow's head and neck until the animal had no choice but to join the procession, and her calf trotted beside her. A slatted crate was secured to the side of Clarissa's wagon with rope, and inside the crate were three chickens that she hoped would continue laying eggs. A rooster sat on top of her wagon, occasionally flapping its wings and crowing, as though king of the wagon train.

Her wagon even carried a crate that contained something that had belonged to her mother—beautiful china from Germany, carefully packed in straw. It was all she had left of the mother she'd lost so long ago, and of the life she'd known in St. Louis.

She could not take her heart or trust with her. Chad had stolen both. It still hurt deeply to think about it, but it was done now, and she doubted she could ever love or trust a man again, let alone ever find it in her heart to forgive.

They guided the three wagons through rows of others still gathered outside of Independence, and after several minutes they came closer to the big oak, where Clarissa quickly counted ten wagons circled around it. Children ran and played, and women cooked in big pots over fires.

Families. That was good. Having other women and children along would make this trip so much easier. The families from Michael's church who'd originally wanted to come with them had decided against the trip. One of the men had been drafted into the Union Army under the new draft law. Another decided to stay behind to help care for that man's family, and the mother in the third family found out she was expecting. They worried the trip would cause her to lose her baby.

And so it was just Michael and Carolyn, the girls and Clarissa. Clarissa breathed deeply for courage. She hated lying, but after discussing the issue of her divorce, the three adults had decided to tell others that Clarissa's husband had been killed in the war. That would avoid problems that might arise with some of the women knowing she was divorced.

It still irked Clarissa that she should be ill-treated just because her husband had cheated on her. Chad was the coward and the adulterer, yet some people treated her as though she was somehow tainted now. It hurt deeply to be treated so. Deep inside she'd reconciled herself to her fate and had decided to be proud and strong and do a good job of raising Sophie on her own. After much prayer and long talks with Michael, she'd come to realize that God surely held nothing against her for the divorce. She'd been a good and faithful wife and mother. She would not allow Chad's foolish decisions to wreck her own faith.

The decision to go with Dawson Clements as their guide had not been easy. The man was certainly a contrast of character and emotions, saving a child one minute, beating a man near to death the next. He obviously had a goodness somewhere deep inside, but he certainly hated showing it. And as much as the man protested talk about God and prayer and professed to have no use for preachers, Clarissa suspected he longed to know Christ, to understand his own bitterness and perhaps find a way to forgive whoever it was who'd brought him to such an attitude.

Because of Dawson's experience with the army and Indians and the way west, and the fact that he had a commanding way about him that could mean a well-organized wagon train, they'd decided to join him.

When they drew closer to the other wagons, Dawson himself walked out to greet Michael wearing simple denim pants and a plaid shirt with knee-high boots. A gun was strapped to his side, and he still wore the wide-brimmed, black hat.

Clarissa watched him greet Michael with a handshake. Good. At least the man was accepting Michael even though he was a preacher. Dawson's attitude toward men of God was strange indeed, and Clarissa wished she knew why.

The men talked for a moment, then Michael nodded to Dawson and called out to the women to follow him to a grassy spot ahead. Clarissa followed, and Dawson stood and waited for her wagon to get closer. He walked up then and grasped the halter of one of the lead oxen, shouting, "Whoa, there! Whoa!" Once the animals stopped, he turned to Clarissa.

"You have no help driving these oxen?" he asked.

"I'll do just fine on my own, Mr. Clements," she answered defensively. "Michael has taught me well."

"It can get pretty tiring, ma'am, and sometimes these beasts get ornery and decide not to obey."

"I'll handle them." It irritated her that he should question her ability.

"What if you get sick or break a bone or something? Who's going to drive your wagon?"

Frowning, Clarissa folded her arms in front of her, a switch still in her hand. "Why do you care, Mr. Clements?"

He pushed back his hat, and Clarissa noticed a lingering bruise on his cheek. He was clean shaven again, and his dark hair brushed his shirt collar. It literally angered her to notice how good-looking he was, which made her feel even more defensive.

"Mrs. Graham, I got this wagon train together, and I intend to see that everyone arrives safely in Montana. Now for the sake of practicality, I need to know you'll have a backup for the days you can't drive these oxen, and believe me, there will be such days."

"I can see you haven't changed when it comes to always looking at the worst of things, Mr. Clements. Tell me, do you ever wake up joyful, and simply grateful for the new day? Have you ever thought about simply trusting God to see you through things?"

He closed his eyes and let out an obviously disparaging sigh. "Mrs. Graham, we haven't even left yet and already you're presenting a problem."

"A *problem*?"

He put his hands on his hips and leaned closer. "Yes. I'll be giving orders on this trip, and I expect them to be followed. Now, I was not trying to insult your ability to lead these oxen. I was simply pointing out a *fact*. The time will come when you'll need help with these oxen, so I'll talk to these families here. A couple of them have older teenage boys who could probably relieve you if necessary."

"I can't afford—"

"They wouldn't expect to be paid. We're all here to help each other out and make sure we all get through this trip without too many mishaps, ma'am. And if the day comes that I tell you someone else is driving your oxen, I expect you to cooperate. Is that understood?"

Ever since Chad left her, Clarissa had grown proud of her ability to fend for herself, proud enough that she resented *any* man's help. She'd show men that she didn't need a man to take care of herself.

"Understood," she answered, holding her chin high. "But only because I faint at the thought of getting on your *bad* side—that's assuming, of course, that you have a *good* side."

He looked her over in a way that made her blush, then grinned. "I do have a good side, ma'am. It pops out every once in a while." He nodded and tipped his hat, then turned away, calling to her as he walked back to the circle of wagons. "Meet us inside the circle in an hour," he yelled, not turning back around. "Big meeting."

Yes, sir, she answered silently. An army man. She should have known that having been an officer, he was accustomed to giving orders. With a man like Dawson Clements in charge, this was going to be a very interesting trip.

Chapter Seven

❦

It was nearly dusk when Dawson's orders could be heard shouted from within the circle of wagons. "Okay, everyone, gather round and listen up!"

Outside the circle where Clarissa was camped with Carolyn and Michael, Dawson's booming voice was easily heard. They took Lena and Sophie's hands and walked inside the circle, where the other families had gathered, all of them encircling Dawson and a grizzly-looking man of about forty-five or fifty who stood beside Dawson, leaning on a rifle.

Several women held babies, while older children standing nearby were ordered to keep quiet and listen. Clarissa lifted Sophie into her arms, and Lena grabbed hold of Carolyn's skirt.

Clarissa thought the bearded man leaning on the rifle looked as though he hadn't bathed in months. His leather vest appeared well-worn, as did his stained, floppy leather hat, and he wore a gun on each hip. She noticed some kind of big knife hung in a sheath from the man's belt.

"Everybody listen up," Dawson continued, using the commanding voice of an army officer. "This is Zeb Artis. I found him today offering to lead a wagon train west, and I took it upon myself to hire him for our train. I know Zeb from when he scouted for the army off and on over the years. He's fought Indians and trapped beaver and hunted bear in the Rockies. The man is experienced. He knows the way west and knows Indians. You will all have to pool together to pay the man, but I hired him because while I'm watching over this entire wagon train, someone needs to scout ahead for good places to stop and rest, look out for Indians, herds of buffalo and the like. This group has grown larger than I'd planned on, and I can't do it alone. Zeb has agreed to help out. He'll be worth every penny you scrape up for him. He doesn't ask much—just whatever you can afford. I'll let all of you decide that amongst yourselves."

No one argued, and Clarissa suspected that was because they knew better. Dawson had a way of stating facts with a strong hint that no one was going to change any decisions he made.

"I've made a list," he continued, pulling a piece of paper from his pants pocket. "There are eighteen children in this group, ranging in ages from one to nineteen. We have twelve men and eleven women, ten wagons, ninety oxen, nine draft horses, twenty head of cattle, one bull, twelve calves, six milk cows, three horses and three mules." He put the paper back in his pocket. "This is a big wagon train and a big responsibility. To make things go smoothly, I expect every one of you to follow my decisions and rules. Is that understood?"

People looked at each other and said nothing, until one man who seemed too well dressed for setting out on a trip west suddenly spoke up. "What if one of us thinks certain things could be done a better way, or thinks we should go on when you say to stop, or vice versa?" the man asked, an arrogant air about him.

"Then he should keep that thought to himself," Dawson answered curtly. He glanced at Clarissa. "Or herself," he added.

The remark made Clarissa bristle. Did Dawson Clements think she was going to be some kind of problem on this trip? How dare he! Dawson looked away, scanning the crowd. "You hired me to guide you west, mainly because I'm experienced and know the country into which we are headed. There is no sense questioning decisions I make when you have no grounds on which to argue about it. If any of you had already been west, that would be another story, but you are depending on someone who knows what he's doing to get you to Montana, and you're paying me well for it. So why argue about anything?"

The well-dressed man shrugged. "Just wondering if any of us will be allowed to speak our mind," he said rather defensively.

"You're an attorney, I believe, Mr. Burkette?" Dawson answered the man.

Burkette, a nice-looking man with a pretty wife and two young children standing beside him, straightened, looking quite proud for people to know his profession. "Yes, I am."

"Well, keep your concerns for peoples' rights and your fancy notions to yourself until you reach Montana, Mr. Burkette," Dawson told him firmly. "When you get where you're going, you can practice law in any way, shape or form you want. You can tout your profession and your college education to anyone who wants to hear about it. But don't do so on this trip. If you want to travel with me, you'll listen to whatever I tell you and you'll do it—or you can travel with someone else. Is that understood?"

Burkette smiled and shrugged.

"I asked if you understood, *Lawyer Burkette.*"

Clarissa did not miss the flash of arrogance and anger in Burkette's eyes before he answered in the affirmative, and she suspected Dawson had not missed it, either. He glared at the lawyer a moment longer, until Burkette nervously looked away.

"I like this," Michael said softly to Carolyn and Clarissa. "Mr. Clements will take no argument or trouble from anyone. That's what a man needs to do to keep a big bunch like this organized. His army training is to our benefit."

Dawson seemed to soften a little then as he casually walked within the circle talking to the rest of the travelers. "I don't mean to put a damper on things, folks, but you hired me to do a job, and I intend to do it right and get all of you to Montana with as few disasters or injuries or deaths as possible. Even though thousands have gone before you, the trip isn't easy. They say some day a railroad will connect this whole country, but that's a long way off. None of us will be so lucky to travel that way, but if it happens, those of you who are already settled out west will benefit greatly from the railroad. A good share of you will end up rich business owners or landowners some day." His gaze landed on Carolyn, Michael and Clarissa. "I hope that happens for you." He turned away. "But first I have to get you there. The rest is up to you."

He pulled out another list. "Now, as I introduce each family, I want you to step forward, tell us your plans for settling in Montana, then step back as I introduce the next family. By the end of this trip you will all know each other well. For now it will help to know a little bit about the others you're traveling with. Let's see here." He studied the list a moment.

"Walt and Bess Clymer and their son Stuart, from east Kansas."

An older couple stepped forward, nodding and smiling to the others. "Ma and Pa and I are gonna build a horse ranch." Their son spoke up for his shy parents.

"Mrs. Graham," Dawson called, surprising Clarissa. "This young man has agreed to help guide your oxen, or Carolyn Harvey's oxen, if either of you can't do it."

Still irritated at the suggestion she'd need help, Clarissa pushed that irritation to the side and nodded to Stuart Clymer. "Thank you," she told him, before casting Dawson a glance that let him know she still did not appreciate his lack of faith in her abilities.

The introductions proceeded: John and Rosemarie Clay, farmers from northern Arkansas, and their children, ages four and three. Robert and Jenny Trowbridge, young newlyweds also from Arkansas, hoping to make their fortune in gold or silver. Florence and Haans Buettner, a German couple from southern Missouri who intended to open a supply store in a gold town. They had three children, ranging from three to eight, and were hauling an extra supply wagon guided by Haans's brother, Eric.

Then came Sue and Samuel McCurdy, the children of Irish immigrants, from southern Missouri, and Sue's sister Betsy and her husband, Ben Gobles. Sam was a blacksmith, Ben a gunsmith and there were five children between the two couples, from one to five years old.

Next came two more German couples. Opal and Otto Hensel had three children, six, eight and nine, and were farmers from southern Missouri. Wanda and Will Krueger, who had no children, intended to raise cattle out west, and they were herding twenty head of cattle, one bull and four calves, with the aid of Will's brother, Bert.

Then came the attorney, Peter Burkette and his wife, Blair, who had two children, a boy of three, and a daughter just one year old.

Carolyn and Michael's turn came. "I am Michael Harvey, and this is my wife, Carolyn, and our daughter, Lena," Michael spoke up. "I am a minister and will be glad to pray with any of you who wishes. If you'd like to have services on Sunday mornings, I'll be glad to conduct them for you. I will start my own church in Montana along with ranching or farming for a living."

Clarissa's heart pounded. She'd have to introduce herself as a woman with no husband, and before she could stop herself, she was telling everyone she was a war widow and explained she was traveling to Montana to help Michael and Carolyn with their ranch, as they were close friends. She glanced at Carolyn with their ranch, as they were close friends. She glanced at Dawson, remembering that the day she'd bandaged his leg she'd told him her husband was not in the war. She'd never given him an explanation of whether Chad was alive or dead, or any reason for her not being with him. She could tell from Dawson's curious look that he realized she was lying and wondered why. For a moment she was petrified that he'd call her out in front of everyone and demand an explanation, considering the mood he was in, but to her great relief he said nothing.

"Well, then," he told them all, "we've got a start at getting to know each other. We will leave here day after tomorrow. That will give all of you one more day to get acquainted and learn which children belong to whom and find ways to help each other look out for the young ones. Once we begin this journey, it's not each man for himself but all of us helping each other. Some of you will have to put up with things from the others that you don't like, but I won't have arguing or lack of cooperation from any of you. Montana is big country, so when we get there, if there is someone among us you can't stand and hope to never see again, including me, you won't have any trouble getting far away from them."

Everyone chuckled at the remark, which eased the minor tension among them. Clarissa thought how nice it was to see that Dawson Clements actually possessed a sense of humor.

"Well, since my claim is right beside yours, you'll just have to put up with me," she told Carolyn and Michael.

The couple laughed, and Michael put out his hands to the two women. "Let's pray for a safe trip, shall we?"

Clarissa held a now-sleeping Sophie in her left arm and put her right hand in Michael's left, and Carolyn took his right hand. They bowed their heads.

"Dear Blessed Father," Michael prayed. "Grant us safety and health on the journey ahead. Bless and protect everyone going with us, and especially bless Dawson Clements with wisdom and wise thinking and the strength he will need to get us to our destination. Lord Jesus, we pray for Mr. Clements's soul and for the secret pain he refuses to share, and we ask You to take away that pain and to guide us in Your way to find the right words that might bring this man back into Your light. And protect all the little children traveling with us, that none will suffer sickness or pain on this journey. In Christ's name we pray."

"Amen," the three of them said softly together.

When they looked up, Dawson Clements was standing not far away, watching them. Scowling, he turned and walked away.

Protect me, oh God;
I trust in You for safety.
I say to the Lord, "You are my Lord,
All the good things I have come from You."

—*Psalms* 16:1-2

Chapter Eight

❧

May 5, 1863

They were on their way! Clarissa felt more joy than she'd known in many, many months, shadowed only by the occasional stab of pain at realizing she'd never seen Chad since the day she read the letter from Susan. How strange that any human being could so suddenly walk away from his own wife and child without looking back. She realized Chad Graham's selfish, insensitive nature was her best aid in putting the man behind her and leaving him there forever. If only she and Sophie didn't have to carry the man's name—and if only she could find it in her heart to truly forgive him. Her heart was too injured for that. God would have to understand that some things were impossible for the human heart.

For now it was time to look only forward, not back. The first three days of travel brought enough excitement to help her forget the reason she was doing this. From now on little Sophie need never suffer stares or hear lies about her mother and father and the trumped-up reasons some people had probably decided caused the divorce. God surely had a plan for hers and Sophie's lives, and heading for Montana was part of that plan.

Everyone on the wagon train was in a wonderful mood. For the first part of the journey there would be plenty of places to stop, even places to stock up on more supplies. It would be a good month before they would have cause to watch for Indians or worry about running out of something. The biggest immediate problem would be crossing rivers. Old Zeb had told them that even the normally shallow Platte River could be very high this time of year.

Clarissa decided not to worry. For now, the countryside smelled wonderful, spring wildflowers blooming everywhere, new grass creating a sea of pungent-smelling green along the well-worn trail that for the most part was flat. The weather remained cool and sunny, perfect for the long hours of walking, and when they camped for a noon break, Sophie and Lena and several other little girls ran through the grass picking wildflowers.

Sophie's cheeks glowed and her blue eyes sparkled. Clarissa's heart soared at the girl's glee and unfettered curiosity. She was full of questions—"Why" this and "Why" that, "What's this?" and "When will we get there?" She and Lena were practically inseparable, and having so many other children along made what might have been monotonous days exciting for Sophie and Lena, as sometimes they would ride with another family and sometimes other girls would ride with them.

Lack of privacy was the one deprivation that took getting used to. Men could just turn their backs or even walk away from the train to take care of necessities. Mothers helped their little girls, and most of the little boys were not bashful about such matters. But because of the danger of getting too far away, women chose not to walk too far for their personal affairs. Instead, they would form a circle and spread out their skirts, allowing a woman inside the circle to take care of business without being seen, and with the other women's backs to them. After the first two days of getting used to no outhouses, Clarissa and Carolyn and the other women learned to set aside modesty and accept the new way of tending to personals. Clarissa thought how incredibly understanding women could be toward each other at such times, most always ready to help another with children or come up with medical remedies for "female" problems.

Other than an occasional ride up and down the long line of wagons to check on things or pass information about the trail ahead, Dawson Clements kept to himself most of the time, never taking people up on offers to have a meal with them. They saw Zeb Artis only in the mornings, before he would ride far ahead of them and usually not show up again until most of the travelers had bedded down for the night.

Clarissa's feet were beginning to blister and ache fiercely, but she'd decided not to complain to Mr. Clements. It still irked her that he'd been so sharp with her about driving the oxen. In her mind he'd insulted her abilities, and after what Chad had done to her, she was not about to admit she needed a man's help for anything, especially one as bossy and arrogant as Dawson Clements.

What an odd sort of personality he had. He seemed to have an extraordinary dislike for any form of discipline, and in his eyes, that could be a simple spanking. Last evening he'd called a quick meeting to add to his list of rules, which was that he did not want to see a child beaten or spanked. They were told that if a child misbehaved he or she was to be brought to him in the evening and he would give them a good talking to and some kind of extra chore that would cure them of misbehaving again.

He told them that one thing he admired about Indians was that they never screamed at their children or physically hit them. Indian children learned discipline through praise for the things they did right. When they did something wrong, the adults would show extreme disappointment and sadness over it so that the child was so embarrassed and felt so sad that he or she never misbehaved in that way again.

"Praise is the key," he told them. "Children love to please their fathers and mothers. Spankings can destroy their spirits."

Destroy their spirits. Later that night, Clarissa, Michael and Carolyn talked about the man's strange new rule, especially his comment about spankings destroying a child's spirit.

"The man was talking from experience. Anyone can tell that," Michael surmised.

"Yes, and since he told us he ran away at thirteen, surely he'd been abused," Carolyn suggested.

"By a preacher perhaps?" Clarissa suggested.

Michael sighed deeply. "I hate to think so, but I'll bet you're right." He shook his head. "How sad. And you know something? That man's own spirit has somehow been destroyed. That explains why he doesn't seem to have any true joy about him."

Carolyn nodded. "I have a feeling that teaching him about true joy will be a bigger challenge than we thought."

Clarissa had to smile now at the thought of their conversation. Michael and Carolyn had taken on the salvation of Dawson Clements as a personal and very important project. That was the kind of people they were, the kind who cared about another's troubles and did what they could about them—the kind who would not turn their backs on a divorced woman with a daughter to raise, the kind who prayed for men like Dawson Clements, who probably cared absolutely nothing for them in return. True, loving, spiritual, honest men like Michael Harvey were rare indeed. He was not good-looking or big and strong or good with his fists, but he was a real man in so many other ways, with a courage of spirit that was brave enough to reach out to those who didn't want and would not ask for his help.

Then there was Dawson Clements, disturbingly handsome, a man who *was* big and strong and good with his fists and probably with a gun—but who wouldn't think of reaching out to those who didn't want his help and who seemed to practically scoff at prayer.

"Who are you, really, Dawson Clements?" she muttered as she switched at the oxen to keep them moving. She hated to admit it, but the man had been right that walking so many miles every day leading the oxen would begin to take its toll. Her feet were killing her!

Chapter Nine

May 8, 1863

The pouring rain brought back memories of Shiloh. Just like that night Sergeant Bridger was shot in front of his eyes, Dawson huddled down inside his rubber poncho. He cursed the turn of events. It had poured for practically the past twenty-four hours. The weather had been better than expected until now, but then, what else could he expect this time of year in these parts? Once farther west, rain would barely be a problem, but they were, after all, not even out of Missouri yet.

What truly rankled him was suddenly wishing he'd never met Mrs. Clarissa Graham and that little girl of hers. More than that, he wished he'd at least not told her and that couple she was traveling with to look him up when they went to Independence. He could have at least told them he had all the wagons he could handle and not allowed them to join this train. Everything was working out just fine until he opened his big mouth and let those three and their little girls join up.

Now he found himself upset over the first minor delay. And why? Because down inside he knew the next few months were going to be difficult and he wanted them over with as fast as possible. Clarissa Graham was going to end up needing help, and he was probably the one who'd end up having to help her. That meant having to associate with her and that preacher friend of hers.

Why did Mrs. Graham upset him? There was no good reason for it. She angered him, interested him, confused him, reminded him how long it had been since he cared one whit about any woman, leastways not a decent one like Mrs. Graham. Saloon women were easy—a man didn't have to care about them. Clarissa Graham was a respectable woman, the kind he admired for her courage and determination—and she had a shape that made a man want to stare at her.

He chastised himself for thinking about that. A beautiful, redheaded, hazel-eyed, slender, single woman on a wagon train with a bunch of married men and jealous wives could only mean trouble, the kind he preferred not to deal with.

He wished he knew the story behind the woman's "dead" husband, whom he knew wasn't dead at all. Was she still married to him? Was she running from him? He supposed he had a right to ask, since her situation could be important to the way she fit in on this train; but asking might be misinterpreted as being interested in her in a way that went beyond just being the leader of this wagon train, and he couldn't afford her thinking that. That could lead to discovering she was no more interested in getting to know him better than a rabbit wanted to get to know a fox.

He'd had all the disappointments he could handle. Memories from boyhood reminded him he was not worthy of anyone's love or concern. The one time he'd allowed himself to truly care enough about a woman to marry her, she'd up and died on him, taking their unborn baby with her. Then, of course, there had been Sergeant Bridger, one man he'd dared to consider a friend, only to see him die right in front of him at Shiloh. That had only instilled in his soul the fact that he deserved nothing good in life, that a cruel God would continually punish him until the day he died.

Why hadn't that Rebel shot him instead of the young sergeant? No, that would have been too easy. God wanted him to live in constant loneliness and with the constant guilt of being responsible for the death of his parents and the constant pain of realizing he could never be forgiven for his sin.

Now he'd gone and allowed a preacher to join this wagon train, a preacher and two women who actually bothered praying for him. He ought to have a good talk with them and tell them what a waste of time that was. They could certainly pray for better things than Dawson Clements, a lost soul who all the praying in the world could not help.

He should have made sure about Clarissa Graham's true circumstances. He'd probably invited disaster by letting her come, but her skills as a nurse could end up being helpful, as well, he supposed as having a preacher along. Those traveling on this train who thought God and prayer would help them survive might at least keep good hope and try harder if they thought God was helping them, and having a preacher along to boost their faith couldn't hurt, he supposed.

He heard a horse approaching in the distant darkness. That would be Zeb, but as a precaution, he reached for his rifle and readied it. Zeb finally rode into the light of the campfire Dawson had managed to keep going by erecting a lean-to with branches and blankets around the side from which the wind-driven rain came down. It provided enough shelter to keep the fire going.

"You're later than usual," he told Zeb.

The old mountain man dismounted and began unloading his horse. "Muddy up ahead. I had to find a roundabout way, and a man can't travel very fast in pitch dark with rain in his eyes. Wretched weather."

"How muddy?" Dawson asked.

Zeb threw his bedroll and some belongings inside the shelter Dawson had built, then set his saddle down and covered it with a poncho. He left his horse bridled and tied it to a young sapling. "*Very* muddy," he answered in his cracked, aging voice. He threw a blanket around himself and sat down near Dawson under the shelter. "You ain't gonna get them wagons through, I'll tell you that much. It'll take a good day of sun to even think about it."

Dawson fumed inside at realizing there would be a further delay. "I guess we're stuck here then, aren't we?" He leaned against his saddle farther inside the shelter.

"It won't be so bad. Gives us time to take up some of these folks on their offers of a good home-cooked meal or two. I've had plenty of invites. Reckon you have, too."

"I'd just as soon keep to myself. You start eating with these people, you start getting attached, and that could lead to problems later when it comes to making decisions, like who has to cross the river first, or who has to throw out their prized belongings in order to get up the side of a mountain. Staying detached from them makes it easier to break their hearts later if it becomes necessary."

Zeb chuckled. "You sure ain't exactly the most friendly sort, are you?"

"Can't afford to be. Besides, I seem to have a sort of curse about me—you get friendly with me and something bad happens to you."

Zeb spit a wad of tobacco juice into the fire. It landed with a hiss. "That's crazy talk," he told Dawson. "You sure have some strange ideas, Clements, but I admire your ability to give orders and keep things organized. What do you intend to do when you reach Montana?"

Dawson shrugged. "I'm not sure. Look for gold, I guess. Maybe look for a job as a foreman or a guard at a mine, something like that. I'm used to giving orders. Or maybe I'll just travel on someplace else. I probably should rejoin the army. I liked it out west, and army life is all I've ever known."

"Then why'd you quit in the first place?"

Dawson could still hear the cries of the wounded at Shiloh, still saw the look in Bridger's eyes when that bullet landed in his back, still saw the bloodshed and heard the exploding cannon and smelled the smoke from rifles fired so repeatedly that their steel barrels grew hot and soft and warped. And he could still remember the pain of that shrapnel ripping into his leg as he was hauled cannon through Mississippi.

"Had enough of war, I guess. A man can take only so much of seeing men walking around with their guts hanging out and seeing arms and legs in literal piles outside of hospital tents. Of all the fighting I did in Mexico and against Indians, nothing matched what I've seen the past couple of years. I had a chance to get away from it all and I took it. But once I get back out west, I don't know, I just might rejoin. Depends what I end up doing in Montana, Wyoming, California, wherever I land."

"Yes, sir, it sure is beautiful country," Zeb spit more tobacco juice. "Ain't you thought of settlin' with a good woman? Havin' a few kids?"

"Not for me. I tried it once. She died. So did the baby."

"Had me an Indian wife once. She missed her people, so she went back to them. I'm a roamer, you know? I couldn't stay in one place, and she wanted me to settle with her tribe. So we went our separate ways." Zeb looked at Dawson. "Me, I've always been sort of ugly, and I'm uneducated, except in the ways of a mountain man, you know? I just ain't the type to be a normal married man like the men on this wagon train. But you, you're educated, Clements, and a good-lookin' man, and not all that old yet, either. Army or not, you ought to think about marryin' again. That there widow woman on this train, she's a looker, for sure. Now there's somethin' you ought to pursue, know what I mean? You ought to at least give it a try. That there is a lot of woman. Seems to me she's brave, goin' west without a man of her own. That woman's got pluck." He nudged Dawson's arm. "And maybe she's lonesome for a man, if you know what I mean. Could make this trip right pleasurable for you," he ended with a chuckle.

The remark brought a quick twinge of desire Dawson would rather not have experienced. It awakened his original ire at allowing Clarissa Graham to join this wagon train in the first place. He shook his head. "A woman like that needs the settling-down type who's willing to work at a real job and provide for his family. I'm just not ready for any of that yet. Might never be."

"Well, I'd sure give that pretty woman some serious thought. If I was your age and had your looks—"

"Drop it, Zeb. You just tend to your scouting and leave the decisions about the people on this train to me."

Zeb spit once more and chuckled again. "Yes, sir, Mr. Clements." He reached over and untied a blanket from his supplies, then fluffed it up and used it like a pillow, lying down inside the shelter. "I'm gonna try to get some sleep. You'd better do the same."

Dawson sat staring at the flickering flames as thunder rumbled in the distance. Again he wondered what the real story was behind Clarissa Graham, wondered why it mattered, and wondered why he hoped she and that little girl of hers were staying dry.

Chapter Ten

❦

May 10, 1863

Clarissa fought an urge to cry, the desire coming from anger more than despair. She was certain that Dawson Clements had placed her wagon toward the end of the wagon train today so that the muddy places in the trail would be churned up the worst by the time she reached them, making her job harder.

After waiting a full day after the rain, everyone voted to get going so they could reach the Kansas River ferry crossing and get it over with. The crossing could take the better part of yet another day, as wagons had to be unhitched, the entire train floated across in parts—children, animals, wagons one by one, oxen, women, men and so forth. One ferry could carry only so much.

They had not even reached the ferry yet, and if her wagon, Carolyn's wagon and the two that followed them could not get through the current mud bath they trudged, they might not even make the ferry by tonight.

She switched at the oxen, shouting orders and calling the beasts by their names as it took every effort of each ox to keep the wagon moving through mud that came a good halfway up between the wheel bottom and the hub. She grimaced and tried to keep the hem of her dress lifted, to no avail. Her black leather lace-up shoes made sucking sounds with every step, and it took every ounce of energy to keep up with the oxen, even though they, too, were not moving very fast. She looked ahead to see her bigger, stronger friend Carolyn trudging forward beside her own oxen.

"How are you doing, Carolyn?" Clarissa yelled.

"I think we'll make it!"

Carolyn's voice sounded distant, as indeed she was several yards in front of her, making good progress now. Apparently the ground was better there, if only Clarissa could reach that point.

Michael had taken the girls and proceeded farther on to leave Lena and Sophie and his wagon with others so he could come back and help Carolyn and Clarissa, but when Clarissa looked past Carolyn's wagon to see a rider coming, she rolled her eyes when she realized it was Dawson Clements.

"Where is Michael?" she fumed under her breath. Dawson was the *last* person she wanted to see her struggling in the mud. She was sure he was just waiting for her to fail.

"Come on, Betsy!" she ordered, giving the ox's rear a switch. "Keep going! Giddap! Giddap!"

Betsy, Jack, Bee, Moo, Sadie and Buck—all six were pulling this time, struggling to keep the wagon from being completely pinned in the quagmire through which they waded. Clarissa glanced up to see Dawson talking with Carolyn. He waved her on and pointed to something, and it looked as though Carolyn was finally free. He rode closer, then past Clarissa to talk to the two remaining wagons behind her own. Clarissa could hear only bits and pieces of what he was saying as he shouted something about veering farther south and around, then back north.

Those two wagons were also moving into deeper mud, but they veered to their left then, and Clarissa saw Dawson, still on his horse, take the harness of one lead ox and help the man with the first wagon urge the oxen to the left to slightly firmer ground.

"Why doesn't he come back here and help *me* do the same?" Clarissa wondered, not that she would have accepted his help. Maybe he knew that. Her own stubbornness could cost her some embarrassment. She used all the leg power she had to pull her left foot from a sucking hole and planted it on a rock, gritting her teeth and pulling up her right foot, then managing to make her way closer to the oxen so she could take hold of the harness of a lead animal, which today happened to be Sadie.

"Come on, girl. Show Dawson Clements what you can do!" Sadie eyed her in a way that told Clarissa the animal was doing all it could. The ox's eyelid was opened extrawide, showing the whites of her eyes in a way that almost seemed to say the poor ox was terrified she might never get out of this muck.

"Ha! Ha!" Clarissa ordered again, switching the animals and tugging at the harness. Then she heard Dawson's deep voice behind her.

"Need some help?"

"I'm fine," she insisted. "Better ground is just ahead. Carolyn made it. So will I."

"Sometimes oxen just respond better to a man's voice," he told her.

A man's voice? The arrogance of him! Clarissa figured that, like all men, this one thought a woman couldn't get by in life without a man. "These oxen are used to my voice," she answered. "They'll respond just fine."

"Nevertheless, I could throw a rope around that lead oxen's neck and—"

"You don't need to do that," Clarissa interrupted. "Come on, Sadie!" she urged the ox, then. "Pull with Moo. Pull! Pull!"

"Ma'am, I don't intend for the rest of the wagon train to be across the river tomorrow before you even reach the ferry landing."

"Just leave me alone and go on about what you were hired to do, Mr. Clements!" she said with obvious irritation. Why, oh why did she feel like crying? She hated it when she cried just because she was mad or embarrassed.

Then the worst happened. She slipped. Facedown she went in the slimy mess, right between the lead ox and the next four. The next thing she knew, someone was pulling her up and hauled her away in one arm, then plopped her on a horse. Her face was plastered with so much mud she couldn't see at first. She wiped it away from her eyes, and that was when she heard the strangest sound.

Dawson Clements was laughing! He was leading his horse to more solid ground, his own clothes splattered with mud, and his high, black boots caked with the brown, unforgiving pudding.

At first Clarissa was furious. The man was laughing at *her!* How dare he! Now the tears really did come, and she fought them wildly. Dawson stopped walking and looked up at her and burst into more laughter, a rich, deep sound. Clarissa was able to control her tears only because it suddenly occurred to her that never once had she seen Dawson Clements do more than barely crack a smile. To see him laughing was astonishing indeed!

"Mrs. Graham, I'm truly sorry," he told her before laughing more. "But that's the funniest sight I've seen in a long time."

Clarissa held her chin high. "You distracted me, Mr. Clements. That's the only reason I fell," she insisted. "And I could have gotten up by myself. You didn't need to play the rescuer."

His laughter calmed to a grin. He stood closer, keeping one hand on his horse's neck. "I suppose you'd rather I let the next couple of oxen walk on you and shove you even deeper into the mud?" Then he sobered completely. "I probably just saved your life, ma'am. A thank-you would be nice."

Their gazes held a moment, and he smiled again. With mud splattered on his face, his teeth looked whiter than ever. Suddenly Clarissa thought that if it took her falling facefirst into the mud to bring out the lighter side of Dawson Clements, maybe it was worth it. She couldn't help smiling herself, then.

"Thank you, Mr. Clements."

"You're welcome, Mrs. Graham." He folded his arms authoritatively. "And while we're out here all alone, why don't you tell me the truth about your husband? It might be important. Back in St. Louis you mentioned that he wasn't dead. He's not trailing us, is he? Are you running from him?"

She lost her smile. "Far from it. *He* ran away from *me*, Mr. Clements, with another woman, a supposedly Christian woman I'd considered a friend, no less. I never saw him again. He had the divorce papers delivered to me, since he was too much of a coward to bring them himself."

She watched his eyes and saw no change, for good or for bad.

"We owned a successful supply store in St. Louis that had been my father's," she added. "My kind husband sold that out from under me and left me practically penniless. Apparently the supply store was the main reason he married me." Why had she suddenly found it so easy to tell him? "And if you don't want a divorced woman on your wagon train, I'll just fall back and travel with someone else."

He studied her a moment. "Why would any man leave a woman like you and a gorgeous little girl like Sophie?"

Clarissa was a bit astounded by the remark, having expected something derogatory. "I don't know. You would have to ask him, but I have no idea where he can be found." How could all that laughter suddenly turn to so much pain? "Have I answered all your questions, Mr. Clements?"

He turned to look ahead, noticing that Michael was coming toward them on one of his draft horses, leading another one with him. Dawson looked back at Clarissa, then reached up and lifted her down from the horse. Clarissa couldn't help but appreciate the feel of his strong hands about her waist, and she realized then that he'd carried her from the mud in just one arm, almost like a sack of potatoes. What a comical sight that must have been, and what a strong man he was.

"You answered them honestly," he told her. "That's all that matters. And no one else needs to know your true situation. Personally, it makes no difference to me, other than I have this strong desire to beat the daylights out of the man who left you and Sophie. He has no idea what a blessing he had."

Clarissa softened even more. "That's a nice thing to say, Mr. Clements. Thank you."

Their gazes held a moment longer, and Clarissa was feeling things she'd rather not feel. Then Dawson put the reins of his horse into her hands. "Don't be so unwilling to ask for help next time," he said. "Take my horse and ride on ahead. Michael and I will get your oxen and wagon out of this mess. When you reach the others you can wade into the river and wash off all that mud."

He grinned again and left her, and Clarissa watched after him as he waved down Michael. She could still hear his laughter, and it struck her again how very unusual it sounded, coming from a man like Dawson Clements. Before that she would have guessed he didn't even know how to laugh.

"Who are you, Dawson Clements?" she muttered. "Where have you been in life, and where are you going?" If she asked him those questions aloud, no doubt he would brush her off like a pesky fly.

Chapter Eleven

❧

"He laughed?"

Carolyn's eyes were so wide that Clarissa had to chuckle. How odd that the fact that someone had laughed could draw such a reaction of astonishment. "Yes," she answered. "Dawson Clements actually laughed, and not just a chuckle."

Clarissa, Carolyn and Michael sat around a campfire relaxing after the long day of getting all the wagons through or around the mud and ready for the river crossing in the morning. Lena and Sophie were already sleeping, and the camp was relatively quiet, with other families working or talking around their own campfires. Clarissa actually felt compelled to keep her voice down so others wouldn't know they were talking about Dawson Clements.

"At first I was furious with him for laughing at me," Clarissa continued. "But then it struck me that the man was actually laughing heartily. He has a wonderful laugh, very deep and genuine. And he's so handsome when he smiles like that."

"Is he now?" Michael asked with a glint in his eye.

Clarissa suddenly realized how the remark sounded, and she hoped the firelight wasn't bright enough to reflect the red she felt coming into her cheeks. She rolled her eyes. "I didn't mean that the way it sounded."

"Sure you didn't."

"Really! It was just such a surprise to see a smile and hear laughter from a man who's normally so serious and grumpy."

Michael chuckled as he poked at the fire with a stick. "Well, Clarissa, I'll tell you something I truly believe, and that is God put us on Dawson Clements's wagon train for a purpose. And He has a purpose for Mr. Clements, too. I believe God is trying to get through to him, through us, all of us, but mostly through you, Clarissa."

Clarissa ran a hand through her long hair, which she'd left undone so it could dry out before she wrapped it back into a bun. "What on earth could I do for the man?" she asked.

"You've already started doing something," Michael answered. "You made him laugh, didn't you? I have a feeling that was quite an accomplishment."

She shrugged. "It certainly wasn't intentional, I can assure you. I was so mad at him before I fell, even madder *after* I fell! I felt so humiliated. I certainly was not trying to make him laugh, especially at me."

"God had a hand in it, I'm sure. He's got something in mind for you, too, Clarissa, and I have a sneaking suspicion Dawson Clements has something to do with that."

Clarissa sighed, adjusting a blanket she'd laid over her lap. "You're a preacher, not a matchmaker, Michael Harvey. You had better stick to your calling."

"Oh, but I am. This is part of it. I've been praying for the both of you, and look what's happened."

"Oh, *nothing* has happened! I fell into the mud, and he laughed at me. *That's* what happened. None of it means anything, and if you're suggesting I am interested in that ornery, cloud-covered man, I'm *not!*" She sobered. "I'm not interested in *any* man—not now, and maybe not ever, after what Chad did to me. I don't think I could ever love or give of myself that way again, let alone trust any man again."

"You trust me, don't you?"

"I'm not *married* to you."

Michael chuckled. "But surely you see how devoted I am to Carolyn," he told her, giving his wife a loving glance. "There *are* other good men out there, Clarissa. You're so very young, and little Sophie needs a father."

Clarissa shook her head. "Surely you aren't suggesting that someone like Dawson Clements is the answer. He's hardly every woman's dream, with that bossy attitude and crusty nature. The man has a huge chip on his shoulder that would take a bull moose to knock off, let alone the fact that he is obviously un-Christian to the point of practically being a heathen. He apparently would rather befriend a murderer than a preacher."

"And eventually we are going to find out why that is," Michael answered. "Before this trip is over I will find a way to bring light into that man's eyes."

Carolyn, who sat beside Michael on a log, reached over and took hold of one of his hands. "I just hope he doesn't end up punching you right in the face for trying," she told him.

Michael chuckled, kissing her cheek. "We'd best be retiring. Tomorrow will be a long day, I'm sure, getting animals and wagons and children and all of us across the river with only one ferry raft."

"And the Cherokee who run the ferry service will be quite rich by the time we're done," Carolyn suggested as she rose.

"It's ridiculous what they charge, and they know they have us over a barrel."

"Which is why they can get away with it," Clarissa commented, also rising.

"Let's pray before retiring," Michael suggested.

Clarissa walked closer, and the three of them bowed their heads. Michael prayed for safe passage across the Kansas River tomorrow, then added a prayer for Dawson Clements.

"May he laugh again, Lord Jesus, for laughter is a balm for the broken heart. Please continue to guide us in helping Mr. Clements by putting Your words into our mouths and making us say the right things. Keep him safe and well, Father, and we pray the same for our little Lena and little Sophie. In Christ's name, Amen."

Clarissa echoed her *Amen*, and she and Carolyn embraced before Carolyn left for the wagon where Lena slept. Michael left to bed down in his wagon, and Clarissa made for her own. Just as she rounded the end of the wagon to climb inside, she gasped when Dawson Clements appeared out of the shadows. "Mr. Clements!"

He stepped closer, and because of the darkness she could not read his eyes. "Thank you for making me laugh today," he told her quietly.

"What?"

"Do you know how long it's been since I laughed?"

His appearance and the admission took her by complete surprise. "I—I suspect it's been a *very* long time."

"I'm sorry it seemed I was laughing at you. I know you were trying your best and trying to do it all on your own. I admire that about you, Mrs. Graham. What you're doing takes a lot of courage."

She folded her arms. "For a woman without a husband?"

By the moonlight she saw him grin. "Yes, for a woman without a husband. But trips like this take courage even for women with husbands along. In fact, most of them are going *because* of their husbands, not because they truly want to go. You, on the other hand, are going of your own accord. That takes guts."

Why was he here telling her these things? What should she make of it? "I suppose I should thank you, Mr. Clements, since that sounds like a compliment. However, I'm not so sure I'm all that courageous, since I'm more determined to leave certain things behind than to strike out for someplace new. You asked me earlier today if I was running from my husband. I guess in a way I am doing just that—running from painful memories and the hurt of rejection and abandonment. And I'm leaving familiar places so that my daughter won't have to suffer teasing and hear lies about her mother and father."

He leaned closer, resting one hand on the wagon gate. He was close enough for Clarissa to catch the scent of leather and fresh air and a bit of what was simply Dawson Clements. A rush of womanly feelings swept through her that made her back off a little.

"I know about abandonment and rejection, Mrs. Graham. You and I have more in common than you might think."

He was trying to talk to her! If Michael was right that God wanted to use her to help this man, what on earth should she say? He was the type that one wrong word could bring back that dark side that was not a pleasure to be around.

"I wish you would share some of the reasons with me, Mr. Clements, but of course your personal affairs are not my business. I am glad you came by, though. I wanted to thank you again for helping me today and not screaming at me for my inadequacies."

He actually chuckled. "There is nothing inadequate about you, Mrs. Graham. I am thinking you're the finest woman I've come across in a long time. I know I seem pretty ornery, but my goal is to make sure I get all of you to Montana safely, and since the army is all I've ever known up to now, I tend to bark orders and accept no nonsense. It isn't aimed just at you."

Clarissa smiled. "I understand, Mr. Clements."

"And please don't be too afraid or embarrassed to ask for help when you truly need it."

"Thank you. I will keep that in mind."

He nodded, then just stared at her a long, quiet, tense moment. Clarissa could tell he was thinking of saying more, but he didn't. For a brief, almost terrifying moment, she even thought he was considering kissing her. The realization caused her to freeze against the wagon gate, especially when she caught a light scent of whiskey on his breath. Although he didn't appear flat-out drunk, she suspected it had taken a few swigs of the demon brew for this man to have the courage to come here and say the things he'd said. Now she worried that the firewater in his blood might give him bigger ideas.

"Good night, Mr. Clements," she said, deciding he'd better leave. Yet part of her didn't want him to go at all.

"Good night, Mrs. Graham."

After he was a few steps away, Clarissa called out to him.

"Yes, ma'am?" He turned to look back at her.

"Speaking of asking for help, do you have any suggestions for—for feet that hurt so bad you'd like to cut them off?"

"Well, I—" He broke into laughter again, that wonderful, hearty laugh that literally made him seem an entirely different man. He stepped closer again. "I'm sorry, but it's the way you said that." He laughed again, and Carolyn called out from her wagon.

"Clarissa? What's going on over there? Is that Mr. Clements?"

"Yes," Clarissa called back, keeping her eyes on Dawson.

"Everything is fine."

Dawson tipped his hat. "Thank you again for a good laugh. No offense meant."

Now Clarissa had to laugh. "None taken."

"And I do have an answer for your feet. Is Mrs. Harvey suffering the same problem?"

"Yes, in fact, she is."

"Then tomorrow I will bring both of you something that will help."

He turned and vanished like a shadow. Clarissa stood there for a moment to collect herself. Mr. Dawson Clements continued to surprise her with his mystifying ability to change moods as readily as a chameleon could change its colors, although she had no doubt that whiskey had played a role in the Dawson Clements she'd just talked to. She found herself wondering what the man was really like. Which Dawson Clements was the *real* Dawson Clements— the bossy, grouchy, demanding one who hated preachers and beat up men who hit their children; or the soft-spoken, apologetic man she'd just talked to; or the robust, almost jolly man who'd laughed so hard when she fell in the mud, as well as just now? Did it always take whiskey to get him to open up even a little? And why had he made a point to come and talk to her alone tonight? He could have come forward when she was sitting with Michael and Carolyn.

She finally found her legs and climbed into the wagon to nestle beside Sophie. She kissed her daughter's hair, and Sophie sleepily said, "I love you, Mommy."

"Love you, too," Clarissa answered, pulling Sophie into her arms. She wished Carolyn had not heard Dawson laugh, although everyone in camp had probably heard him. Now Carolyn knew he'd been here talking to her, and she and Michael would both be full of questions in the morning. She didn't feel like being teased about something that was becoming much too serious a matter. Worse, what might the other travelers be thinking?

Chapter Twelve

❧

May 11, 1863

Clarissa tied Sophie's slat bonnet, determined that her daughter's fair complexion would not be destroyed by the prairie sun. The hats also provided wonderful relief from the sun's glare, and she wore one herself during all daylight hours, as did most of the women along the journey.

Today would be exciting but long. All wagons would first be floated across the river one by one. Clarissa would have her job cut out for her helping Michael tend the eighteen oxen, two draft horses and Trudy the cow along with her calf, while Carolyn's job today would be to keep watch on the two girls and take the ferry across with them.

"You and I will take turns going across and coming back until we get all the animals across," Michael told her, handing her the leather straps that were buckled to the bridles of the two draft horses. "On the other side young Stuart Clymer will help watch those we deliver over there."

Neither Michael nor Carolyn had asked one question this morning about Dawson Clements having been at her wagon last night, something Clarissa deeply appreciated. Michael Harvey always seemed to know when to talk and when to say nothing. She suspected he'd told Carolyn not to bother her about the visit. Clarissa could just hear the man telling his wife that Clarissa would tell them about it in her own good time. She had to smile at the suspicion that Michael feared pressuring her might disrupt something good that was happening between her and Clements.

The trouble was, she had no idea if last night meant anything at all, either good or bad. If she'd not caught the scent of whiskey on Dawson Clements's breath, she might make more of his visit, but she'd grown up being told that whiskey was a demon drink and made men do things they would not normally do, making them feel brave when they really were not, and stirring sinful desires in them. Thank goodness she did not know firsthand if that was true or not. Neither her father nor Chad drank a drop, one of the few good points she could score for Chad Graham. At the moment she wondered if a drink now and then would have been much less a sin than cavorting with another woman. She thought about Stanley Swenson, a shoemaker across the street from her father's store in St. Louis. Everyone knew Mr. Swenson liked to tip a bottle fairly often, but he was a friendly man, a hard worker and devoted husband with six children. Drinking now and then seemed hardly a sin at all for men like him. It seemed to her that it was a man or a woman's heart that mattered, the love and devotion they carried there.

She looked up then to see the man riding toward her, carrying something.

Walk by Faith

"Hi, Mistoo Clement," Sophie called to him, waving.

"Hello there, Sophie," he answered with a smile. "I brought you something."

"Me?" The girl clapped her hands, and Clarissa walked closer as Dawson dismounted, but he was looking only at Sophie as he handed her a pair of small, knee-high moccasins.

"Indian shoes!" she said.

Dawson sobered slightly when he looked at Clarissa, then handed her a bigger pair of the moccasins. "You wanted something for sore feet," he told her. "No one knows better the best kind of shoes for walking on rough ground and through weeds and thickets than Indians. You wear these, and your feet will feel a lot better. And the knee-high legs will protect you from scratches and bruises," he added.

Clarissa took the moccasins as Carolyn and Michael both approached.

"Are you sure it's proper to wear these?" Clarissa asked, looking over the fringed and beaded footwear.

"Well, ma'am, I would hope you've learned by now that out here properness and protocol don't much matter. It's practicality and survival that matter, and those moccasins fit both needs. Besides that, who's going to see them under your long skirts?"

She met his eyes, seeing a hint of the dark cloud there again. "Well, then, thank you very much, Mr. Clements. This was very thoughtful of you. I wasn't sure you would even remember."

"What's this?" Michael spoke up before Dawson could reply. "Are we dressing like Indians now?"

"Just footwear for the women and little girls," Dawson answered, remaining sober as he handed more moccasins to Carolyn. "A pair for you, ma'am, and for little Lena. Mrs. Graham told me last night you both had sore feet. I got these from the Indian trading post down by the river. They will be much more comfortable than leather shoes." He turned to Michael. "And, Mr. Harvey, wearing these will help protect the women and little girls from scratches and snakebites."

"Well, now, Mr. Clements, that's very kind of you. What do we owe you for these?"

"Don't worry about it. Just make sure the women and girls wear them for their own protection." Dawson turned to Clarissa. "Will you step away with me for a moment?"

Glancing at a grinning Carolyn and Michael, she felt her face redden a little as she turned back to Dawson. "Certainly." She walked closer to her wagon, and Dawson followed. He folded his arms and remained quite serious.

"Mrs. Graham, I'm sorry for coming over to your wagon last night with you standing there alone. If anyone saw me, which they most likely did after hearing me laugh, they might get the wrong idea, you being alone and all."

"I thought the same thing, Mr. Clements, but I'm not going to worry about it. I haven't noticed anyone treating me any different."

"Even so, I don't want to cause you to suffer stares and gossip. Last night I was—well, not drunk, mind you, but I'd imbibed somewhat, and whiskey can cause a man to be, well, a little unwise, I guess you'd say."

"So I've been told," she answered. "But you were a gentleman and did absolutely nothing wrong. I hope you were serious about the things you told me—about feeling free to ask for help—and how it felt good to laugh."

He rubbed at the back of his neck, appearing very uneasy. "Well, it did, ma'am, and I meant what I said. I just want you to know that won't happen again, coming around at night like that. I mean no disrespect, and from now on I won't show you any more attention than anyone else. I think it's best that way."

"Yes, it probably is best," she answered. "I appreciate your thinking about my welfare, so to speak. And thank you again for the moccasins. I will wear them and see if it's true that they are better than leather shoes."

He tipped his hat. "Ma'am." He walked away then, leaving Clarissa full of questions and doubts. Apparently he'd woken up this morning angry with himself for showing her his softer, vulnerable side.

"And you do have one, Mr. Clements," she said softly.

"How you hate to show it."

He mounted his horse and rode ahead to begin directing the river crossing.

"Mommy, look!" Sophie was already sitting on the ground holding up the moccasins. "Put them on me, Mommy!"

Clarissa smiled and walked over to kneel down and unbutton the girl's worn leather shoes so she could remove them.

"My, my, how thoughtful of Mr. Clements," Carolyn said with a gleam in her eyes.

"Carolyn, mind what I told you this morning," Michael told her. "Don't be teasing Clarissa. Let God work in His own way."

Clarissa looked up at him. "I'm not so sure that God was working at all last night, Michael. I smelled whiskey on Mr. Clements's breath. It's more likely it was the whiskey working on the man than any divine intervention."

Michael chuckled. "Perhaps. But then whiskey can cause a man to speak the bold truth when he ordinarily would not. You know of course that my Carolyn is dying to know just what he told you."

Clarissa pulled the small moccasins over Sophie's feet and legs. "There. How's that?" She helped the girl to her feet.

"They feel good, Mommy! Put Lena's on," she said excitedly.

Lena came and sat down in front of Clarissa, and Carolyn handed Clarissa the other pair of small moccasins. "You're not going to say anything more?" she asked Clarissa.

"Maybe this evening. There is just too much to do right now," she answered. "Put on your moccasins, Carolyn." Clarissa was beginning to feel like a fool for being rather flattered by Dawson's visit last night, for lying awake half the night thinking about him—wondering about him—wishing she could find a way to break down the wall he kept built around himself. He seemed to be suffering so on the inside, but it was absolutely stupid of her to care. Her emotions were in terrible condition because of Chad. She would have to watch out more for her heart and feelings on this trip than for her physical well-being.

She removed her shoes and pulled on her own moccasins, and to her dismay they were even more comfortable than Dawson Clements had claimed they would be. He was absolutely right. Indians certainly did know the best way to dress. She couldn't help wondering about the loose Indian tunics she'd seen some Indian women wear. They had to be more comfortable and practical than white women's corsets and camisoles and slips and stockings and formfitting dresses.

She stood up and walked around, getting a feel of her new "shoes." "These are wonderful," she told Carolyn, who was in turn getting a feel of her own moccasins.

"Yes, they are." Carolyn walked closer, grasping Clarissa's arms. "Quick, before we get involved with the river crossing! What happened last night? What was Dawson Clements laughing about this time?"

Clarissa gently pushed her away with a warning look. *Nothing* happened. He simply came over to apologize for laughing at my fall in the mud, and to thank me for making him laugh. He said it felt good. As he left I told him my feet were so sore I'd like to cut them off, and that's what made him laugh again. And like I said, he'd been drinking, Carolyn, so none of it meant a thing. This morning he apologized for that, too, and he said he would never again visit me after dark like that. He's afraid it could cause problems for me with the others on the train, and I completely agree. So the matter is settled, and none of it means anything at all, so don't look at me like that."

"Like what?"

"You know what I mean. Come on. You take the girls and get them across and I'll help Michael with the oxen. Maybe you can take Trudy and the calf with you and the girls. That will help."

Carolyn breathed a sigh of obvious disappointment. "I was so hoping we—you at least, were starting to get through to Mr. Clements."

"Well, I'm not—and none of us has any business caring one way or another about the man. Let's turn our attention to getting ourselves to Montana and just quit talking about him, all right? I doubt he will as much as give us the time of day after this, and I don't want to talk about it anymore."

Clarissa walked up to Michael and took the reins of the draft horses again. "Let's get the oxen down to the river."

Michael gave her a serious look. He was so short that he was able to look her straight in the eyes. "You know of course that it's impossible for you to tell a good lie."

Clarissa couldn't help but break into a smile.

Chapter Thirteen

May 20, 1863

The river crossing took a full day, and thankfully, after that the weather improved greatly, with warmth and sunshine helping dry out the muddy places farther along the trail.

Clarissa paged backward to reread her diary account of falling in the mud. Secretly, she liked reading it because it reminded her of when Dawson Clements behaved like the rest of the wagon train and actually laughed. Now, since telling her he would not allow any further conversations or special attention, he'd kept his word.

Why did she wish he had not?

She set the diary aside and climbed out of the wagon, thinking again how grateful she was for the moccasins Dawson gave her. They still felt wonderful on her feet, the triple-hide soles buffering her feet from stones and the high legs protecting her shins from scratches and bruises. Her feet and legs finally felt stronger. She was growing more adjusted to the long daily walks and the daily chores of hitching and unhitching teams, cooking over campfires, loading and unloading supplies daily for meals and feeding the chickens and livestock, hauling water and finding ways to at least wash the dust from her face and keep Sophie clean.

Nothing about this trip so far had been easy. She could already see that she could manage as long as the weather cooperated and she and Sophie and the animals stayed healthy, but a change in either situation could cause big problems. She'd found a way to keep netting around Sophie at night to protect the child from being eaten alive by the pesky insects, which would start biting as soon as supper was finished and the sun was nearly set. People mingled and talked—except for Dawson Clements, who as usual was camped in a tent several yards beyond the circle of wagons.

Michael and Carolyn walked off to join another couple they'd befriended, the Buettners. Their three-year-old daughter, Ruth, and their eight-year-old daughter, Elizabeth, played with Lena and Sophie often, the girls darting under and around wagons now as they played hide-and-seek. The Buettners' six-year-old son, Raymond, was off playing with other boys, and Walt Clymer was strumming on a banjo, his teenage son greasing the wheel axles of their wagon.

People talked and laughed and visited. Clarissa had stayed in her wagon to make her daily diary entry, and now, watching the others, a keen loneliness brought an ache to her insides. With everyone else part of a couple, she suddenly felt like an outsider, in spite of Michael and Carolyn's kindness.

Walt Clymer began strumming a tune to the rhythm of a waltz, and the newlyweds, Robert and Jenny Trowbridge began dancing to the tune. People smiled and clapped, and then two other couples joined in, turning to the simple banjo music while others watched and laughed and talked, enjoying a chance to relax for a short while before retiring and then waking up to another long, arduous day of chores and walking.

"Would you like to dance, Mrs. Graham?"

Clarissa turned to see Haans Buettner's brother, Eric, one of two single men on the wagon train besides Dawson and his grizzly old guide. She guessed Eric to be around thirty, and he was neither handsome nor ugly, a sturdy German man who was hardly any taller than Clarissa.

No, she didn't want to dance with him, but she did not have the heart to turn him down. Still, she worried how it might look if she accepted his request. She graciously agreed, and Eric turned rather clumsily to the music.

"I'm not so good at this," he told her.

"You're doing fine, Mr. Buettner."

"You can call me Eric," he told her with a strong German accent. "But I will call you Mrs. Graham. It's only proper."

Clarissa found herself hoping Walt would not play the tune for too long. She nodded in agreement, looking away from Eric's eyes so he would not get any wrong ideas, which she feared he might already have because she was a "widow." Neither seemed to know what to say to each other, so they danced silently, and after another turn Clarissa noticed him—Dawson Clements—standing near a wagon, watching her.

What was he thinking? Why did it bother her to be seen dancing with a single man? Why did she wish it was Dawson Clements who'd offered a dance? Then again, she doubted he'd ever danced a day in his life. After all, dancing was a joyful act, and Dawson Clements had no idea how to be joyful.

Now Michael and Carolyn started dancing, looking rather comical with Michael's head coming only to Carolyn's shoulder. Everyone was having a good time—everyone but Clarissa, who could not keep herself from glancing at Dawson whenever she got the chance. With the setting sun at his back, he was little more than a dark, shadowy figure. Between that and the way his wide-brimmed hat was pulled down, Clarissa could not see his face. Was he smiling or frowning? Did he approve or disapprove of her dancing with Eric Buettner? Why did it matter to her?

She had to stop this nonsense. She had to start praying more, beg God to show her what He wanted of her. If the Good Lord meant that there be something more serious between her and Dawson Clements, she wished He would give her some kind of sign, show her the way. Either that, or help her stop thinking and wondering about the man and get on with her life. God knew better than anyone that she was far from ready or willing to care about anyone of the male species. She wasn't sure she could ever again survive the kind of pain Chad Graham had caused. Maybe all He wanted of her was to help Dawson Clements find the saving grace of Jesus Christ and learn how to be happy.

Her thoughts were suddenly interrupted when there came a scream from the direction of where the girls were playing. Instant panic filled Clarissa when she heard Sophie yell for her mommy. She tore away from Eric Buettner to run and see Dawson Clements had already reached the girls and was bent over little Ruth, who lay on the ground screaming at the top of her lungs.

Clarissa grabbed Sophie into her arms, embracing her tightly. "Sophie, what's happened? Are you all right?"

"A snake bit Ruth." Sophie sniffled.

"Oh!" Clarissa hugged her tight. "It didn't bite you, too, did it?"

"No, Mommy. It crawled away in the grass."

Michael and Carolyn reached them, Carolyn sweeping Lena into her arms. Clarissa kissed Sophie and handed her to Michael to hurry over to where sweet, chubby little Ruth lay being consoled by her panic-stricken mother while Dawson studied two little red marks on the girl's wrist.

"I saw the snake slither away," Dawson said in concern. "It was a rattler."

Ruth's crying quieted as her eyes rolled up, and she appeared to pass out.

"Do something," Florence Buettner screamed. "She'll die!"

Clarissa knelt beside Dawson. "We have to try to suck out the venom."

"I know." He reached toward his belt and pulled a large hunting knife from a sheath hooked there. Florence screamed and wept as he deftly sliced an X across the bite marks. Clarissa knelt beside Florence, putting an arm around the woman while Dawson began sucking out blood and venom from Ruth's wrist, spitting it out on the ground. Over and over he repeated the rescue attempt as a crowd gathered. Peter Burkette demanded to know what Dawson was doing.

"He's sucking out the venom," Clarissa answered. "It's the only thing he can do for now. Someone get some whiskey to clean the wound when he's done."

"Are you sure?" Haans Buettner asked.

"Yes. I'm a nurse, Mr. Buettner. And since the bite is on her wrist rather than her foot or ankle—" Her voice caught in her throat. Such a pretty little girl! This could have been Sophie! "With her so small, the venom will reach her brain much more quickly." She looked up at the Buettners, swallowing back her own tears. "You'll have to pray very hard."

"Keep her head elevated," Dawson said, spitting more venom.

A sobbing Florence lifted the child's head more.

"I wish we had some moss," Clarissa commented. "Sometimes it helps draw out the poison."

"Good idea," Dawson answered.

Clarissa looked around the crowd. "Someone go to the river and see if you can find moss growing on anything or on the ground. Look around the trees there."

"I'll go," Eric, the girl's uncle, offered, running off.

"I'll help," added Walt Clymer, a huge man who lumbered away like a plow horse.

"Ruthie, my Ruthie," Florence lamented. The stout, plain woman's body shook with sobs. "What would I do without my baby?" She leaned down and kissed the little girl's cheek.

Wanda Krueger came running with whiskey and a cloth bandage. Dawson wiped at his mouth with the sleeve of his calico shirt he wore, then took the whiskey and dumped some over the wound. Little Ruth gave no reaction. Dawson then rinsed his mouth with some of the whiskey and spat it out, then drank some down before handing back the bottle and wrapping the wound with the cloth. Clarissa saw a strange terror in his eyes.

"If someone finds moss we'll unwrap this and cover the wound with the moss." He glanced at Clarissa. "You were right. The Indians use moss on wounds to help healing, especially for drawing out puss or poison." He got up and lifted the girl, handing her to Haans while Clarissa helped Florence to her feet.

"Put her in your wagon with plenty of pillows under her head so she's elevated," Dawson told Haans. "That helps a little as far as keeping too much poison from going to the brain."

Haans carefully took the girl into his arms, the sturdy German's eyes filling with tears.

"I don't know what else to tell either of you," Dawson said to Haans and Florence. "Right now it's a matter of waiting. We'll know by morning if she's going to be all right."

Florence pulled a handkerchief from her apron pocket and broke into heavy sobbing. Wanda Krueger put an arm around her and led her to the Buettner wagon, and the crowd went on their way, the happy dancing they'd previously enjoyed now ended with an air of gloom.

Dawson turned to Clarissa. "Thanks for your help," he told her.

Clarissa wiped at tears. "I didn't do much. You did the right thing. I just can't help thinking how that could have been Sophie."

"We need to tell the children not to play under the wagons anymore," Dawson said. "Snakes like to crawl into the shadows of wheels and barrels and such."

Clarissa nodded. She met his gaze then, seeing his own sadness.

"Gather around, everyone," Michael called out then. "Let's all pray together for little Ruth. There is power in numbers." He waved his arms to call people together, and they circled around, leaving Dawson no choice but to stay in the circle. To leave would look as though he didn't care, and Clarissa suspected that was the only reason he stayed put as the others reached out and held hands to pray together. Daringly Clarissa reached for Dawson's hand, and she could tell he gave it to her quite unwillingly. The man did not want to pray; but he had no choice now but to stand there while Michael prayed ardently for the Lord Jesus Christ to spare the life of the Buettners' daughter. When everyone said their Amens, Dawson let go of Clarissa's hand.

"I'm going to see if I can find that snake," he said, quickly leaving. Clarissa suspected it was an excuse to get away from an uncomfortable situation.

"Look how he runs from Jesus and all things that concern the heart," Michael said quietly aside to Clarissa. "Mark my word, he'll do his own praying later that no one will see or know about. I saw the look of desperate worry in his eyes when he was sucking out that venom."

People quietly parted, and a few minutes later a gunshot made them all jump. Moments later Dawson came back to call out that the snake was dead. He ordered everyone to retire for the night. Clarissa walked past the Buettner wagon, and she could still hear Florence sobbing. She wondered how Dawson even knew he'd shot the right snake. Perhaps he'd simply shot the first rattler he'd spotted, just to relieve his own frustration over what had happened to little Ruth. The man seemed to have a penchant for feeling responsible for anything bad that happened to those around him.

Hear my cry, Oh God;
Listen to my prayer!
In despair and far from home I call to You!
Take me to a safe refuge, for You are my protector,
My strong defense against my enemies.

—*Psalms* 61:1-3

Chapter Fourteen

❧

May 21, 1863

"Little Ruth Buettner died last night." Clarissa stopped to wipe at tears that threatened to stain the fresh ink on today's page of her diary.

It was now two o'clock in the afternoon, and Dawson Clements had allowed the weary, grieving travelers to finally stop for a while. Today's trek covered country that was much hillier than they'd experienced up to now, hills that were high enough to be the first real strain on animals and people alike. Twice they'd crossed creeks that melt-off and spring rains had turned into something more like rivers.

We buried the little girl early this morning, and then Mr. Clements insisted we had to leave. It's been very hard, since most of us got little sleep for worrying about little Ruth and then listening to Florence Buettner's bitter weeping from 4:00 a.m. until the girl was buried. Florence had only a half hour to sit by her daughter's grave, then had to be dragged away sobbing wretchedly because we had to go. I pray for her tortured heart, and I beg God to please never let me have to face such a loss myself. Little Sophie is all I have, and it was my decision to make this trip. I could never live with the guilt if something happened to her.

She felt sick at the memory of the burial, poor Mrs. Buettner having to leave that little grave behind, never to see or visit it again. Michael, of course, read from the Bible and prayed, and he assured Florence that Ruth was not in the ground at all. She was sitting at the feet of the Lord, and her spirit would always be with Florence.

Clarissa shuddered at the memory of Florence's tirade against Dawson Clements as she fought those who pulled her from the grave site. She screamed that he was a cruel, heartless man for making her leave so soon. Then she shouted that Ruth's death was his fault. She claimed he should have warned them not to let the girls play under the wagon. Everyone knew it was just a grieving mother lashing out, but the look on Dawson's face was one of total devastation, a reflection of something that surely went deeper than Florence's accusation.

"Let's move!"

The words came from Dawson, who rode up and down the line of wagons, ordering them to get going again.

"We'll travel till dark this time."

Clarissa heard his horse ride past her wagon. She put away her diary and climbed out, her back and legs aching. Even though she'd grown more accustomed to the walking, this was the first day they'd encountered so many hills. So much climbing was a new exertion. She grimaced when she picked up Sophie to put her in Carolyn's wagon. She gave the child a hug and kiss first, hardly able to hug her enough since watching little Ruth being put into the ground.

Carolyn walked up beside her then, lifting Lena into the wagon. "I can't get over the sight of that lonely little grave," she told Clarissa. "Poor Mrs. Buettner. Michael tried talking to her a little while ago, but she just sits in their wagon and stares."

Clarissa looked up at her friend, whose brown eyes reflected her own grief. "I can't imagine losing Sophie or Lena like that," she told Carolyn. "But for Mrs. Buettner to blame Mr. Clements—" She shook her head. "Did you see the look on his face?"

"Yes. It was like he took her words to heart. Michael says it's natural for someone who's lost a loved one to try to blame someone else. Everybody knows this wasn't Mr. Clements's fault."

"Mommy, is Wooth all bettoo now?"

Clarissa turned to see Sophie and Lena both watching them with wonder in their eyes.

"Did Mrs. Buettner stop crying yet?" Lena asked.

Clarissa thought that the girls understood Ruth had been in the little homemade box that was buried this morning, but apparently neither girl grasped what had really happened.

"Ruth went to heaven to be with God," Carolyn told the girls. "Remember? I told you that He made her better, but she's going to stay with Him. She won't be back. That made Mrs. Buettner sad, but she understands that Ruth would rather be with Jesus now. Her mama will stop crying after a while."

They turned when Dawson rode back in their direction. "Let's get going, ladies. You can finish your visiting tonight."

"We'll be too sore and tired by then," Clarissa answered with a smile, hoping to wrestle a smile out of the man in return, but to no avail.

"If you want to get where you're going before the snow flies in the mountains, you'll have to put up with the hardships getting there," he answered coldly before riding off.

Clarissa looked at Carolyn. "I think he was referring more to burying loved ones than being tired and sore," she commented.

Carolyn nodded. "Let's just pray neither of us has to leave a little grave behind at any time on this trip, and that Mr. Clements gets over this himself." She gave Clarissa a hug and walked around to the front of her wagon to switch her oxen into motion. Clarissa did the same, and for the next several hours she forced her aching legs to keep moving, up and down more hills, climbing into the wagon seat and shouting and switching the oxen to get them to wade through yet another cold, deep creek.

Up and down the line of wagons, others shouted, and those leading cattle whistled and yelled. Wagon wheels creaked, cattle bellowed, horses whinnied, oxen snorted and the rooster atop Clarissa's wagon crowed once every couple of minutes. Everyone could hear Florence Buettner crying. The woman had insisted on staying out of sight inside the wagon, even though it caused more weight for the oxen that pulled it. She kept her other two children in there with her, and Clarissa thought how hard this must be on those little ones to know their little sister was gone and their mother was so horribly sad.

A pall of grief hung over all the emigrants, and Clarissa suspected each one of them was wondering if they would in turn have to bury any of their loved ones on this journey. What started out as an exciting adventure with minor hardship was beginning to turn into a long journey through an unforgiving land, with civilization falling farther and farther behind them.

By the time they circled the wagons for the night, the sun had nearly disappeared beyond the western horizon and there was barely enough light left by which to unhitch the teams. The girls had played hard jumping around inside Carolyn's wagon, and a couple of times they got out and walked and ran beside their mothers because they were bored. Because of that, both the children had already fallen asleep by the time they stopped to make camp, and the women decided not to wake them.

"I'll find a way to make room for myself," Carolyn told Clarissa. "I don't want them in there alone all night. If Sophie wakes up and wants you, I'll bring her over."

"Thank you, Carolyn, and let's not cook tonight," Clarissa suggested. "I'm too tired to even eat, but I know I should eat something. Let's heat coffee and just eat cold biscuits and dig some ham out of the larder."

Carolyn looked at Michael. "Is that all right with you, dear? If you'd rather have a full meal—"

"Ham and biscuits is fine," Michael told her. With a groan of exhaustion he sat down on a crate, making a remark about his weary bones. Clarissa knew his heart was heavy for Florence Buettner.

The women built a fire and heated coffee, day-old biscuits and some ham, all of them gobbling down their food quickly, anxious to go to bed. The women cleaned up and set the coffee away from the fire so it would not boil away overnight. There was enough left to heat in the morning.

Clarissa walked to her wagon and climbed inside, half falling into the feather mattress centered amid crates and trunks and sacks of food. She decided she would not even put on a nightgown. She was simply too tired, as much from the grief she'd experienced the night before and all day today as from the long walk.

"Mrs. Graham?"

Puzzled, Clarissa sat up and pulled aside the canvas at the back of the wagon. Dawson Clements stood there. "What is it, Mr. Clements? You said you wouldn't come to my wagon at night anymore."

"I know," he answered softly. "Just don't light a lantern."

"You haven't been drinking again, have you?"

"No, ma'am, although I find it very tempting, the way I'm feeling." He moved closer, resting his forearms on the top of the wagon gate so he could quietly talk directly inside the wagon. "I, uh, I'd like to ask you something."

Clarissa scooted closer, a little angry with Clements for seeking her out this way again just when she'd decided she was better off not giving him another thought. "Well, I may not have the answer, Mr. Clements, but I'm willing to listen."

He sighed with hesitation before continuing. "Do *you* think that little girl's death was my fault?"

Clarissa was flabbergasted at the question and the fact that he cared what she alone thought. "Of course not! And neither does anyone else, Mr. Clements. Mrs. Buettner is a grieving mother who wants to blame someone for her child's death. It's a way of trying to make ourselves feel better. I have a feeling she's just trying to avoid her own guilt for letting Ruth play unsupervised. In fact, I feel the same way. I should have been watching my baby girl more closely instead of dancing with Eric Buettner. That will never happen again."

"Which one? Not watching your little girl closely, or dancing with Eric Buettner?" he asked.

The question embarrassed her, and she was glad for the darkness, but she also saw the humor in the remark. "Both," she told him. She could feel him smiling then.

"I'm glad."

"Glad I don't blame you for Ruth's death, or glad I won't dance with Eric Buettner again?"

"Both," he said, joining in the teasing.

Clarissa was rather stunned at the answer. Was the man saying he was interested in her and didn't want her looking at another man? She wished he would explain himself so her emotions wouldn't be tossed in every direction every time he talked to her. "Why did you think I would blame you for Ruth's death?" she asked, deciding it'd be better to get off the subject of who she might dance with.

He paused a moment before answering. "It's a long story, but I was raised believing I was responsible for the deaths of my own parents. It's a horrible guilt to live with."

"Who on earth told you their deaths were your fault? How did they die?"

"In a fire. I started it accidentally, playing downstairs while they slept. I was eight years old. I ran out, scared, thinking they'd hear the noise and smell the smoke and get out by themselves." He swallowed before continuing. "They never came through the door. By the time I realized they needed help, the flames were too hot for me to go back inside. I just stood there in shock and watched the house burn down. I never heard a sound out of either of them. A neighbor found me standing there watching, and when I broke down sobbing that I had accidentally started the fire, he decided I was evil and must have set it on purpose. No one would have anything to do with me after that except a preacher who took me in—out of the kindness of his heart, he told others. But there was nothing kind about the man. He beat me regularly with a wide belt, saying that was the only way to beat the devil out of me."

"That's terrible! Surely you don't really believe it was your fault!"

"I don't know what to believe," he said, his voice now strained. "I only know that my life has been miserable since the night of that fire. I ran away at thirteen and joined the army because I didn't have any place else to go. I needed a bed to sleep in and food in my stomach. The army gave me both, certainly not the best, but I survived. Since then things have happened that make me wonder if I truly am cursed and if it's really true I can never be forgiven for that fire."

"Never be forgiven? By God? Did the preacher tell you that?"

"Practically every day of the five years I lived with him and his family."

Clarissa couldn't help reaching out and touching his arm. "That's not true, Mr. Clements. God is *very* forgiving, and *no* child is held accountable by God for anything he or she does before the age of twelve. Children are born naturally innocent, Mr. Clements. What happened was an *accident,* plain and simple, and you were only eight years old! You panicked and didn't know what to do."

Compassion swept through her when he put his free hand over hers. "A lifetime of guilt is not an easy thing to get over, Mrs. Graham. What Mrs. Buettner said today didn't help."

"Of course not. You need to pray about this, Mr. Clements. It's Michael you should be talking to, not me."

He stiffened and let go of her hand, pulling his arm away. "No."

"Just because he's a preacher? He's a wonderful man, Mr. Clements. He's nothing like that man who raised you. That man might have *claimed* to be a preacher, but I assure you, there wasn't a Christian bone in his body, the way he treated you. And God *is* a forgiving God. That's why He sent Jesus Christ to us, to die for our sins, so that by believing in Him, all sins are forgiven. You didn't do anything wrong. You have to stop blaming yourself and letting that guilt make you so angry and impatient and frustrated with life."

He paused, then suddenly announced, "I have to go. Thanks for the talk, and for not blaming me for that little girl's death. You'd better get some rest."

He disappeared. Clarissa peeked out from the canvas flap and couldn't hear a sound. She sat back down, feeling terribly frustrated. She would have liked to talk to him longer about God and prayer and forgiveness. She wished he would talk to Michael, who she believed could do a much better job than she could helping a man like Dawson Clements. Now she understood why he'd insisted parents not beat their children. Now she understood why he'd lit into that man who was beating his son. Now she understood why he hated preachers and turned away from prayer and talk of God. He'd grown up believing God was unforgiving, directing preachers to beat evil children. What else had happened in his life that left him feeling so unworthy of love and forgiveness and led him to believe perhaps he truly was evil in some way?

She lay down, realizing she'd have to tell Michael what she'd learned and ask him what she should tell Clements if he came to her again to talk. Why had he chosen *her* to spill out his story to? She remembered the feel of his big, strong hand over her own. The man had actually reached out to her. But why? How should she feel about that? Where was all this going, and did God have anything to do with it? Was she simply supposed to help the man find God again, or was there more to this situation? She was the last person to help someone else with their faith, when her own had been nearly destroyed when Chad left her. It had taken a long time for her to bother praying again, to trust God again. It was easy for her to tell someone else about faith and forgiveness, but what about her own faith? What about her own inability to forgive Chad?

A coyote yipped somewhere out on the prairie, and it reminded her of how far they still had to go. Dawson Clements's attentions were making this trip more difficult for her than all the bad weather and snakes and deep rivers could possibly make it.

Chapter Fifteen

❧

May 30, 1863

They reached the Platte with no more catastrophes, much to Dawson's relief. Throughout the long trek he worried about how difficult the trip was becoming for Clarissa Graham, but he did not visit her again alone. He was angry with himself for going to her a second time, let alone telling her something he'd never told another person in his entire adult life.

He couldn't even use the excuse this time of being drunk. What was it about that woman that made her so easy to talk to? Why did he think she would understand? Maybe because, like he'd told her, they had some things in common. She knew about rejection and abandonment and the inability to trust.

What interested him most was that what happened to her did not seem to have affected her faith in God. And now she'd planted the idea that God actually forgave a man's sins. She'd made him realize that forgiveness was what he wanted more than anything, a way to shake the awful guilt he'd lived with his whole life, as well as his hatred of Preacher Carter and all men who professed God's love, a love he'd doubted since his parents died in that fire.

He'd almost reached the point of abandoning God completely, until Sergeant Bridger asked him if he believed in God and heaven. As though God Himself heard the young man, He'd apparently decided to take Bridger then and there. Dawson still felt pain at the memory of the stunning way Bridger died—smiling and talking with him one minute, dead the next. Now he wondered if God meant for him to do something special with the money he'd inherited from Sergeant Bridger. It wasn't a huge sum, but it was enough to buy some of that land in Montana under the Homestead Act if he wanted, or to afford the equipment he'd need to look for gold.

He didn't deserve that money. In addition to being told he was responsible for his parents' deaths and then the death of little Ruth, he'd felt somewhat responsible for Bridger's death. If he'd been more alert, he might have noticed that Rebel sneaking up on them. He needed forgiving for the way he'd literally shot the face off that already-dying Confederate soldier. Ever since his parents' deaths, he'd experienced periods of uncontrollable rage, like the day he beat the father who was hitting his son with a belt.

All that and more were why he had no business letting himself become interested in a fine woman like Clarissa Graham. What did he know about loving a woman like that and taking care of her and a little girl? Even his Mexican wife had married him more for the prestige of marrying a gringo who could take her to America legally, than for love. Even a soldier's life was better than the way Estella had been living when he met her while stationed in Texas. He'd taken leaves to Mexico, where he'd found Estella working her young life away in a laundry.

He realized now that he'd married Estella more for companionship and to have a woman in his bed than out of love. Nothing in his marriage had taught him about real love and devotion—the kind of love a woman like Clarissa Graham would demand, especially after what her ex-husband had done to her.

It seemed true happiness would forever elude him. He'd hoped he'd find it when he quit the army and headed out on his own. Maybe he'd find gold in Montana and get rich. Maybe he could *buy* happiness. Trouble was, he'd met Clarissa Graham, and that woman was changing all his plans. She was beautiful. She was strong. She had courage. She was alone. She cared about people. She was raising a beautiful daughter by herself. She had a way of drawing him to her without even trying. He fought that feeling as hard as he could, and again he'd stayed away from the woman since that last time he visited her and told her things he had no business telling her.

He wanted that woman in every way he could think of. He wanted to touch her, hold her. He wanted to protect her, provide for her, be a father to that wonderful little girl. But experience told him he was a fool to be thinking such things. She probably wanted nothing to do with any man after what her husband did to her. Plus, nothing in his life had ever gone right for him. What made him think pursuing Clarissa Graham would be any different? He had no idea if she was even interested, other than to treat his wounds and maybe save his soul. If he fell in love with her, no doubt God would take *her* from him, too. It was time to stop fantasizing about

God and forgiveness and about making a life with Clarissa Graham. He had to face reality. He was not meant to live like ordinary men. He wouldn't even know *how* to live like that.

From a high bluff he glanced back at the travelers. Clarissa looked so small, walking bravely beside those big oxen, never complaining. The man who'd left her and little Sophie should be drawn and quartered.

Suddenly he spotted movement coming over a bluff to the left of the wagon train. Quickly he counted eight horses, being ridden fast and hard, headed for the wagon train. He could tell from here they were white men, and instinct told him they had no good intentions in mind. He turned and whipped his horse into a hard run to summon Zeb.

He cursed under his breath. All he'd thought about was trouble that might lie ahead. He'd given no thought to trouble that could be lurking behind them, but with the country at war, marauders, mostly Rebels, ranged everywhere in the south and the west, mostly looking for goods and supplies to furnish their men and their war efforts. At least that was their excuse, but there was no excuse for killing and pillaging innocent people.

Suddenly he heard gunshots. He crested another rise, then spotted Zeb. He pulled the six-shooter he wore at his waist and fired it into the air. Because of the bluffs that buffered them, Zeb probably had not heard the gunshots back near the wagon train. He signaled Zeb to ride back to him, and Zeb kicked his Appaloosa into a fast run.

"The train is being attacked," Dawson told him. "I saw about eight men riding hard toward them."

"Let's go!" Zeb said, kicking his horse into a hard gallop. "The wagons ain't camped far from the river. Let's ride back through the trees there so's they don't spot us. We'll give them what for!"

Dawson felt a rush of dread. Already he was attached enough to Clarissa Graham and her little girl to feel a real loss if something happened to them, and the urge to protect them surged stronger inside than any other emotion. He and Zeb charged over a hill, down the other side of it out of sight, into the trees along the river. A slight rise separated the wagon train from the river, and both men quickly dismounted and checked their ammunition as they retrieved their rifles. They scuttled up the hill and flattened themselves on the top of it.

Below them the marauders were circling the wagons shouting orders. Dawson noticed a woman lying on the ground. Could it be Clarissa? *Please, God, don't let it be her.* What had made him pray like that? He hadn't prayed in over twenty years!

"How's your aim?" he asked Zeb.

"Pretty good. I've shot Indians, bears and buffalo, as well as just huntin' rabbits and such. I ain't gonna miss and hit one of the emigrants, if that's what you mean."

Dawson leveled his rifle. "Count four wagons from the left. I'll take every bandit from there going left. You aim for the ones from there going right so we don't waste bullets on the same men. Once we start shooting, that will draw their attention away from the travelers. That should give our people time to take cover, maybe even grab guns of their own, although I'm not so sure any of them knows much about how to use one."

The bandits were shouting for the emigrants to throw certain supplies out of their wagons—potatoes, flour and such, and wrap them in blankets. A couple of the children were crying, and one man screamed for them to shut up.

Dawson took aim. "You ready?"

"Ready as I'll ever be." Zeb also took aim with his rifle.

"Fire," Dawson said quietly. He pulled the trigger, and the man he'd zeroed in on fell from his horse. He hated having to shoot toward the emigrants, but they had no choice. One of Zeb's victims also went down. Before the men could react, Dawson had shot yet another one from his horse. Zeb's shot missed, and they heard a loud ding when the bullet hit a pan hanging on the side of a wagon.

Women screamed and grabbed their children, ducking under wagons. One man jumped at one of the bandits but was kicked away.

Dawson fired again, hitting that intruder. "Five left," he told Zeb, who again fired his own gun.

"Now there's four," Zeb said gleefully.

"Let's get out of here!" someone shouted.

"Don't let them get away!" Dawson told Zeb. "They might come back with even more men!" He stood up and started down the hill, Zeb on his heels. He stopped and leveled his rifle at yet another bandit, who cried out and fell from his horse when Dawson's bullet caught him in the back.

"Three!" Zeb yelled. He took aim and fired. A bandit fell from his horse but got up and started running. Dawson took a second shot at him, and he went down with a scream.

The last two were now riding hard, almost out of rifle range. Zeb and Dawson both fired, and one more man went down. The last man finally disappeared over the ridge.

Supplies were scattered everywhere. Children were crying and men and women were running around, shouting to others and asking if they were all right.

Dawson knelt beside the woman who lay on the ground. He turned her over. It was Florence Buettner.

He moaned, thinking of her two remaining children and her husband. Just then Haans Buettner knelt on the other side of his wife, then leaned over and broke into tears.

"That was some shooting!" Ben Gobles exclaimed. "It's good you two got here when you did."

Dawson rose. "I didn't expect trouble to come up from behind. From now on I'll be more diligent in keeping an eye behind us as well as ahead of us."

"Some leader you are!" Peter Burkette came storming forward. "We could have all been killed!"

Dawson cast him an angry glare. "Maybe you'd like to be the one to ride at the back of this train and eat our dust, Mr. Burkette. Are you volunteering?"

Burkette stiffened. "Well—no. I—I don't have a horse."

"I can get you one!"

"Watching out for this train is not my job, Mr. Clements."

"That's right! It's *mine.* And I'm doing the best I can. If you don't want to help, then keep your mouth shut or I'll shut it for you!"

"You're doing a fine job, Mr. Clements."

Dawson turned to see a teary-eyed Preacher Harvey standing nearby. "That was great shooting. None of us could have done something like that."

Dawson stepped closer. "What is it? Has something happened to your wife or Mrs. Graham?"

Michael swallowed. "It's Sophie. She took a stray bullet when they first attacked us. She's in Clare's wagon."

Dawson felt as though someone had slugged him hard on his chest. He groaned. "Some of you keep an eye open in case they come back with more men," he ordered. "They might have given up, but we can't be sure!"

He headed for Clarissa's wagon, the lawyer's words ringing in his ears. Another disaster, and maybe he was to blame.

Chapter Sixteen

❧

Dawson found Clarissa and Carolyn both inside Clarissa's wagon, tending to a crying, terrified Sophie. A sniffling Lena sat at the end near the wagon seat, terror in her eyes.

"Come on out so I can get in there," Dawson told Carolyn. "Take Lena out of here."

A sobbing Clarissa looked at him with devastation in her eyes. "How did this happen? They came out of nowhere!"

Dawson helped Carolyn down, and she hurried around to lift Lena down from the front of the wagon while Dawson climbed inside. "Zeb and I got most of them," he told Clarissa. "One got away. I've told folks to circle the wagons, and Zeb rode after the one who escaped to do a little spying and see if there are more camped somewhere over the bluff."

Clarissa held Sophie close, a blood-soaked bandage on the girl's left arm, a lot of the blood also staining Clarissa's blue gingham dress. "I'm so glad you're here," she sobbed. "I've treated all kinds of wounds, but when it's your own daughter—" She couldn't finish.

"I know," Dawson answered, his heart aching for her. "I'm sorry, Mrs. Graham. I was only looking ahead for trouble, not behind."

She shook her head. "You couldn't have known. I'm just glad you and Zeb got here and shot most of them before they could do more harm. Poor Mrs. Buettner. I think they killed her."

"Let me look at Sophie's arm."

"I think it's a flesh wound. I don't think it broke the bone, but she's so terrified I can't get her to let me look at it good."

"Sophie." Dawson spoke her name. "It's Mr. Clements. Can I look at your arm?"

"It hoots," the girl said, her body jerking in sobs.

"Maybe I can fix it. Remember when I kept you from getting hurt by those horses back in St. Louis? Can I help you again? If you want your arm to get all better you have to let your mommy and I bandage it better."

Pouting, Sophie looked at him with big blue eyes that tore at his heart.

"I wouldn't want to live without my Sophie," Clarissa told him, leaning down to kiss the girl's tears. "It will be okay, sweetie. Please let us fix your arm. We can make it feel lots better."

"Okay," the girl answered in a tiny, pathetic tone that made Dawson want to hug her. In his army career he'd not had much chance to be around children, and her innocence stirred him. Being around her helped him start to believe what Clarissa had told him, that little children can't be held responsible for things they do in total innocence. Was there really hope he could be forgiven?

Carefully he unwrapped Sophie's upper arm and felt along the bone. She cried harder, but she didn't pull away. "You sure are a brave little soldier," he told her. "I've seen grown men cry over a wound like this, and they wouldn't let me touch them." He looked at Clarissa. "I agree. It's a flesh wound. We should wash it out with whiskey and wrap it tighter. As long as she doesn't get infection she should be fine, except for a scar, which I hate to see on such a pretty little thing." He sighed. "Give her to me and find some more bandages and some whiskey."

Clarissa met his eyes as he took Sophie. "Thank you," she told him.

"Don't thank me. If I'd been more alert this wouldn't have happened."

She wiped at her tears. "You've got to stop blaming yourself for every bad thing that happens to others, Mr. Clements. I don't blame you for this."

He pulled Sophie close, as she shook quietly, her crying now ended. "Lawyer Burkette does," he told her.

Clarissa dug into a small trunk and pulled out clean bandage material and a small bottle of whiskey. "Lawyer Burkette likes to pretend he knows everything. He's an arrogant man who doesn't like having to answer to anyone. It bothers him that someone other than himself is in charge, so he's looking for any excuse to call you out."

Dawson thought how beautiful Clarissa was even in her current disheveled state, her hair coming undone, her hazel eyes puffy and red from crying. He imagined how beautiful she would be with that rich auburn hair falling around bare shoulders. Don't be a fool, Clements!

"Here's the whiskey," she said. "Sophie, sweetie, this is going to sting, but after that your arm will feel better, I promise. Remember, Mommy is a nurse. I fix people's owies."

Quiet tears trickled down the sides of her face then as she lay face-up in Dawson's arms. "I'll be a bwave soldoo," she answered.

Clarissa and Dawson both grinned, but then Sophie screamed when the whiskey hit the open wound. Dawson held her tightly.

"It's okay, Sophie," he told her. "I remember how bad it hurt when your mommy put that stuff on my leg. Remember when I came to your house?"

"Yeah," the girl replied through sniffles.

Clarissa began wrapping the arm. "Once this is on nice and tight, you'll feel lots better," she told Sophie.

Dawson could only imagine how terrified she must have been to see her daughter shot. He could well imagine what a horror it would be for her to lose her little girl.

"I was so afraid it was worse than this when Mr. Harvey told me Sophie had been shot," he told Clarissa. In the confines of the wagon she was so close, the only thing between them being Sophie herself.

"How is she? Shall I come in and pray?" Michael Harvey was standing at the back of the wagon.

"Yes, do pray," Clarissa answered, "but don't come inside. There isn't room, and Mr. Clements seems to have a calming effect on Sophie. I want him to stay a few more minutes."

"It's just a flesh wound," Dawson told the man. "You'd be better off praying for Mrs. Buettner, and we'll need you to pray over all the graves when they're ready. Personally I wouldn't offer any prayers for those no-goods out there who did this, but I suppose you think everyone needs praying over, so do what you think is best, Mr. Harvey."

Michael nodded. "Thanks for helping with the little girl. She likes you, you know."

Michael left, and Clarissa and Dawson could hear him telling someone to get a shovel. "Let's get these men buried before dark so we can be on guard during the night."

Clarissa finished wrapping Sophie's arm. "Do you think they'll come back?"

"Hard to say. They were probably rebels looking for food and supplies. A lot of them are starting to get desperate. Zeb will be back by night with a report."

"You must be pretty good with that rifle."

"Sixteen years in the army requires it. When a pack of Indians are after your scalp, you learn to shoot straight."

Sophie was calm now. Clarissa smiled at his remark. "Do you think we'll have Indian trouble, Mr. Clements?"

"You never know. They're probably feeling pretty confident right now, what with half the western army involved in the war. Some forts have been completely abandoned. The Indians might think this is a good time to raise some he—uh, to do some raiding and such."

Clarissa tied off the bandage. "How's that, Sophie? Feel better?"

"A little." The girl nodded, then looked up at Dawson. "You my daddy now?"

The question astounded both of them.

"Sophie!" Clarissa exclaimed. "What on earth made you say that?"

"Mistoo Clement fixed me like a daddy would. I can tell. He's holding me like a daddy." She looked into Dawson's eyes. "I want a daddy like Lena has." She looked at Clarissa, all innocence. "Can Mistoo Clement be my daddy?"

Dawson cleared his throat nervously, and he saw color come into Clarissa's cheeks. "It's all right," he assured her. "She's just wanting a daddy. She doesn't understand what that involves."

Clarissa put her hands to her cheeks. "I'm so embarrassed. And so sorry."

"Don't be." Their gazes held a moment, and Dawson longed to tell her he'd like the chance to be Sophie's daddy, but poor Clarissa would probably be shocked and insulted and kick him out of the wagon. Still, there was something in her eyes that almost made him tell her how he was feeling.

No. He didn't deserve a woman like Clarissa Graham, or the happiness a little girl like Sophie could bring him, or children of his own.

Fearing Clarissa would read his thoughts, he looked down at Sophie. "Sophie, as long as we're on this trip, I'll be your *pretend* daddy, but I can't be around much, you know. I have to help everybody, not just you and your mommy."

"That's okay. Can I call you Daddy?"

Dawson frowned. "How about Dawson? That might be better."

The girl actually smiled. "Okay."

Dawson looked at Clarissa. "Why don't you call me Dawson, too? Mr. Clements is beginning to sound too formal, what with you fixing my leg and the couple of little talks we've had, and now this."

"Then you must call me Clare."

He smiled. "All right. And to make sure people don't get the wrong idea, I'll address Mr. Harvey as Michael and his wife as Carolyn, and start calling a few others by their first names."

Clarissa nodded. "Yes, we certainly wouldn't want the others to misunderstand."

"Right."

Again her big, beautiful eyes held his gaze. What was she trying to tell him? Did he dare think she had feelings for him that went beyond a simple friendship?

"Thank you again, Mr. —I mean, Dawson."

"I'm so sorry it happened at all, Clare." He looked down at Sophie, deciding he had to get out of this wagon. It was too painful being so close to Clare Graham. "Sophie, you lie very still now for a while. Try to go to sleep, will you? We'll camp right here the rest of the day and tonight. I don't want you jostled around in this wagon." He looked at Clarissa again. "Besides, we have some graves to dig." He scooted out from under Sophie and gently laid her into the comforter she used for a bed, then moved to the back of the wagon. "You'd better stay in here and rest yourself. Did you unload any of your supplies for those men?"

"I didn't have a chance because of Sophie."

"Good. Then I don't have to worry about looking for what belongs to you. I'll tell Carolyn to make you and Sophie something to eat."

"Thank you. You're a good man, Dawson. And this wasn't your fault. Believe that. Neither are the other things you blame yourself for. God loves you very much. He even loves those bandits, and if they asked His forgiveness, He would forgive them. There is nothing man can do that cannot be forgiven, Dawson. Remember that."

"Oh, I wouldn't be so sure of that, but it's a nice thought."

He gave her a smile and left, thinking how just minutes ago he was furious and terrified, shooting men down with not a thought to taking the lives of such scoundrels. But as soon as he climbed in that wagon with Clare Graham and little Sophie, he softened up like a biscuit soaked in milk. What was happening to him?

Trust in God at all times, my people.
Tell Him all your troubles, For He is our refuge.

—*Psalms* 62:8

Chapter Seventeen

❧

June 8, 1863

Haans Buettner left the wagon train, taking his remaining two children with him. He was simply too brokenhearted to continue the journey, for he'd planned to settle in Montana and build a new life with his beloved wife. Now that she and his little Ruth were both gone, he didn't have the heart to go on. He took Florence's wrapped body with him when he left, planning to find Ruth's grave and bury her mother beside her.

It was painful to watch the man leave them, and it reminded Clarissa how lucky she was that Sophie was alive. Eric Buettner decided to go on with the supply wagon and open his supply store as planned. After a matter of time, Haans would come back west, after the children had time to heal and get over their mother's and sister's deaths.

Zeb and Dawson both spent the next eight days after the attack riding ahead and behind the train, keeping watch both ways and staying in the saddle from dawn to dusk. Dawson was right in telling Sophie that she wouldn't see much of him, and Clarissa suspected he was glad for the excuse to stay away. Sophie's remark about wanting him to be her daddy had embarrassed him as well as herself, although there were moments when she could not help wondering how nice that might be, if Dawson Clements truly knew what he wanted out of life.

Sophie recovered well, thank goodness. The girl had begun talking about Dawson often, asking when he would stop and talk to her again. After having her own daddy walk out on her, Clarissa wondered how Sophie would handle it when this trip was over and Dawson Clements went his own way. She wasn't sure how she would feel about that herself. It was becoming more and more difficult to picture him riding out of her life, and that was a dangerous way to feel about a man.

They followed the Platte day after day, allowed to take one afternoon to wash some clothes in the river and take a halfday's rest. Clarissa could tell her clothes were beginning to hang on her. All the walking had caused her to lose weight. Most everyone else was looking the same, mostly tired and gaunt despite having enough food.

Most of the travelers had never done so much walking or worked so hard day after day. There were no front porches to sit on, no casual evening socials, no comfortable beds to sleep in, no tables to sit at, no way to wash or for a woman to fix her hair fancy or wear a pretty dress.

It had come to the point where no one much cared how they looked, and it had grown so hot that most of the women had given up wearing several underslips. Mosquitoes were becoming a huge problem, so much so that people seldom sat around long at night. They preferred getting into their wagons or wherever they chose to sleep and covering themselves with netting. Some even slapped mud on their necks and faces as a deterrent to the pesky, whining, stinging insects.

Finally they were camped at their next major stop, the junction of the North and South Platte. Here they would cross the river again and follow the North Platte. This time there were no ferries, and Clarissa did not look forward to the arduous, dangerous crossing, although Dawson had assured them that although the Platte was swollen, it still shouldn't be more than three or four feet deep at the most. He told them that later in the summer it was practically no more than mud in some places.

Now I truly can see we are entering the great western desert, as they call it. Already the land is more arid, the grass not quite so green. Other than along the river, there are no trees. The horizon is as endless as if one were looking out over an ocean. I know there are high, rocky mountains ahead of us, but for now there is not a hill in sight since we left the bluffs we've followed the past several days. Mr. Clements says that by the end of June we should reach Fort Laramie, where we can enjoy a good day's rest and refresh our supplies before going on into much hillier country again.

"Mommy, it's Dawson!" Sophie spoke up.

Clarissa closed her diary and looked up from the log she sat on to see him approaching the area along the river where she was camped with Carolyn and Michael. A cool breeze had kicked up, helping ward off the mosquitoes, and Lena and Sophie were playing by drawing pictures in an area of damp sand nearby.

"Hi, Dawson!" Sophie literally ran to the man. "Look at my owie!"

Dawson knelt down and studied the new bandage there. "Well, it looks like you're doing just fine, little soldier."

"Yeah! You fixed me!"

"Well, I'm glad."

"Will you pick me up?"

Dawson hesitated.

"Now, who could turn down an invitation like that?" Michael asked jovially.

Dawson grinned and lifted Sophie.

"Look, Mommy, I'm high!"

"I see that."

"Come and sit down a while," Michael offered. "We have some coffee left."

Dawson looked around, appearing somewhat uncomfortable. "I guess it would be all right." He carried Sophie to a food crate that served as a chair and sat down, letting the little girl sit on his knee. Lena ran over and insisted on sitting on the other knee.

"Well, now, if that isn't a sight!" Carolyn exclaimed.

Both little girls hugged Dawson, who looked embarrassed. "Hey now, people are going to think I'm a big softie," he told the girls. "I can't have them thinking that if I expect them to take orders from me," he teased.

"Dawson's my daddy," Sophie said in a rather bragging way to Lena. "Now I have a daddy, too!"

The girls giggled, and Clarissa reddened. "Sophie, stop saying that."

"It's okay, I guess," Dawson told her. "If it makes her happy. No real harm done."

Clarissa raised her eyebrows. "Until we reach our destination and you ride off into the sunset," she answered. "She knows she had a daddy before and that he's gone. I'm not sure she'll like seeing you leave, too."

Dawson lifted both girls down and told them to go draw him a picture in the sand so he could drink his coffee. They ran off, and he took a tin cup of coffee from Clarissa.

"Well," he answered, "maybe I *won't* ride off into the sunset."

"Now there's some words I like to hear," Michael said. "You need to settle, Dawson, and I sure would like it if you claimed some land near me so I could call on you for help now and then."

Did he mean it? Was Dawson really considering staying in Montana? Why did that make Clarissa so happy?

"Help? I thought you were going to build a church," Dawson told him. "Don't expect me to help with that or help you raise money or something."

Michael laughed. "Yes, I'll build a church. But in the meantime I have to provide for the family. I'll likely be looking into ranching, raising cattle or something."

Dawson rested his elbows on his knees, holding the cup with both hands. "You've got to have a good plan to settle in land like that," he told Michael. "It's pretty harsh and unforgiving. If I were you, I'd settle in town somewhere first, maybe get a job while you build a congregation—get yourself used to the country and learn a little more about cattle and ranching or farming."

Michael sobered. "Well, I appreciate the advice. If you stay around maybe we could find a way to work together. If you stay around maybe we could find a way to work together. You know the land better than I do."

Dawson shrugged. "I've never ranched, but I guess I could learn quick enough. I know about horses and what they need. I'd have to do some studying when it comes to cattle."

"Speaking of studying, did you get any schooling in the army? You seem a pretty well-spoken man," Carolyn said.

Dawson studied the cup he held as he talked, and Clarissa again wondered at his mood changes. This was the most talkative he'd been so far.

"Finished the equivalent of high school and a little college," he told them, "by the good graces of a major whose life I happened to save in the Mexican War. He sent me to his home in Philadelphia for more schooling. He was killed fighting Indians a couple of years after I returned to the army. Army life is all I've ever known, till now."

"And during all that time you've never married or been in love?" Carolyn asked.

Dawson pursed his lips and thought a moment before answering. "I married once—a Mexican woman—more out of loneliness than love, and she just wanted out of the miserable conditions she was living in. She ended up dying only a few months later. She was carrying. The baby died with her."

"Oh, how sad!" Carolyn commented.

Dawson stared at his coffee cup. "Death and loss seem to follow me. I haven't dared care much about anyone since. I had one pretty good friend in the army, but he was shot down right in front of my eyes at Shiloh. Like I said, it's almost dangerous getting close to me."

After another moment of silence, Michael spoke up. "You've got to get such thoughts out of your head, Dawson. God loves you too much. I'm sorry you've never known the joy of having a real family around you."

Dawson glanced at Clarissa, then at Michael. "Up until I was eight years old I did. It's hard to remember most of it now, but from what I can recall, my parents were good people." He cleared his throat. "I, uh, I suppose Clare told you how they died."

Michael nodded. "Yes, she did. I'm so sorry you lost both parents at such a young age, but it was an accident, and you're not to blame. No child that age is capable of such a deliberate action."

Dawson suddenly gulped down the rest of his coffee. "I'd better go."

"Dawson, come look!" Sophie called out.

He rose and handed his cup to Clarissa. "Thanks for the coffee." He walked over to look at Sophie and Lena's drawings, telling them they were very good, then hurried away.

"You got too close to the subject of his childhood," Clarissa told Michael.

Michael shook his head. "Some day he'll come to me and let me pray for him, and he'll understand that he's forgiven—more important, that he doesn't *need* forgiving. You mark my words. And that man is giving a lot of thought to you, Clarissa Graham. That was a pretty big hint, talking about settling in Montana."

Clarissa smiled bashfully. "Maybe. But I'm not sure it matters, Michael. I've been disappointed once in the worst way. I'm not sure I could ever trust someone that much again."

"You would if you could find a way to forgive Chad for what he did to you and Sophie. That's the only thing that will keep you from loving again, Clare. Dawson Clements is a lot of man to turn your back to, and look how much Sophie likes him. Chad Graham couldn't hold a candle to that man."

She waved him off. "It might not even matter. Dawson might have something else in mind completely, something that doesn't even involve me. And don't forget how strong the smell of gold can be. It's silly of us to talk about this. We are taking far too much for granted, and I'm not interested anyway."

Michael shook his head. "My, oh my. You are the worst liar who ever walked the face of the earth. And Dawson? I can see right through that man. He's interested, all right. He just doesn't feel worthy of you, or of happiness. When he learns to quit blaming himself for things that aren't his fault, he'll be able to open his heart and truly love someone. I told you, Clare. God is working in His own way, on you and Mr. Clements both."

"Since when did you become such a romantic?" Clarissa teased.

"Just calling it as I see it," Michael answered.

Clarissa folded her arms. "Then you're looking through rose-colored spectacles." She walked over to join Sophie and Lena, praising their drawing.

"See, Mommy?" Sophie pointed to her drawing, a man and a woman and a little girl, drawn as stick figures. "It's you and me and Dawson. And this is the house we'll have someday."

"Is that so?" Clarissa thought how it was going to break poor Sophie's heart—and maybe hers—when Dawson left them....

Chapter Eighteen

❦

June 16, 1863

Crossing the Platte to get to the north branch was indeed a frightening experience. The fork was so wide we could not even see the other side, but as Mr. Clements promised, it was hardly any deeper at the center than at the edges. I have never known such a shallow river, even when it is swollen in spring, although several times the water touched the wagon beds. To keep them safe, Dawson rode across with Sophie and Lena, as well as taking some of the other youngest children, making several trips back and forth.

We will soon reach Fort Laramie, where we will get a much-needed rest. Everyone is anxious, especially Otto Hensel, who accidentally shot himself in the foot two days ago while cleaning a handgun he thought he might need because we are in Indian country. Mr. Clements was very upset with him and said that no one who is not accustomed to using guns is allowed to handle one at all.

Clarissa had to smile at the memory of Otto hopping around on one foot yelping like a wounded coyote. She felt sorry for his pain, but the picture was comical indeed, and she was not the only one who'd had to turn away and laugh. Even Dawson, upset as he was over the incident, had later laughed about it when he agreed to eat supper with her and Michael and Carolyn later that night.

"Buffalo!" someone shouted.

Clarissa had been standing at her open wagon gate and using it like a table for her writing. She blew on the ink as more of the travelers started shouting, "Buffalo!" She closed the book and set it and her pen and ink inside the wagon to join others who were running outside the wagon circle. She'd heard a great deal about buffalo, but had never seen one, and she was just as curious as everyone else. She ran to catch up, spotting Lena and Sophie with Carolyn and Michael. The girls were pointing, their eyes wide with excitement.

"Look, Mommy! Michael calls them bufflow."

"I see them!" Clarissa lifted the girl so she could see better. They were camped on a low rise, and ahead of them in a lower section of land moved a sea of dark bodies, so many buffalo that it appeared one could literally walk through that valley on top of their backs.

"Look how big they are!" Lena exclaimed. Even from where they stood, it was obvious that many of the shaggy beasts were as tall or taller than the average horse, with much shorter legs and much bigger girths than an equine.

They looked solid and strong and a little frightening. She saw Dawson riding toward them from the direction of the herd.

"No guns and no shouting," he said when he reached them. "If that herd were to decide to stampede this way, you'd never get out of the way in time. They are amazingly fast for their size and those short legs. A herd that size would destroy everything in sight."

"What magnificent beasts," Michael commented.

"And great game," Dawson added. "There's enough meat on one buffalo to feed a family for weeks, maybe months. That's why they are so valuable to the Indians." He directed his attention to the others. "There is a hunting tribe of Sioux right behind those buffalo, so don't be alarmed when you see them come into view. They aren't out to make war. They're just hunting. They have women along to do the gutting and skinning."

"Indians!" Young Robert Trowbridge commented, "You sure they aren't dangerous?"

"Yes, how *do* you know for sure?" Lawyer Burkette questioned Dawson.

Obviously peeved at him, Dawson scowled at Burkette. "Because I served out here for years," he answered. "I know a war party from a hunting party."

"You're sure they're Sioux?" Otto Hensel asked.

"Yes, and they know we're here. Zeb and I have already talked to them. They'll leave us alone as long as we leave them alone, so don't anybody go getting any ideas."

"What if they try to turn that herd toward us to stampede us to death?" Burkette asked arrogantly.

"They won't."

"Why shouldn't they?" Burkette asked. "We have plenty of supplies and women along. Don't they lust after white women?"

To everyone's surprise, Dawson flat-out slugged Burkette, sending him sprawling on his back. A couple of women screamed and others, men and women alike, gasped and stepped back.

"You know, Burkette, for all your fancy education, you sure do talk like an ignorant man," Dawson told him. "You don't need to talk like that in front of the ladies here, and you don't need to be planting frightening thoughts in their heads. I told you I have already talked to them. It's a *hunt-ing* party. You hired me for what I know about the land out here, so listen to what I tell you."

Burkette wiped at the blood on his lip, his face beet-red as he got back to his feet. "What's wrong, Clements?" he fumed. "You afraid I'll offend the woman you're sweet on?"

"Peter, that's enough." Burkette's wife spoke up. Blair Bur-kette was an elegant woman who was friendly but reserved, and some suspected she was abused by her husband. He'd raised his hand to her more than once, but so far no one had seen him hit her.

"Shut up!" Burkette barked at the woman. "Or I'll *shut* you up!" He turned back to Dawson. "*No one* calls me ignorant! If you're going to single me out, Clements, how about ad-mitting your own indiscretions—like seeing the widow woman on the side. Everybody knows about it and we don't intend to put up with it!"

More gasps. Clarissa felt the color coming to her cheeks, more from anger than embarrassment. "How dare you!" she exclaimed. "There is nothing going on between me and—"

"Don't say another word," Dawson ordered before she could finish. He kept his eyes on Burkette. Suddenly he grasped the lawyer around the throat with one strong hand and turned to slam him against a wagon. "Apologize to Mrs.

Graham!" he growled. "Or I'll drag you to those Indians and tell them to practice their latest torture on you!"

Burkette stood there panting, his dark eyes bulging from fear and anger. He looked sideways at Clarissa. "Sorry," he said quietly.

"Louder!" Dawson insisted.

Taking a deep breath, Burkette repeated, "I'm sorry."

Dawson let go of him and he slid to the ground, grasping his throat. Dawson turned to the others. "I'm sorry you had to see that, but I'll not have one person on this wagon train wrongly accused of *anything*. Mrs. Graham is one of the finest women I know. I don't want to hear one other person suggest otherwise. And if I choose to properly court her—" he looked at Clarissa, who stood speechless and amazed "—I'll court her," he finished.

The entire group became momentarily silent. Clarissa felt a wonderful warmth move through her entire body at the revelation that Dawson Clements was indeed interested in her as more than just one of the members of the wagon train.

Blair Burkette ran over to her husband, who angrily shoved her away and told her to leave him alone. He glowered at Dawson before storming away from the crowd. His wife followed. The sound of whooping Indians broke the odd silence, and suddenly everyone was turning their attention again to the sea of buffalo in the distance, where a good twenty or so Indian warriors rode swift ponies directly into the buffalo herd. The animals began to run, thankfully in the opposite direction.

"There is a sight you may not see again," Dawson told them, "but one you'll want to savor to tell your grandchildren about—watching wild Indians on a buffalo hunt. In a few years there won't be many buffalo left...or Indians."

"You sound like you sympathize with them," Otto commented. The man used homemade crutches to stand.

"Sometimes I do," Dawson answered, "but not when one is headed toward me with a raised tomahawk."

People laughed nervously. Clarissa could hardly keep her attention on the spectacular sight before her. Sophie watched as though mesmerized, and now they could hear gunfire. One by one several of the lumbering beasts fell.

"Might as well sit on the ground and watch," Dawson told them. "We have to go right through there, and we can't until they're through with the hunt. Pretty soon the women will come in and start gutting and skinning the downed buffalo. They'll use pretty much every part of the animals, not just the meat. And by the way, everybody, once the herd and the Indians are gone, you can hang buckets on the sides of your wagons and start picking up buffalo chips."

"Buffalo chips? Vat are dose?" Otto asked.

Dawson chuckled. "'Chips' is just a nice word for, let's say, what the buffalo leave behind when they're gone. From here on you'll see plenty of those leavings, and those that are dried-up make excellent fuel for fires. The smoke stinks, but we're headed into country where wood won't be all that plentiful, so start gathering, folks." He walked away and mounted his horse, and everyone looked at each other until finally Otto started chuckling. The others joined in then, realizing what Dawson had been talking about.

"Yes, sir, life sure is different out here." Michael laughed.

Dawson rode back down the hill, circling some of the dead buffalo while the hunters continued the chase, practically disappearing on the horizon as they followed the stampede. Everyone sat equally fascinated, and about an hour later Indian women with horses pulling sledlike contraptions behind them made an appearance from wherever they were camped to the left of a rise where they couldn't be seen by the emigrants.

One woman at a time stopped beside a buffalo and dismounted, and it was obvious they were beginning the cumbersome project of gutting and skinning the animals. They all watched as Dawson spoke with one of the women, then rode back to the emigrants.

"I need a couple of volunteers," he told them. "Preferably men. I spoke with the wife of one of the hunters who told me they are offering us one buffalo. All we have to do is go down there and skin it and leave the hide for them. There's enough meat there to share with all of you, and we're close enough to Fort Laramie to get the meat there in time to smoke it while we're there so it will last. Who wants to come with me to clean the thing?"

"I will!" Robert Trowbridge piped up enthusiastically, obviously eager to impress his young wife.

"So will I," Michael told him.

"Michael, if we can ride your two draft horses down there, we can use them to drag the meat back. It will be a pretty heavy load. Bring about three blankets."

"Sure thing." Michael left to untie his horses, and Dawson glanced at Clarissa, who was still somewhat dumbfounded at his remark about courting her. He tipped his hat to her and rode away.

Chapter Nineteen

❧

Everyone's spirits rose when they reached Fort Laramie, and Clarissa could tell that Dawson was most certainly in his own realm here. Since their arrival two days ago he'd spent most of his time talking with Major General Bartley Trundell, currently in charge of the garrison.

Clarissa shook out quilts and hung them outside over barrels, over the wagon seat and tongue, using any means she could to air them out. Shaking the quilts helped her vent her frustration over Dawson's talk of courting her. He'd not talked to her alone or even joined her and Michael and Carolyn for a meal since the day of the confrontation with Burkette during the buffalo hunt.

She wiped perspiration from her forehead with the back of her hand, feeling covered with dust from the quilts and perplexed over what to think about Dawson. Perhaps he didn't mean to court her at all. Maybe he'd just said that to make his visits to her appear appropriate. Apparently someone had seen him come to her wagon a couple of times after dark and had made the visits into something more than they were. That, too, frustrated and angered her.

The wagons were circled just outside the fort, which consisted of several buildings and a huge, two-tiered barracks with a porch and railings shading both stories, all of which covered a large, sprawling area of land in Nebraska Territory. Soldiers milled about in constant activity everywhere—some drilling in formation, some in fenced corrals training fresh horses, some working a blacksmith shop, some serving clean-up duty by shoveling horse manure into wheelbarrows to be hauled away, some practicing on a firing range, some sitting outside the mess hall peeling potatoes. Today two men marched around the parade grounds carrying heavy logs, apparently some kind of punishment for disobeying an order or perhaps trying to desert.

Dawson always seemed to be at one of those places when he was not with the major general, and Clarissa doubted more and more his hints that he wanted to settle into a different life. The man was a soldier, through and through.

She brushed herself off and looked toward a shade tree where Sophie and Lena played with straw dolls. Seeing that they were fine, she climbed back into the wagon to straighten more items and decide which clothes needed washing. She'd decided to risk a little of what precious money she had to pay a laundress at the fort to wash them for her, feeling somewhat guilty for the indulgence but needing the respite from scrubbing her own clothes in the river.

Plenty of hardship lay ahead, and Dawson had told everyone to take as much rest as they could get. They would leave the day after tomorrow for the next jaunt of their journey, through country even more dangerous as far as Indian worries. Besides that, the next stretch would be nothing but a gradual climb, even when the land seemed flat. They would be a good mile above sea level when they reached the foothills of the Rockies. Then came the most treacherous part of the journey.

She tried not to think about the danger ahead. She would take these three days to pretend all was well. The only thing she couldn't get off her mind was Dawson Clements. Her hardest decision was whether or not she even *wanted* the man to court her. Was he taking too much for granted? Did he think that just because she was a woman alone she was naturally looking for a man to woo her and take care of her? Certainly not. She didn't want to be patronized, nor did she want Dawson Clements's pity.

She gathered some clothes into a pillowcase and tossed it toward the back of the wagon, too late to realize Dawson had come around the corner. The pillowcase full of clothes landed in his face.

"Hey!" he exclaimed, laughing as he grabbed the case full of clothes. He threw them playfully back inside.

"Oh! I didn't know you were there," Clarissa told him, embarrassed. She instantly forgot all her self-warnings about allowing another man into her life. Feeling suddenly flushed, she wondered how she must look. "I'm afraid I'm a mess," she excused herself. "I've been shaking out quilts and straightening things in here. I've decided to take my clothes to the laundry here at the fort, if they'll wash them for me."

Dawson pushed back his hat. "I've already set that up for you and paid for it."

"What?" Clarissa crawled to the back of the wagon and sat down on the gate. "You don't need to do that. I am perfectly capable of—"

"I know what you're capable of. And *I* am capable of doing things for you if I want to, and I wanted to."

"You shouldn't be spending money on me. I've always heard soldiers make hardly any money to begin with. Surely whatever you have is important for your own future plans."

He sobered. "A man I met at Shiloh left me some money when he was killed. It wasn't a tremendous amount of money, but enough to get me started at something new. I felt like it was a sign that it was time to do something different with my life." He put out his arms. "So, here I am, leading a wagon train to Montana and wrestling with some very strong feelings for a beautiful woman I still hardly know and who hardly knows me. How's that for fate interceding in a man's life? An unexpected inheritance, a war wound that gets me discharged and leads me to you, a trip to Montana that you just happen to end up joining. Don't you think that means we need to explore these chance encounters?"

She nervously pushed back some wild strands of hair, thinking again how terrible she must look. She was starting to have feelings for him, and she couldn't do a thing about it. "I suppose it does."

Dawson stepped closer, grasping her hands. "So do I. And I have begun my quest to win your heart and your trust by setting things up with the wife of Major General Trundell to let you and Carolyn go to their frame house, over there at the end of the barracks—" he nodded toward the spot "—where Mrs. Trundell will let you use her bathtub to clean up. It's the only real, porcelain bathtub on the fort site, so it's a privilege to use it. She doesn't mind, and the woman would enjoy your company. Her husband tells me

Clarissa sighed. "I don't know what to make of you. You can be so thoughtful, and then I don't see you for days. You won't open up to me or Michael or anyone, and then you turn around and talk about courting me, but there is so much about you I don't understand."

He held her hands tightly, total seriousness in his eyes. "I meant what I said about wanting to court you. I stayed away the past few days till we got here because I wanted to make sure people understood we weren't up to anything improper."

He suddenly broke into a grin so handsome that it disturbed Clarissa in very *improper* ways. He gripped her about the waist then, lifting her down as though she weighed nothing. Clarissa was amazed at his good mood, probably from being in such familiar surroundings.

"I have arranged for a dance to be held here tomorrow," he told her, "from late afternoon until however late people want it to continue. The fort will provide food and music. They even have a portable wooden dance floor they can set up for us, something they often do for wagon trains or visits from generals and senators and the like. So, go take a bath and fix yourself up, and tomorrow put on your prettiest dress, because you will be dancing every dance with me."

This was too wonderful, and happening too fast. Her trip to settle on her own was not supposed to include meeting a man and falling in love with him.

"What if I would rather dance with Eric Buettner or Bert Krueger?"

He frowned. "*Would you?*"

His grand stature made her feel very small. Could she truly trust such a big, strong man about whom she still knew so little? "No, but I don't want either of us to—I don't know," she met his eyes again; they were so very blue. "I don't want you thinking I *need* a man to survive, or feeling sorry for me because of what my husband did."

He answered in all seriousness. "I don't for a minute think either of those things. You're a strong, determined woman who will do just fine all alone if that's how it ends up for you. And it isn't you I feel sorry for. It's your ex-husband, who made a grave mistake when he walked out on you and Sophie. And just for your information, I in turn don't want you allowing a courtship because you feel sorry for *me*, because of my past. I don't want your pity any more than you want mine. Agreed?"

She took a deep breath. "Agreed."

"Good. Get some things together and I'll escort you to the major general's house. Bring Lena and Sophie. I'm sure they'd enjoy a bath, too."

"Dawson!" Sophie and Lena were both running toward him then. Dawson turned his attention to the girls, picking them up, one in each arm. They each kissed a cheek, and Dawson turned back to Clarissa. "I'll go tell Carolyn about the bath. You get out a clean dress and some soap and a brush for that beautiful red hair. And by the way, your face is filthy, Mrs. Graham."

He walked away, and Clarissa put her hands to her face, wondering just how dirty it really was. She climbed back into the wagon and dug a dress and underwear and towels out of a trunk. She found a hand mirror and held it up, gasping at how she looked. If Dawson Clements was still interested when he saw her looking like this, there most certainly had to be something genuine to it. She closed her eyes, thinking how kind it was of him to think about arranging baths for her and Carolyn and the girls.

God help me make the right decisions. Show me Thy way, and give me courage and understanding to know when my heart speaks true. Help me learn to love again, if that is what You mean for me, and help me find a way to forgive Chad Graham. Until I can forgive him, I can never give my heart freely to another.

Your lips cover me with kisses;
Your love is better than wine.
There is a fragrance about you;
The sound of your name recalls it.
No woman could keep from loving you.

—*The Song of Solomon* 1:2-3

Chapter Twenty

✤

June 21, 1863

The army band consisted of two fiddles, one guitar, a trumpet and a drummer. Together they managed to play waltzes surprisingly well, and for a change of pace, they called out a lively square dance, a sergeant shouting moves that kept the emigrants skipping and turning and changing partners so swiftly that they sometimes got confused, ending in uproarious laughter.

Not far away, a side of beef, turned on a spit by two more soldiers, roasted over a pit of hot coals, and nearby a table sat loaded with sweet potatoes, boiled regular potatoes, bread, a ham and even berry pies, some made by the army cooks, most of the pies by the few soldiers' wives who lived at the fort. Clarissa had not felt so beautiful or enjoyed herself so much since before giving birth to Sophie. It was after that that Chad had seemed to lose interest in her and had begun turning away from her in the night.

Now here was Dawson, who kept one hand firmly at her waist, held her other hand and whirled her around the makeshift dance floor more adeptly than she'd expected. He looked wonderful in black dress pants, high black boots, a white shirt, black vest and black string tie. It was obvious he'd had the army's barber give him a shave and a haircut, and now his thick, dark hair was slicked back neatly and had a slight curl to it where it met the collar of his shirt.

This was the first time Clarissa saw him for how truly handsome he was, and the way he looked at her made her feel beautiful in this dress she'd brought with her, a pale green velvet that was fitted at the waist. The front buttons of the bodice were hidden under white lace that decorated the scooped neckline and the edges of the puffed sleeves.

Now Dawson turned her to another waltz, and when she rested her left hand on his right arm she could feel the hard muscle beneath his shirtsleeve. Everything about the man spelled safety and security, but so had Chad when he'd consoled and comforted her after her father's death.

"Have I told you how beautiful you look?" Dawson asked, drawing her away from negative thoughts. "Yes," she answered with a light laugh, meeting his eyes. "And you have never looked more handsome."

He actually looked embarrassed. "If you say so." He glanced away from her. "Looks like Sophie and Lena are having fun."

Clarissa looked to see the girls dancing together and giggling. "Thank you for arranging this," she told Dawson. "It's a wonderful break for everyone."

Their gazes met again. "You all deserve it," Dawson told her. "We have a long way to go yet."

"What are they telling you about the Indians?" Clarissa asked.

Obvious concern filled Dawson's eyes. "The Cheyenne are causing a lot of problems south of here and around Denver. Up north the Sioux are causing havoc along the Bozeman road that leads to western Montana. That's where men are starting to dig for gold. Right now we're between the two, but we'll have to be vigilant. We'll probably have bigger problems the closer we get to Montana."

"I have to wonder if we made the wrong decision. The Indian problems frighten me."

"As soon as the war is over a lot of soldiers will be sent back west and things will be safer. Meantime, it might be best at first for you to claim your land and then settle closer to a town where there is safety in numbers."

He'd said "you," not "we." Clarissa couldn't help being a bit confused over what this man's intentions really were. As though he'd read her mind, Dawson stopped dancing and led her off the wooden platform.

"Let's go someplace where we can talk." They walked past the others to the long porch of the barracks building and a wooden bench there. "Sit down, Clare," he told her.

Clarissa obeyed, not sure what to expect or even sure what she wanted to hear him say. He sat down beside her, and in the distance they could see Carolyn and Michael dancing together awkwardly. "They make a rather comical couple, don't they?" Dawson said. "With Carolyn taller and even a little broader than Michael."

Clarissa laughed lightly. "They certainly do, but they are very happy together. Two people of strong faith and convictions. Carolyn used to help at the store, and after my divorce, she and Michael became my most loyal friends. They even pulled out of the Light of Christ Church when some of the women and deacons there nearly shunned me from church activities, as though I'd committed some terrible sin. That's when Michael started his own church. He and Carolyn are the most forgiving and nonjudgmental people I have ever met."

Dawson leaned back, moving an arm across the bench behind Clarissa and putting one foot up on his knee. "Too bad that isn't the kind of family I ended up with after my parents died in that fire."

Clarissa turned and faced him, afraid to lean back, afraid his arm might come around her, afraid of how good that might feel. "It must have been awful for you, being so young and thinking it was all your fault, and then living with that— that horrible man who raised you. He was *not* a man of God at all, Dawson. I hope you realize that. The lessons he beat into you about God and forgiveness were all wrong. Just look at Sophie. What if she accidentally caused my death? Do you honestly think that beautiful little girl should be held accountable and called evil and full of sin?"

He sighed, watching Lena and Sophie. "Of course not," he said quietly.

"And neither are *you* evil and full of sin. It's time to forgive yourself, Dawson."

He closed his eyes. "I should have run to them and got them up, but I ran out instead."

"You were a terrified little boy. Your first instinct to run was natural, and at that age you had no idea how fast a fire can spread. You've grown into a good man, a man who can surely think reasonably, who can watch other children and realize you did nothing wrong. God sees the goodness in you, too."

"I just don't understand why God had to let it all happen."

"It's not our place to question God's ways, Dawson, and God might not have had anything to do with it. Satan can sometimes use evil ways to win a soul away from God. Believe me, I've questioned God plenty of times myself the past several months. Now I realize that I never should have married Chad Graham in the first place. He would never have been a truly good father and he was never a good husband. I was in mourning for my father when Chad turned on the charm, professing his love and convincing me we should get married so he could take care of me." She turned away. "I was so young and vulnerable, and such a fool."

They both sat quietly for a few seconds, digesting each other's words. Dawson leaned back again. "And that's why you're so afraid to fall in love or marry again," he said matter-of-factly. "You hate the fact that he took advantage of you and convinced you you needed taking care of. You hate the thought of marrying again for that reason. You're bound and determined to take care of yourself and never depend on or trust a man again."

Clarissa remained sitting straight and rigid. "You understand people better than one would think," she answered. Finally she met his eyes again. "And you in turn are afraid to love for fear of that love slipping out of your grasp, like with your parents, and the man who sent you to school but then was killed, and the wife who died and took your baby with her, and the young man who befriended you and then was killed. You've never known true love and friendship since your parents died, have you, Dawson? Not only that, you've always believed you don't even *deserve* to love and be loved. You're so unsure of your worthiness, and yet you're the most worthy, deserving, capable man I've ever met."

He held her gaze. "We both have a lot of obstacles to overcome, don't we?"

"Maybe it's those obstacles that help us understand each other." She looked away again, afraid he would read the rush of emotions she was feeling. "Maybe we could…help each other. I can help you learn to forgive yourself, and you could—" Was she really saying this? "You could help me learn to forgive Chad Graham by showing me that a man can love completely and can be trusted."

There came another moment of silence, then Clarissa heard him sigh deeply. "You sure know how to put things in perspective," he told her. His strong, sure hand came over hers. "Look at me, Clare."

She felt herself literally tremble as she turned to face him.

"I think I'm falling in love with you," he told her flat-out. "And that scares me. All I know is the army life. When I first decided to head for Montana, it was just a lonely man who didn't know what to do next with his life. I have no idea if I can even provide for you and Sophie like a husband and father should. All I want for now is for you to know how I'm feeling, and to be patient with me while I figure out if I can do this right—be a husband and father, I mean.

"And I know you need time to sort out your own feelings. But believe me when I say that I'm not after something you own or playing on your vulnerability or thinking a woman can't survive without a man. I have no doubt what a strong, able woman you are. This isn't because I think you need me, Clare Graham. It's more that—I think I need you. You make me laugh. You make me feel confident and worthy. You make me see that I need to do something with my life beyond riding a horse and positioning cannons and shooting Indians.

"One thing I remember about my parents is that they were happy together. Before the fire I had a loving family and a good life. I want that again. I'm asking you to think hard about all this, because when we reach Montana, we need to decide, together, whether I should stay, or ride out of your life."

Clarissa swallowed, searching for her voice. "I—don't know what to say. I'm afraid to love again, but when I'm with you something happens inside of me that makes me hate it when you don't come around. But it scares me to death to think it could be love. After what happened with Chad, I'm not even sure how love is supposed to feel. I thought I loved Chad, but now I know it wasn't love at all."

"I didn't ask you to say you love me, not right now. I'm just asking you to think about maybe—maybe marrying me when we reach Montana, but to have patience during the times I seem to be staying away from you. It's partly to save your honor, and partly because I've never had such a time wrestling with my feelings before. I've never cared before about what lies ahead in my future. Now I care. I see *you* in my future, but I'm scared that somehow I'll let you down or be responsible for something happening to you."

Clarissa searched his troubled eyes. "That's where faith comes in, Dawson. If God means for this to be, He'll show both of us the way."

He lifted her hand, and kissed her palm. She yearned to hold him, but all the doubts Chad Graham had instilled in her kept her in check. What if she did give her heart to this man, and then he realized he wasn't made to live a normal family life and ran off to rejoin the army, or decided to go look for gold?

Still, she could not bring herself to pull back when he came closer. In the next moment his lips covered hers in a warm kiss that lingered, but when he began to press her close, she turned her face so that his warm breath was on her cheek.

"I can't yet," she said in a near whisper. "I don't want to let love be nothing more than need and want." She lowered her head and turned away. "We both have to be sure it's not just those things bringing us together. It has to be something much deeper than that. And we have a long way to go yet. So many things could happen."

He didn't reply right away, but finally he moved an arm around her. She hated admitting how good it would feel to lean on someone strong, to feel those arms wrapped around her.

"I understand," he told her. "Just knowing you have deep feelings for me is enough for now. Promise me you will give serious thought to the things I've told you."

She nodded. "You know I will. Thank you for being so honest about your feelings. And I hope—" Finally she faced him again. She still felt his kiss on her lips. "I hope you will pray about it as I will. You need God in your life and your heart, Dawson. Let God take away all the anger and show you His love. That is when you will know what is right, and will be totally free to love wholly and completely."

He rose, giving no reply to the remark, and she realized he still had tremendous reservations about God. The preacher who'd raised him had all but destroyed his trust in a forgiving Lord.

"We'd better get back to the others," he told her, now grinning again, "before they start gossiping about us." He put a hand to her waist, then leaned down and kissed her cheek, whispering "thank you" in her ear.

They walked back to the gathering, and found that the soldiers were serving food to the emigrants, some of whom turned and stared at Clarissa and Dawson. Dawson immediately left her side and began talking with the soldiers. He left with some of them, and Clarissa did not see him for the rest of the night.

Chapter Twenty-One

❧

June 28, 1863

Lawyer Burkette has left us, choosing to travel south with a regiment of soldiers headed for Denver. He feels he can do well there, and most of us are glad to be rid of him, because he often caused problems for Mr. Clements.

Clarissa breathed another sigh of relief to have Burkette off the train. He stayed behind when they left Fort Laramie, and no one missed him, although Clarissa felt sorry for his mouse of a wife.

She leaned back against the side of the wagon, keeping a quilt over her knees and writing by lamplight. They were moving into ever-higher country now, and the nights were much cooler.

The trail since leaving the fort is much rougher, and we are not always close to the river, so we now are more careful how much water we use. We climb much higher hills, which slows us down so that we are not making as many miles a day as we did coming through Nebraska. We are moving through what Mr. Clements says is the southern end of the Black Hills, not high enough to call mountains, but certainly high enough to cause great exertion on oxen and people alike. There are thick pines and cedars here. The smell is wonderful, but the journey has become harder.

Dawson seemed to be everywhere, in front of them, behind them, beside them, ever watchful for possible Indian trouble.

We are in Sioux country, and at any time wild Indians could come upon us and demand supplies. Mr. Clements says we must put on a good show of firearms and not allow them to bully us into giving up more than we can afford; however, we must try to be friendly. Will Krueger and his brother now must keep a closer watch on their cattle, since Indians sometimes steal them for meat.

We will stay on this trail to a place called Red Buttes, and then to Independence Rock, where I plan to carve my name as one of the earliest settlers headed for Montana. From there we will leave the common Oregon Trail and head north, following the Powder River into Montana. Mr. Clements says that will be the most dangerous part of our journey because of both mountains and Indians.

She stopped writing when she heard what sounded like arguing from the direction of the McCurdy wagon. She heard a woman scream, "Get out!" Then came what sounded like a slap, then a woman sobbing. A man started cursing profusely, and Clarissa set her diary aside, frowning with worry. Sophie slept with Lena and Carolyn tonight. If there was going to be some kind of trouble—

"So, there you are!"

Clarissa gasped when Samuel McCurdy suddenly appeared at the back of her wagon and was already half climbing inside before she could climb out. "What on earth—?"

"You think it's fun, don't ya?" Sam told her, his face beet red and making his hair look redder than normal. He'd grown a beard since beginning their journey, and lately he'd been drinking.

"What are you talking about?" Clarissa said, scooting away from him.

"I'm talking about the way ya entice the men on this train, us knowing you keep company with Dawson Clements while the rest of us got wives that won't give us the time o' day!"

Astonished, Clarissa moved her hand under a quilt to grasp a handgun Dawson had given her for use only in case of an Indian attack. "You're drunk!" she seethed. "Get out of my wagon!" she screamed.

He just grinned. "Sure, 'n' first I'll be gettin' what Clements gets! My wife ain't given me no relief in all these weeks!" He leaped for her, shoving her down into the quilts and grasping at her.

"Stop it!" she screamed at him, turning her head when the drunken man tried to kiss her. "I have a gun!"

"You'll not use no gun, missy," he groaned, "on account of you're wantin' this as much as me. I know how you intend to make a livin' when you reach them minin' towns in Montana."

Desperate, Clarissa put the gun in his side. Suddenly someone grabbed the man off her, and in the turmoil her gun went off. She heard Sam cry out and saw him being literally thrown out of the wagon at the same time. She heard a scuffle outside, heard several hard punches.

She lay in shock as she heard other men's voices now. "Stop it, Dawson! He's been shot!"

Clarissa looked at her gun. She'd shot a man! But what else was she to do? She didn't mean to pull the trigger. She was going to warn him again first. The gun simply went off. "Okay! Okay!" someone else yelled. "Let's handle this the right way."

It sounded like Ben Gobles, Sam's brother-in-law.

Now she heard a woman sobbing. "He was drunk," she cried. "He hit me and left the wagon."

That was Sam's wife, Sue. Now Clarissa heard a child crying, probably one of their children.

There came more talk of "frontier justice" and holding a hearing about what just took place—to see who was really guilty of what. Did some of them actually think *she* was guilty of something? She sobbed, sitting up, shivering at the memory of Sam accosting her. She looked down at the gun, then raised her gaze when Dawson climbed into the wagon, dark rage in his eyes.

"Clare! What did he do?"

Bewildered, she looked at the gun again. "I didn't mean to shoot him. It just...went off. He—" She looked at Dawson again. "He kept touching me...saying ugly things. He was...drunk."

Dawson moved closer, carefully taking the gun from her hand. He sat down and pulled her close. "It's all right. You didn't have any choice, and you only wounded him in the thigh. He'll live."

Clarissa curled against him, relishing the safety of his arms. "He said terrible things, Dawson…about you and me."

He held her tighter. "He's drunk and he's angry with his wife. We all know they've fought before and he's got an Irishman's temper. What he said was all in his drunken head, Clare, but I assure you, he's off this wagon train."

"But what if others think the same thing? Maybe they do."

"We'll straighten it out." He kissed her hair. "Tell me he didn't…get far."

She buried her face in her hands. "No. Dawson, why does it have to be this way?"

"It doesn't. McCurdy and his family will be left behind tomorrow. And if his sister- and brother-in-law don't like it, they can stay behind, too. This might not have happened if he wasn't drunk, but I don't intend to take the chance again."

"Clarissa!"

Dawson turned. "Look," he told her. "Here's Carolyn. I'd better get out of this wagon. Carolyn will help you."

"No. Just send Sophie over. I'll be all right. I just want to hold my little girl and pretend this never happened."

Dawson kissed her forehead, and with a sigh of anger he climbed out of the wagon, telling Carolyn to get Sophie and bring her over.

"Tie him up!" he told someone. "Then pour some whiskey on that leg wound and bandage it. Tomorrow we'll have a hearing about this, but I can tell you right now, nothing anyone says will change my mind. Sam McCurdy is off this wagon train! Tomorrow he gets left behind!"

"No! We've come so far!" Sue objected.

"Your husband is a drunken troublemaker," Dawson told her. "I don't want the worry of this happening again."

"Then kick Clarissa Graham off the train!" Sue McCurdy yelled at him. "*She's* the troublemaker! You shouldn't have brought a single woman along, and the things you two do are no worse than what my husband tried to do. It isn't fair to have a pretty single woman flaunting herself in front of the men."

The air hung silent for a moment.

"Ma'am." She heard Dawson speak up then. "Never in my life have I given one thought to hitting a woman, but you sure make it tempting. Get out of my sight!"

"You're a cruel, unreasonable, demanding, unfair man, Dawson Clements!" the woman screamed at him. "My husband and I will *gladly* leave this wagon train!"

There came a moment of silence.

"I want to know right now if any of the rest of you are thinking about what that woman said," Dawson demanded. "And I'm telling you for the last time that Mrs. Graham has done absolutely nothing wrong. She's a fine, moral woman, and it takes guts to come out here alone like she's done."

"That's so," Michael interjected. "I've known Mrs. Graham for a long time, and she's not got a sinful bone in her body. This ugly mess is not fair to her."

Clarissa felt sick. Now poor Michael had been dragged into this. Were people claiming she was sleeping with him, too? How cruel and disgusting!

"We're putting an end to this," Dawson announced. "Tomorrow we will record what happened, talk about it and then take a vote. Either Sam McCurdy will be off this train, or I'll leave *all* of you behind and go on alone with Mr. Harvey and his wife and Mrs. Graham. Either way, I am asking Mr. Harvey to marry me and Mrs. Graham tomorrow. Maybe *that* will put an end to the sinful and unfair visions some of you have conjured up in your dirty minds!"

Marry! Clarissa's eyes widened in amazement. How did he know she would agree to such a thing? Was the man crazy?

"We don't all think that way, Mr. Clements, please believe us." Wanda Krueger spoke up. "I like Mrs. Graham very much. She's been a big help, nursing cuts and bruises on the children and helping watch them and all. I assure you we've never seen you or she act disrespectfully. You mustn't judge all of us by what a drunken Irishman and his angry wife have done and said."

"Nevertheless, what's done is done. The idea has been planted, and I won't have it! We'll be married tomorrow and that's all there is to it! Now, take care of that drunken excuse of a man and get some sleep!"

Clarissa heard the crunch of gravel beneath Dawson's boots as he walked away. Then the wagon rocked slightly as Michael climbed onto the wagon gate. "Clare, are you all right?"

Clarissa swallowed, still stunned over every unexpected action that had taken place. "I…didn't mean to shoot him, Michael. Please pray he doesn't die."

Michael smiled. "He won't die. I saw the wound. It's just through the flesh of his thigh, and I don't doubt he deserved worse. What about you?"

Clarissa shook her head, running a hand through her hair. "I don't really know. I need time to absorb all of this."

"I'm so sorry, Clare. Maybe my wagon should be between yours and Carolyn's, instead of in front of hers. That way I can hear better what's happening with the both of you."

"You have enough to worry about. I'm the one who's sorry. I've been a burden to practically everyone, especially you and—" Her eyes widened and she moved closer. "Michael, did you hear what Dawson said?"

"About marrying you?" He rubbed at his eyes. "Of course I did."

"Do you think he means it?"

"I expect he does."

"But I don't *want* to marry him. At least not now, not this way, for all the wrong reasons. What on earth makes him think I would do such a thing?"

Michael shrugged. "Well, now, I guess you'll have to ask him, won't you?"

"Michael—"

"Carolyn is here with a very sleepy Sophie," he deliberately interrupted. He took Sophie from Carolyn and lifted her inside. Clarissa took her and laid the girl into the quilts.

"Mommy," Sophie said drowsily before falling right back to sleep.

"Clare, are you okay?" Carolyn asked, her brown eyes full of concern and sympathy.

"Yes, I'm fine. I'm so sorry, Carolyn, to be the cause of all this commotion."

"Nonsense! You weren't the cause. That drunken Irishman was. You get some rest now. We'll pray about this and we'll all talk in the morning, honey." She stepped up on a footrest and leaned farther inside the wagon. "Are you going to marry him tomorrow?"

"No! The man must be out of his mind!"

Carolyn smiled. "I think he knows exactly what he's doing. Goodnight, Clare." She left before Clarissa could reply, as did Michael.

Frustrated and angry and embarrassed and completely sickened over what had just happened, Clarissa pulled the cord that brought down the canvas flap over the back opening of the wagon and leaned against the side of it again.

"Dear God," she prayed. "Forgive me for shooting that man, but I can't believe it's wrong for a woman to defend herself against such ugliness. Why do these things happen to me? Why, God? Why did Chad leave me? Why do people turn on me just because I'm without a husband? All I want is to get to Montana and make a new life for my Sophie. I never asked for Dawson Clements or any other man to come into my life. I just want to be left alone." The tears came. "Lord Jesus, help me know what to do."

Chapter Twenty-Two

❧

June 29, 1863

Sam McCurdy sat on a wooden chair in the middle of the circle of wagons, his head hanging. His wife and children, as well as his sister- and brother-in-law, Betsy and Ben Gobles, and their children, all stood behind Sam in an obvious effort to win the travelers' sympathies so they would be allowed to continue the journey to Montana.

"We all know what happened last night," Dawson announced. "Samuel McCurdy got drunk and beat his wife, then left their wagon and went directly to Clarissa Graham's wagon where he assaulted her and was accidentally shot by Mrs. Graham, who was only trying to defend herself. Then Sam and his wife both insulted Mrs. Graham in the most reprehensible way a woman can be insulted. I won't stand for lies and false accusations on this wagon train. We are approaching a time when we will need to work together more than ever. Lack of cooperation could cost lives. Nor will I abide by a respectable woman being ridiculed and lied about. I feel the McCurdys should be kicked off this wagon train, but all of you insist on taking a vote on this, so be my guests."

Clarissa stood with Michael and Carolyn and the girls, wearing a simple green gingham dress with a high neckline, her hair wound into a tight bun. She wanted to look as prim-and-proper as possible. She kept her chin high, glaring at Sam and his wife. In spite of sporting a black eye, Sue Mc-Curdy now staunchly defended her husband.

"I am a Christian man who believes in forgiveness," Michael declared, "but Mrs. Graham is a fine woman and a good friend to my wife. She was wrongly accosted and insulted. Still, we have to think of the McCurdy children."

Will Krueger stepped forward. "Wanda, Bert and I vote them off."

"Us, too." Walt Clymer spoke for himself and his wife.

"Ve don't vant no trouble," Otto Hensel said. "Za vife unt I say zey should go."

Robert Trowbridge declared rather nervously, "Well, uh, we don't want any more trouble, either. Me and the wife have never seen anything questionable going on between Mrs. Graham and anyone else on this wagon train. She seems like a nice woman and a good mother, and she mostly minds her own business." He looked at his wife, who smiled shyly. "My wife and I, well, we can't help wondering if there could be some other solution to this situation."

"We don't like to be judgmental," John Clay told them. "Rosemarie and I abstain. We'll go along with whatever the rest of you decide."

Dawson turned his attention to the Gobles. "You staying or leaving?" he asked Ben.

The man hesitated, glancing at his wife and then his sister-in-law. "Well, naturally my wife wants to stand by her sister. And we do have to think of the children, Sam's and mine both." He cleared his throat before continuing, as though to muster up some courage. "Mr. Clements, I know Sam did wrong, but you can't muster a man out of this wagon train like a soldier who's disobeyed an order. I mean, I know you're used to giving orders, but it seems your mind is pretty well made up."

"I'm giving all of you a chance to vote on this, aren't I? And as far as running this wagon train like a troop, that's the only way to make sure we all reach Montana safely. I told you before we left how it would be."

"Should we really leave them here?" John Clay asked.

"They could be attacked by Indians, or run out of supplies before more wagons come along."

"Sam McCurdy should have thought of that before he started drinking," Dawson answered, still looking and sounding angry from the night before.

"Well, Dawson, maybe we could let them sort of lag behind, stay a distance from us," Michael told him. "After all, there *are* little children involved here. Maybe the answer is to make them keep a bit of a distance, but close enough where we can help them if they run into trouble. As far as Sam getting drunk and abusing his wife, well, that's something the two of them and the Gobles need to do something about. Sam himself has to answer to the Lord for his wrongdoings, not to us, or to you, Dawson."

Dawson cast him a scowl. "He can't control his drinking. And there stands his wife with a black eye, defending him."

Sue put a hand on Sam's shoulder. "That's my right," she answered. "A woman has to stand by her husband."

"Mr. Clements." Clarissa spoke up then, keeping her address to him formal in front of the others. "Much as I detest Samuel McCurdy, I agree with Michael. We have to think of the women and children. Let them stay, but at a distance."

Dawson's irritation was obvious in the long sigh he emitted. "All right, we'll take a final vote. Everyone who wants them to stay, but farther back, raise your hands."

A few hands went up, then more, and more, including Clarissa's.

"On one condition," Dawson said. "Sam McCurdy owes Mrs. Graham a genuine apology for the way he treated her last night."

Sam kept his head bowed. "I'm...sorry," he said softly.

"Stand up and come closer, and face her like a man," Dawson ordered. "And speak up."

After a moment of hesitation, Sam rose and limped closer, facing Clarissa with bloodshot eyes and bruises on his face from Dawson's sound beating the night before. He looked rightfully remorseful and embarrassed. "I said I was sorry," he told Clarissa.

"I still don't think it's right for a single woman to be along with us," Sam's wife said loudly, an obviously feeble attempt at somehow putting some of the blame on Clarissa. "Mr. Clements, you said last night you would marry her today. Are you going to do it? Seems to me that would solve a lot of problems."

"The only problem here is your drunken husband," Clarissa fumed. "Why do you let him abuse you? Don't you have any pride?"

"Don't talk to me about pride, you hussy!"

Clarissa gasped and headed for Sue McCurdy. Dawson grabbed her. "This meeting is over." He held on to Clarissa as he spoke. "McCurdy, get your family away from here, now! I want you a good hundred yards behind us. Hitch your teams and get moving!"

Sam nodded and turned, walking up to his wife and telling her to shut her mouth. "Help me get the teams hitched!" he growled at her.

"We took a vote, so don't say I run this outfit unfairly," Dawson told the others. "Go on about your business. Since we've wasted part of the morning because of Sam McCurdy, we won't leave until one o'clock." He kept hold of Clarissa's arm and led her away from the others to a stand of pines.

"I think they're right about one thing, Clare. We *should* get married," he told her bluntly.

"What! Are you *crazy?*" She put her hands to her face, still trying to erase the urge to put her hands around Sue Mc-Curdy's neck. *Dear God, forgive me for such animosity!* How could she even consider Dawson's suggestion when she was in such an emotional state?

"I'm not crazy," Dawson answered. "I simply can't tolerate any of those people thinking badly of you because of me. The best way to stop the talk and calm things down is to let Michael marry us."

Clarissa jerked away. "How romantic." She folded her arms and walked a few feet away, seething inside, mainly angry with herself because deep inside a little part of her liked the idea. But the practical side of her told her it was ridiculous. She whirled and faced him. "I still hardly know you. After what I've been through, do you really expect me to turn around and marry a near stranger?"

He put his hands on his hips and stood there in his blue calico shirt with the sleeves rolled up to reveal muscular forearms, a gun belt around his hips, his dark, wavy hair blowing in strands over his handsome face. Why did he have to look so handsome? Clarissa turned away again.

"Let's see," he said. "You already know I was eight when my parents died in a fire I set by accident, and that a crazed preacher raised me and beat me until I was thirteen—and I still have a couple of scars on my back to prove it. You know I ran off and joined the army, fought in the Mexican War, got some schooling in Philadelphia, then back to the army and served in Texas where I married a Mexican woman who died, taking my baby with her. I was transferred farther north, served at Fort Laramie, fought Indians, then got called to the Civil War, fought at Shiloh, where a man I'd befriended willed some money to me before he was killed. I was wounded in the leg in later fighting, was sent to St. Louis to mend, where I also retrieved the money willed to me, then grabbed little Sophie from under the hooves of a team of horses, which is how I met you. You know I decided to leave the army for good and take a bunch of homeless families who'd lost everything in the war up to Montana to start new lives, and you decided to join up with me. What else do you need to know? Where I lived before I ran away? I was born and raised in Springfield, Illinois, which is where the preacher who took me in also lived. I don't think I've left anything out."

She finally faced him again. "Those are just facts. They don't explain the real Dawson Clements. How do I know *you* won't turn out to be a drunken wife beater? You *were* drinking the first night you came to my wagon, if you will remember."

"That was for courage. I'm not exactly the most self-confident man who ever walked, you know."

Clarissa rolled her eyes. "You're the most confident man I've ever met. You give orders like a—like a drill sergeant!

Do you intend to order me around? I've learned some hard lessons, Dawson Clements, and one of them is I'll never let a man walk all over me again—ever!"

He grinned. "Good. That pride is part of what I love about you."

She waved him off. "Stop saying you love me. You don't know me any better than I know you."

"You don't always need to know every last detail about a person to love them, Clare. What else do you want to know about me?"

"What about other women?" she asked, facing him again.

"It was a long time ago that you served in Texas. What about between then and now? Have there been other women you thought you loved?" She saw instant pain in his eyes and regretted the question.

He walked closer, sobering. "No. There have been no other women who meant one whit to me."

She turned away. "Just the kind who follow the soldiers wherever they go, I suppose. How do I know you aren't carrying some dreaded disease?"

"What?"

She covered her face. "I'm sorry. I don't know what made me say that."

"Maybe it's because you don't like the thought of me being with other women."

She gasped. "Oh, the gall. I—I don't know how I feel about you at all! One minute you're nothing more to me than a guide for this wagon train, and the next minute I—"

He stepped closer. "You what?"

She just shook her head.

He grasped her shoulders. "Clare, I don't have any disease. And if you want to know so much about me, sure, I've succumbed to being human a few times. I never told you I was perfect. I'm far from that. But you do something to me. You've made me think about my life and what I want. I know you aren't even sure you love me, and I know the last thing you're ready for is to trust a man again. For now I just want Michael to marry us to quiet things down. It will just make the rest of the trip easier, because I intend to spend more time with you and Sophie, so that you *can* get to know me better. If you're my wife, people won't care how much time I spend with you."

She turned from him again, her emotions tumbling in a cascade of fear and anger and frustration and confusion. "If we do this…don't expect any—you know—conjugal rights, I think they call it."

There came a moment of silence. "Who wants to be with a woman who doesn't really want him?" he finally answered.

She swallowed. "I…didn't say that. I mean—I just need to know it's all for the right reasons. I'll need you to sign a paper that gives me the right to have the marriage annulled at any time, as long as we haven't truly been man and wife. I— This is just to make things look better, right?"

"Right."

"And you won't—you won't think you have…husbandly rights…just because of a piece of paper?"

"Well, let's see. We're out here in the middle of nowhere, with only canvas-covered wagons to sleep in. Do you really think I'd climb in your wagon and force myself on you and have everybody on this wagon train hear the ruckus you'd raise and embarrass me beyond recovery? No, thank you."

She covered her face, hiding a smile that for some strange reason turned to tears. In the next moment his arms were around her, and she didn't mind. He held her close, and she turned to him, taking comfort in his strength.

"When and if we make this a real marriage, Clare Graham, it will be the right way, in private, and for all the right reasons, just like you want it. Will you trust me that much?"

Hard as she tried, she couldn't stop the sobs that poured forth without notice. "I try to be so brave and confident, but I'm scared of everything, Dawson. Outlaws, the Indians, the buffalo, the deep waters, the weather, snakes, wolves, what could happen to Sophie, what I'll do when I reach Montana. And it's not just you—I'm scared I did something wrong in my marriage, that maybe it's partly my fault Chad left—only, I can't understand what it was. What if that happened with you? And what about the army? It was your whole life. How do you know you won't want to go back? I don't want that life for Sophie. I want to be settled. I want her to have a real daddy—who's with her every day."

"I guess that's where the trust comes in, when I tell you I will give you all those things. And Chad Graham, from what you've told me, was a poor excuse of a man who was probably scared to death of responsibility. My guess is she's already thinking of leaving the woman he ran off with. He'll never be settled and happy with one woman. Some men are like that. I'm not one of them. I know it in my heart, even though up to now I've never lived that way."

Clarissa pulled away. "This is terrible. I'm so sorry. Here you're asking me to marry you and telling me you love me, and I'm bawling like a baby and acting like you've asked something horrible of me."

"You have a right to cry."

It struck her then, and she faced him, wiping at her tears. "So do you, Dawson."

A strange look came into his eyes. "I did my crying, after my first beating. After that I made a vow to never cry again."

He put on a smile that obviously masked something much deeper. "Now, are you going to marry me?"

She couldn't think of one thing about Dawson Clements that any woman wouldn't be attracted to or want. He was handsome, able, caring, brave....

"Marriage is the last thing I came out here for. It's one thing I believed would not happen again for a long, long time, if ever. Yes, I'll marry you, but only to make it easier for us to spend time together, with the agreement that I can end the marriage if I so choose, and that you don't demand any husbandly rights without my consent, and that you understand, Dawson Clements, that it's quite possible we'll reach Montana and have to go our separate ways. I don't want you blaming yourself for that. It wouldn't be a rejection of you or because you aren't worthy. It will be because of my own doubts and fears."

He stepped closer again, grasping her face and wiping at her tears with his thumbs. "Then I will have to do my best on the rest of this journey to erase those doubts and fears, won't I?"

She closed her eyes as he leaned down and lightly kissed her lips. She grasped his sturdy wrists. "I don't want Sophie calling you Daddy. We have to think of her, too. She doesn't truly understand what marriage means yet, so nothing has to change where she is concerned. I don't want her growing any more attached than she already is—just in case."

He kissed her eyes. "Agreed. Just in case. And, uh, regarding tonight—no one will believe our story if we don't go off alone together, if you know what I mean."

She stiffened and pulled away. "What are you suggesting?"

"I'm suggesting you camp with me away from the wagon train. You can sleep in my tent. I'll sleep outside, which I do most of the time anyway. I seldom put up that tent, but I'll do it for you."

She put a hand to her forehead. "I suppose we don't have much choice. What about Zeb? Will he know the truth?"

Dawson grinned. "Zeb has done and seen it all. He won't care one way or another, although he's told me that he's known total strangers to get married on trips like this. A man loses his wife and a woman loses her husband—he needs a woman to help with his children, she needs a man to provide for hers, so they get married because it's the practical thing to do. Funny thing is, most of those marriages end up successful. And just look how much more we have to go on. This might work out a lot better than you think."

She met his gaze, determined to give him a warning and doubtful scowl, but his teasing grin made it impossible. "We shall see, Mr. Clements."

"Yes, we shall, Mrs. Clements." He walked up and put a hand to her waist. "Shall we go see Preacher Harvey?"

Chapter Twenty-Three

✤

"I feel like I'm sixteen," Clarissa told Carolyn a short time later, as her friend pulled Clarissa's thick hair into one big braid through the crown and down the back. "This whole thing is so silly."

"I think it's wonderful," Carolyn answered, tying a pink ribbon at the end of the braid. "And I don't believe you will regret this one bit. Who knows? Maybe before we reach Montana you'll face the fact that you really do love Dawson Clements, and by the time we get there you won't be able to legally annul this marriage."

"Carolyn Harvey!"

"He's more man than you'll ever come across again, and you know it. And the poor man loves you dearly, so give this marriage time to become truly real and lasting. It's God's will, you know."

"No, I *don't* know that, and I didn't say I wouldn't give the marriage a chance."

They stood behind Clarissa's wagon, away from the others, so that no one would see Clarissa until the ceremony began. Clarissa turned around and faced Carolyn. "How do I look?"

"You know you're beautiful, no matter what you wear or how your hair is done. Good thing you brought at least one fancier dress along. Pink is perfect with your hair and complexion. And those little white ruffles around the neck and sleeves and down the buttons—why, for all the hard work of traveling this far, a person wouldn't know it by the look of you. You look like you've just stepped out of Sunday church. Dawson will be very pleased."

Clarissa scowled. "I don't care if he's pleased or not."

"It's a sin to lie, Clarissa."

Clarissa smiled, taking Carolyn's hands. "You look very nice yourself today, with that blue ribbon in your hair and that pretty blue dress."

The taller, much more robust woman blushed and smiled. "Well, now, you know it takes a lot to make this plain gal pretty, but I clean up pretty good, I'd say."

Both women laughed, and Sophie came running around to them, carrying a handful of wildflowers. "Look, Mommy! Dawson helped pick them! He said you should cawwy them."

"We're ready, Carolyn!" Michael called from the other side of the wagon.

Clarissa felt her heart rush faster. She took the flowers from Sophie, who wore a yellow ruffled dress for the occasion. "You look so pretty, Sophie."

The girl smiled and skipped off. "Huwwy, Mommy!"

Clarissa glanced at Carolyn again. "Are you sure this is right?"

"You know it is. This is all God's doing, as far as I'm concerned. Now, come on. I've never been a matron of honor before!"

The two women walked around the other side of the wagon, where the rest of the wagon party stood waiting, headed by Michael, who held his Bible open, Otto Hensel, who'd agreed to be the best man—and Dawson, who watched Clarissa lovingly as she stepped closer.

One thing Clarissa did not doubt—she was marrying one of the most handsome men she could ever have found, but she'd learned handsomeness meant nothing when it came to loyalty and true love. And there Dawson stood, wearing a white shirt and black string tie and black jacket, his boots cleaned up as best as he could get them, his face clean-shaven, his thick, dark hair clean and slicked back. Nothing but love and sincerity showed in his dark eyes, as well as a look there that only a woman could appreciate. It made her feel beautiful, and she almost felt sorry for him that this marriage would not be consummated…certainly not right away. They had a lot to learn about each other—and if all the learning meant they would discover this was not right after all, she wanted no regrets, no physical ties.

Dawson reached out, and she placed her hand in his big ones as he folded both of them around her hand reassuringly. Clarissa handed the flowers to Carolyn, and Michael began reading from the Bible.

"Though I speak with the tongues of men and of angels, and have not love, I am become as sounding brass, or a tinkling cymbal. And though I have the gift of prophecy, and understand all mysteries, and all knowledge; and though I have all faith, so that I could remove mountains, and have not love, I am nothing.

"'Love suffereth long, and is kind; love envieth not; love vaunteth not itself, is not puffed up, doth not behave itself unseemly, seeketh not her own, is not easily provoked, thinketh no evil; rejoiceth not in iniquity, but rejoiceth in the truth; beareth all things; believeth all things; hopeth all things; endureth all things.

"'Charity never faileth; but whether there be prophecies, they shall fail; whether there be tongues, they shall cease; whether there be knowledge, it shall vanish away. And now abideth faith, hope, love, these three; but the greatest of these is love.'"

Michael proceeded to have Clarissa and Dawson speak their vows, and for all her doubts, Clarissa could not help feeling sincere. Deep inside she knew this was right after all. If only she could rid herself of the nagging hurts and fears that would not leave her. For his part, Dawson's look could not possibly display more sincerity.

For Clarissa, everything proceeded as though in a strange dream. She was speaking marriage vows, something she didn't believe she'd do again for a long, long time, if ever. It seemed like no time at all before she heard the words, "I now pronounce you man and wife."

The little group of travelers cheered and clapped, as did little Sophie. Michael was beaming, and when Clarissa looked up at Dawson, so was he.

"You may kiss the bride," Michael announced.

Grinning a smile that would attract any woman, Dawson leaned down, and Clarissa allowed the kiss, a warm, soft, deep kiss of promise and reassurance that calmed her. "I love you, Mrs. Clements," he said softly in her ear.

She wanted desperately to reply with the same sincerity, but not yet…not yet. They turned to greet everyone, shaking hands, accepting a few gifts, mostly homemaking items other women were willing to give up. However, the merry-making couldn't last long. Dawson did not want to give up travel time, and within an hour they were changed back into their everyday wear and were again on their way.

At the end of a long morning Dawson shared lunch with Clarissa and Sophie, giving Clarissa a hug and a kiss before they were under way yet again. Throughout the long afternoon Clarissa couldn't help worrying about how the night would go, if Dawson would keep his promise. Early evening brought a long-needed rest to the strangest day Clarissa could remember. Dawson joined them for supper, telling Clarissa he would go set up his tent on a nearby hill and wait for her. Giving her a quick kiss, he left, and Clarissa nervously helped Carolyn scrub dishes and put them back into a wooden box attached to the side of Carolyn's wagon.

"Have a nice night," Carolyn told her with a wink.

"Oh, Carolyn, stop it. Nothing is going to happen. And please don't tease about it. I honestly don't want to be pushed or questioned."

Carolyn smiled. "I understand, and I'm sorry. It's just that Michael feels this is so right for you, and that God wants this, too." She gave Clarissa a quick hug. "But for now you do have to convince everyone else on this train that this is for real, so pack a flannel gown and be on your way, Mrs. Clements."

Clarissa smiled and shook her head. Nervously she packed a few supplies, gave Sophie a quick kiss and headed toward Dawson's campsite.

He was waiting by a lit fire, drinking coffee. "Well, there you are, Mrs. Clements. How do you feel about this day?"

She set down her bag. "Very confused."

He chuckled. "I don't blame you. Want some coffee?"

"No. If you don't mind, I'll go inside the tent and go to sleep."

He shrugged. "Whatever you want. I set up my bedroll behind the tent. That way no one will know I'm not in the tent. And I'll be right close by in case of danger, or—uh—in case you call out to me."

Clarissa rolled her eyes. "Don't get your hopes up, Mr. Clements."

He laughed harder. "Oh, my lovely Mrs. Clements, I told you that was part of the reason I wanted to marry you—the way you can make me laugh. Good night, Clare."

She stared at him a long moment. "I'm sorry, Dawson. This isn't what a man expects on his wedding night."

He just stared at the fire. "We already talked about it. Everything in its own time, Clare. You just sleep well knowing I'm not going to bother you."

In that moment Clarissa decided this man was too good for her. She smiled. "Good night, Dawson. And—thank you. I love you all the more for this."

"Well, then, it's worth it." He still would not look at her, and she guessed that made it easier for him. She ducked inside the tent and quickly got into her flannel gown and crawled into the bedroll he'd laid out for her. A tiny part of her ached to be held in the night again, but Dawson Clements kept his promise, and she awoke the next morning feeling relaxed and refreshed. The smell of fresh coffee and frying bacon met her nostrils, and she peeked outside to see Dawson dressed and making breakfast.

"Well, well, well," she muttered.

Go throughout the whole world and preach the gospel
To all Mankind.
Whoever believes and is baptized will be saved.

—*Mark* 16:15-16

Chapter Twenty-Four

June 30, 1863

"She's right, Michael. I *am* crazy." Dawson sat on a log in front of his tent, and Michael sat across from him, both men with blankets around their shoulders against the unusually cool night. "I marry a woman who's a far better person than I am, inherit a kid I'm now responsible for, agree not to consummate the marriage—" He stared at the firelight. "Now *there's* something I never thought I'd agree to with *any* woman. Then I let her sleep in my tent last night while I slept out in the cold. I told her I'd find a way to support us, and I have no idea what that will be—and craziest of all, I told her she could annul the marriage at any time and that if she asked, I would ride out of her life when we reach Montana." Michael listened quietly. "I already know I could no more ride out of her and Sophie's lives now than I could go the rest of my life without water," he added. "Oh, and then I go and ask you to come out here tonight so we can talk alone. You—a preacher and Clare's good friend. I can just imagine what your opinion is of me right now."

Michael cleared his throat before speaking. "I have a very high opinion of you, Dawson. If I didn't, I would have refused to marry you and Clare yesterday. It seems to me that *you're* the one doubting yourself and claiming not to be worthy of Clare. I'm just here because you asked me to be here. Maybe you should be honest and tell me why you *really* asked to talk to me tonight."

Dawson sat quietly, thinking before answering. "That's the craziest thing of all, and it's hard for me to say it, especially to a preacher."

Michael shrugged. "I am a good listener. Carolyn says that's one of the reasons I make a good preacher. I have no doubt that Jesus himself was also a good listener."

Dawson stared at the fire, almost angry with Clare for the changes she'd brought about in his soul. "I want you to know I'm doing this for Clare, not for me. I mean, I know the kind of man she needs, and I'm not that man yet. I want to be. Part of that means, well, getting myself right with God, I guess you'd say. Now that I've committed myself like this—well, I want to do and say the right things, so that I never lose Clare. I mean—maybe I need a little help over the next few weeks."

"Help?"

Dawson sighed, watching little embers drift upward when a piece of wood in the fire popped. "You know—from God." He was feeling a bit of an idiot, wondering if this was really Dawson Clements sitting here saying these things—to a preacher, no less!

"I—uh—I made a vow, Michael, back when I was maybe ten years old," he continued. "Actually it was two vows, and they came after one of Preacher Carter's many beatings. One was that I would never cry again, and I haven't, not even when my first wife died. The other was to never, ever, ask for help for anything from any man, and certainly not from what I saw as a cruel dictator of a God. It's not that I ever stopped believing in God. Preacher Carter made sure I knew there *was* a God, and that I should fear Him greatly. I hated that God, and there was no way I would ever ask such a Being for help. Carter never said a word to me about God's son or him dying for my sins or any of those things. From the bits of things you've said to me, and things Clare has said, I'm realizing I really don't know anything about God, certainly not about Jesus and all that. So I'm asking you to teach me, for Clare's sake, because she's a good Christian woman. And I'm asking you to—" He hated this. "I'm asking you to pray for me—and to teach *me* how to pray. I want to pray for help in being a good husband and in showing Clare she made a wise choice in marrying me. I want her to love me as much as I love her, and I don't want her pity or feelings of obligation. I just want her to truly love Dawson Clements, with no strings attached."

Both men sat quietly for a moment. Michael took a deep breath before answering. "Well, now, that's quite a request. I have to tell you I am honored to be asked by someone who has doubted and hated God for years, because that tells me you have a lot of confidence in me and my faith. I have had a feeling since the first day I met you when Clare brought you home to treat that leg that God had brought you into our lives—especially into Clare's life—for a reason. I could see right off that you needed God in your life, and Clare needs someone in her own life who can teach her to trust again, not just trust another man, but trust God Himself. Chad Graham hurt her about as deeply as a woman can be hurt, and in her he instilled doubts about her ability to be a good wife, even though that is exactly what she was and none of what happened was her fault. I think she is beginning to see that, but she still has some obstacles to surmount. I firmly believe you will help her there, and that one day you will both see that you were truly brought together by God and should always be together.

"Now, as for teaching you about Christ and prayer and such, you first have to truly believe that God is kind and just, who forgives all sins through the death of his only beloved Son, Jesus Christ, who was sacrificed like a lamb for the people of the world. Through belief in Jesus, all sins are forgiven, Dawson, the minute a man sincerely asks for forgiveness. But it isn't your parents' deaths for which you need forgiving. God knows what happened, and He knows it was an accident, caused by an innocent child. What you need to be forgiven for is hating God all these years, and for being too stubborn up to now to pray and ask for help. You need help with all the anger you carry. God is always ready to listen, Dawson, and simply by voicing to me the things you want to pray for, you have already offered up a prayer, through me. You are already closer to God than you realize. He is working miracles, *in* you and *for* you. Bringing Clare into your life is one of those miracles, and at the same time He's working miracles for Clare through you."

"Through me? That's unlikely."

"Oh, but it's already happening. God thinks highly of you, Dawson. That's why He chose you to bring happiness into Clare's life again. Eventually she is bound to give herself to you, body and soul. The only thing she lacks is trust, and you will teach her about that. And I have told her that she needs to truly forgive Chad, deep in her heart and with all sincerity. That is the only way she will feel truly free to love you. I want to add that I admire the way you are honoring her person and her wishes. These are the things that will gradually win her total trust. I believe you already have her love, Dawson, even if she won't admit it. It's her fear of trusting another man that is holding her back."

Dawson pondered Michael's words. "You're a good man, Michael. I appreciate you coming out here. You have no idea how I wish it was a man like you who'd taken me in after that fire."

"And so do I, but what's done is done, and it's Preacher Carter who was the evil one, not you. Satan worked through him to try to win another soul to his own cause, but down inside you were too strong and too good for him to ever totally control you. And if it's possible for you to accept, Dawson, if you want to truly feel God's grace, I would like to baptize you. Baptism can bring miracles to your life, and peace to your heart."

Why was this so hard? He contemplated telling Michael the *whole* story. But he couldn't bring himself to admit to what he'd done to Preacher Carter. Maybe he'd find a way once he was baptized and did some praying. "I, uh, I don't know if I'm worthy."

"All are worthy, Dawson. We can walk to the river, just you and me. No one else needs to know, if you prefer it that way. We can give some explanation."

Dawson had no explanation for what had come over him, except that God must be controlling his thoughts and movements. "Yeah, sure, why not, if it will help cure what ails me."

Michael rose, and feeling insecure and a bit confused, yet strangely compelled, Dawson followed him to the Platte. Wolves howled in the distant hills and coyotes yipped, yet strangely no mosquitoes bothered them tonight. The two men removed their boots, and Dawson removed his hat. They stepped into the river.

"You're a little tall for me, Dawson," Michael told him. "If you will get on your knees it will be easier for me to pour water over you."

"Sure." Dawson obeyed, an awesome humbleness overtaking him. He closed his eyes, and Michael scooped water into his hands and poured it over Dawson's head.

"Dawson Clements, I baptize you in the name of the Father—" Another scoop of water. "And the Son." Once again he poured water over Dawson's head. "And the Holy Spirit." He kept a hand on Dawson's head then and prayed. "Heavenly Father, this man before me comes to You more as the child he was when his parents were taken from him than the man he is now. That child was taught lies about You, so that Dawson could not come to You and open his heart to You. Teach him that we are all Your children forever, even when we are grown, and that You love us much more than any man can love any child of his own flesh. Forgive this man's true sins, but show him he needs no forgiveness for the one thing he was led to believe was an act of unforgivable evil.

"Help him, Lord, to realize he is worthy of every good thing that comes his way, including Clare, Lord. Fill his heart with love and his soul with your spirit and with truth.

"We pray for all of this in the name of Your son, Jesus Christ. Amen."

Wolves howled again, and Dawson remained kneeling in the water. Michael put a hand on his shoulder. "I'll be glad to talk more whenever you tell me you have the time, Dawson. And be assured that anything we talk about is between you and me. I don't share a man's private needs and feelings with anyone but God. God bless you, Dawson Clements. I'll leave you here alone for a while."

Michael left, walking up the bank. Once he was gone, Dawson broke the second vow he'd made all those years ago. He wept.

Chapter Twenty-Five

July 5, 1863

Clarissa watched nervously as a large band of Sioux followed the wagon train almost side by side. The pioneers made their way over more hills of such long, gradual grades that they sometimes had to stop and rest the oxen before they even reached the tops of the hills. To her they were mountains, but according to Dawson they hadn't seen true mountains yet. The thought was daunting.

Dawson kept his promise about leaving her alone other than to join them during every break, contributing some of his own food supplies to support theirs. He helped her hitch and unhitch her oxen whenever he was able, but since the appearance of the band of Sioux two days ago, he'd stayed at a distance, he and Zeb often keeping themselves between the Indians and the wagon train.

She was falling in love with him. He'd changed since they were married, more so since his talks with Michael. It seemed now that most of the time that dark cloud behind Dawson's blue eyes was gone. He didn't seem uncomfortable when Michael prayed over their meals. She was grateful that Michael had kept his conversations with Dawson to himself. If Dawson thought for a moment that Michael had betrayed his confidence, he would stop talking to him and again lose his trust in preachers.

In spite of her deepening feelings for Dawson, she still couldn't bring herself to give of herself totally and fully trust him. After all, they had a long way to go, and Dawson Clements still had a lot to prove to her once they reached Montana. Until they got there, Dawson had a job to do that kept him busy and constantly on the move. The hardship of this journey, the constant, endless walking, weary bones at night, all simply made it difficult to relax together and talk about all the things they still needed to discuss.

Still, she was Mrs. Dawson Clements, and in the few moments when she wasn't wondering if she'd lost her mind and committed the most ridiculous act ever, she actually liked the idea. Sometimes in the deep of night she fantasized what it would be like to truly take the man as a husband, but somehow Chad Graham's face would always replace Dawson's. Chad's betrayal still burned in her soul, destroying thoughts of truly sharing her soul with any other man.

One thing she did know—it was becoming difficult to imagine life now without Dawson in it. She cared enough that she knew she'd be devastated if something happened to him. It frightened her that the Sioux could decide to shoot him down at any moment, and she couldn't help constantly watching for him to make sure he was still there.

It was late afternoon when men began shouting, "Hold it! Hold up there!"

Clarissa immediately looked for Dawson, who'd given instructions that the minute any of the Indians broke from their band and rode toward Dawson or the wagon train, they were to stop and form a circle. Her heart beat faster when indeed, she saw four warriors riding in their direction. Zeb was riding fast toward Dawson from farther back on the train, where he'd been keeping an eye on the McCurdys as well as watching for more Indians that might be lurking farther back.

God, keep him safe, she prayed silently as she switched her oxen and gave a command for them to begin veering left along with wagons ahead of her, which came around to join up with those toward the rear, leaving an opening for the McCurdy wagons once they caught up. As soon as wagons found their positions, men grabbed rifles and handguns and made ready behind the wagons on the inside of the circle.

Clarissa told Sophie to stay inside the wagon, and as Dawson had ordered, she and other women climbed into the wagons out of sight, ordering their children to do the same. Clarissa hurriedly dug out her handgun from deep inside a trunk she kept locked so that Sophie could not get to the gun. She nervously checked to make sure it was loaded, then moved to the side of the wagon that faced the Indians. She lifted the canvas enough to watch.

Dawson and Zeb were now parlaying with the four warriors, whose horses and faces were painted. She saw Dawson shake his head, apparently refusing something. Her stomach ached with fear and worry. Thank goodness he and Zeb had experience with Indians, but that didn't mean there wouldn't be trouble, and there was Dawson, right in the middle of it. How could she not love that kind of courage and experience? For all his inner doubts, Dawson Clements knew how to take care of himself and others. Surely that kind of conviction would make him a good husband after all.

She had so much to think about, and so little time to do the thinking. Right now she felt the sweat of fear trickle down her neck. Sophie asked her a question and she told the girl that Dawson said she should keep very still. Once she told her that, Sophie didn't say another word. Clarissa continued watching what looked like a literal argument between Dawson and one of the Indians who was apparently some kind of leader.

"Be careful, Dawson," Clarissa whispered.

Finally Dawson shared some kind of hand signal with the Indian and turned his horse. He headed toward the wagon with Zeb and all four Indians. He removed his rifle and held it up sideways, his signal that no one from the wagon train should fire a shot. As they came closer, Clarissa could see the warriors better. The fringes of their clothing danced with the rhythm of their horses. Their black hair hung long and straight and was decorated with feathers and beads, and the paint on their faces and an array of formidable-looking weapons made them frightening indeed. Clarissa could hardly believe Dawson dared to turn his back on them.

By the time they stopped near the wagon train, the McCurdys were just then pulling into place. Dawson turned his horse and faced the Indians again, shoving his rifle through the loop that held it on his saddle. He said something to the Indians and gave them another hand signal before dismounting and walking inside the circle of wagons.

Clarissa hurriedly moved to the other side of her wagon so she could lift that side of the canvas to watch and listen.

"I need a few blankets that can be spared," Dawson told the men. "Some tobacco, some flour, and anything colorful your women can give me—ribbon, lace, buttons, beads, things like that. They wanted a lot more, including a few head of the Kruegers' cattle, but I told them no. I said they either take what we give them, or opt for a fight. I told them we have a lot of guns, many more than they have." He smiled slyly, helping relieve the tension.

"I also told them there is a large regiment of soldiers coming up behind us. Of course I lied, but I think they believe me." He glanced toward Clarissa's wagon, then around at the men. "I don't think this bunch is looking for trouble. They have women and children along and are simply moving their camp north. They happened to cross our path and decided to see what they could get out of us, so don't get itchy trigger fingers. Just do like I said. Somebody lay out a couple of blankets that we can tie some supplies into."

Today Dawson had deliberately worn his army pants and shirt, hoping the uniform would give him an air of authority in the eyes of the Indians, more than if he were simply a common traveler. Apparently it had worked. Quickly Clarissa grabbed a blanket and moved to the back of the wagon, throwing it out without sticking her head out.

"You stay down, Sophie," she warned, terrified the warriors might take a liking to her little girl's bright red hair and beautiful blue eyes.

She laid the gun aside carefully and opened a trunk that held sewing items. She hated the idea of giving away lace and ribbon—which she would need once she settled—to these people who surely couldn't appreciate such things in the same way she did. Still, Dawson had given the order. She shoved the items into a woolen sock and threw in some buttons and the second sock, then tied off the top of the sock and threw it out of the wagon.

Dawson walked over and picked up the blanket and sock, then took it to the center of the circle, where men brought more blankets, sacks of flour and plugs of tobacco and other items. Clarissa heard someone curse the heathens, and someone else said it might be fun to use them for target practice.

"Fire one shot and I'll shoot the man who does so," Dawson warned. "Better to kill one of you and appease those warriors out there than let them wipe out this whole wagon train."

Clarissa had to smile at how easily the army officer in him showed itself. She knew the men believed every word he said, and no one raised a gun as Michael and the Krueger men tied the blankets so that the items inside wouldn't fall out.

"Carry them out and hand them to the Indians," Dawson told them.

"I'm not going out there!" Bert Krueger told him.

"It's all right, I assure you. One thing about Indians is they don't go back on their word, unless one of us does something stupid, like insult them or shoot at them. Come on. I need your help with all this."

Wiping at sweat on his brow with his shirtsleeve, Bert picked up one of the blankets, and he, Michael, Will Krueger and Dawson carried the supplies outside the circle of wagons to the waiting Indians. Each arrogant-looking warrior took a blanket, and Dawson remounted his horse while the other three men made a hasty retreat back to their wagons.

"Dawson won't let them get us, will he, Mommy?" Sophie whispered.

Clarissa smiled at the girl's trust in the man. "No, he won't let them hurt us."

Dawson rode with the warriors as they left, stopping about halfway between the wagons and the rest of the tribe. He and Zeb waited there until the leader of the band of Indians raised a hand in farewell.

Dawson raised his hand in return, and the long procession of natives got under way again. Dawson said something to Zeb, who nodded his head and got his horse into a slow walk, moving ahead of the wagon train to follow the tribe, probably to make sure they kept going. Dawson turned and rode back to the emigrants, dismounting and tying his horse to one of the wagons, then rejoining the circle.

"We shouldn't have any trouble," he announced. "We'll stay here and make camp for the night. Zeb is riding on to make sure the Indians keep going for a ways and to see that they don't regroup into some kind of war party. I don't think that will happen."

"What makes you so sure?" a still-resentful Sam McCurdy spoke up.

"I'm *not* sure. I'm simply going on experience. They have women and children along, and I convinced them there are soldiers behind us. They don't want their women and children hurt any more than we want ours hurt, so just be glad they took the supplies and left. That's a good sign."

"Those dirty savages took some good supplies from us," McCurdy answered. "What gives them the right?"

Dawson's disgust with the man was obvious. "Because, McCurdy, in reality there are more of them than us, and I guarantee they're a whole lot better at a fight than any of you are. Even if they don't have guns, which some of them do have, they'd get through this circle of wagons and kill every one of us. They would burn everything in sight and ride off with your children. Don't you think it's better to try to get along with them, even if it means swallowing a little pride and losing a few supplies?"

McCurdy's lips moved into a pout as he folded his arms and leaned against his wagon, shaking his head.

"You can stay with the circle of wagons for tonight," Dawson told him. "If Zeb comes back in the morning and says things look good, you'd better fall back again once we get started. The last thing you want now is to be left behind with Indians lurking around, so don't do something stupid to make me change my mind about sticking to the vote we took."

Sam glowered at Dawson but said nothing. Dawson walked over to Clarissa's wagon, leaning on the gate.

"Hi, Dawson!" Sophie said in a near whisper. "Can I talk now?"

Dawson grinned broadly. "Yes you can, carrot cake."

Sophie giggled. "I'm not a piece of cake!"

"Sure you are. You're sweet like cake and your red hair reminds me of carrots, so you're carrot cake."

Sophie covered her mouth and giggled again, and Dawson glanced at Clarissa. "You okay, Mrs. Clements?"

"I'm a nervous wreck, but fine," she answered with a smile. "I was scared for you."

"Good. That means you care, at least a little bit."

"You know I do."

He brightened more. "Then how about just one kiss?" he teased.

"Okay!" Sophie thought he meant her. She crawled to the wagon gate and put her arms around his neck, planting a sloppy kiss smack on his mouth. "Pick me up, Dawson."

Dawson cast Clarissa a look of disappointment and despair as he took Sophie into his arms. "Well, I tried," he told Clarissa with a teasing sigh. "If only her mommy loved me as much." He walked away with Sophie in his arms, who yelled to Lena that Dawson had called her a carrot cake.

Clarissa sat back with a sigh. "You're using that child to get to me, Dawson Clements…and it's working."

Chapter Twenty-Six

❧

July 8, 1863

"These waters are deeper than our last crossing," Dawson told his ever-more-weary group of travelers. "I've discussed this with Zeb here. I'll let him tell you what we're going to do."

They all stood at the edge of the swollen North Platte, nervous about getting to the other side.

"We'll tie guide ropes to each wagon," Zeb told them, "and take the ropes by horse to the other side where we'll tie them to oxen or draft horses we've taken over first. If a wagon starts to float, the team on the other side will keep the current from taking it away."

Clarissa rubbed at her aching lower back. Stress from the encounter with Indians, followed by tortuous climbs up ever-steeper hills, had taken a toll on everyone, man and animal alike. Mrs. Krueger was forced to unload a heavy oak headboard her father had made by hand and leave it behind to rot from the elements. She'd cried as though she'd lost a loved one, and Clarissa didn't blame her.

Now they all faced another river crossing, this one more daunting in spite of not being as wide as when they crossed the South Platte. The North Platte was more swollen from spring melt because it was closer to mountains. Several of the travelers had already voiced concerns over the fact that they did not know how to swim. Clarissa was one of them, but she was more afraid for Sophie.

Dawson moved to her side as though sensing her worry. He leaned close to keep his voice from interrupting Zeb's. "I'll take you and Sophie across with me," he told her.

"Lena, too. My gelding is bigger than average and a strong swimmer."

"Dawson and I will both make special trips with any little ones you want to give us," Zeb was telling the others. "Dawson will take his wife first so's she can watch the children on the other side as we bring them over. After the kids, the women and the wagons, we'll help get the cattle across." He looked at Bert Krueger. "Just so's you know, we won't be held accountable for the cattle that panic and drown. Them animals can be pretty unpredictable when they get excited, but we'll do our best." He directed his attention to the rest of the group. "Each wagon will be hitched to the draft horses or oxen on the other side. We'll also tie a rope to the back of each wagon as we float it across. All you men will hang on to it from this side, gradually releasing it as the wagon is floated over. If we can keep the rope taut both ways, we should be able to hang on to the wagon even if the current grabs it. When the draft horses keep pulling, the wagon will eventually reach shallower waters again and roll up the opposite bank. When all is said and done, the remaining men on this side can ride—or I should say swim across—on my and Dawson's horses and mules. If you can't swim your-selves, just hang on. Horses *can* swim. Just keep kickin' their sides and urgin' them on. This is gonna be an all-day proj-ect, folks, and another day of dryin' out on t'other side."

"I'm not so sure about this," Sam McCurdy spoke up. He'd been allowed to join them because they all needed to hear Zeb's instructions.

"Well, unless you know how to fly, McCurdy, I wouldn't be sayin' much, 'cause this is the only way we can keep goin'. Thousands of others have crossed here, includin' me more 'n once, so t'ain't as though it's not possible."

"How many have drowned?" McCurdy asked with ob-vious mockery.

"Well, now, I don't know the numbers, McCurdy. You'd just better hope you ain't one of the statistics."

Dawson put an arm around Clarissa's waist. "Let's get this thing started."

"Now?"

"Now is as good a time as any." He led Clarissa to his horse, a beautiful black gelding with a broad chest and a steady nature. Dawson had already unloaded everything from the horse but the saddle itself and put his gear as well as his boots into Clarissa's wagon. Now he wore only sim-ple cotton pants and a cotton shirt, with only stockings on his feet.

He grasped the pommel of his saddle and mounted the horse, then reached down for Clarissa, taking his left foot out of the stirrup. Clarissa quickly removed her shoes and handed them to Carolyn. "Wish me luck," she said with a deep breath.

"You don't need it. Dawson knows what he's doing," Car-olyn assured her.

"Thanks for the confidence," Dawson told her with a grin. Clarissa got her foot into the stirrup and Dawson took her arm, helping her mount behind him on the horse. "Hang on tight!"

"I'm scared to death!"

"Just hang on to me. I'd never let anything happen to you, Mrs. Clements."

Clarissa realized Chad had never told her something like that. She'd never had to trust her life to him, and she imagined he would have thought of his own life first. Something told her Dawson would give his own life for hers, if necessary. She clung tightly around his middle, thinking what a solid man he was.

"You'll get mighty wet," he yelled to her. "Thank goodness it's plenty warm today." He rode into the river, and in moments they were in cold water that grew ever deeper until Clarissa could feel the horse was no longer touching ground. She squeezed her eyes shut and hung on for dear life as Dawson leaned forward and gave gentle commands to his horse. Soon the water reached nearly to Clarissa's shoulders. She wanted to scream from terror, but a voice inside told her not to be so afraid.

This was Dawson. If she floated away he would swim after her. She began to wonder how she could have made this trip without him, and she pressed her face against his strong, muscled back, praying they would reach the other side quickly. After several long minutes in the strong, cold current, she could tell the horse's hooves were touching ground again. Gradually they made their way up and out of the water, both of them drenched.

Clarissa breathed a sigh of relief. "We made it!"

"I told you we would." Dawson turned slightly, reaching around and pulling her partway in front of him and kissing her lightly. With one hand to her neck he held her fast, kissing her again. His touch made her shiver, but she blamed it on her wet clothes. He moved his lips across her cheek—

"Dawson, you have children and more women to bring across," Clarissa reminded him.

"I'm just celebrating that I got you across all right." She searched his eyes. "Be careful. I hate to see you do this all day long."

"I'd rather be doing this than taking shrapnel in the leg fighting Confederate rebels," he answered with a grin. He kept an arm around her to catch her under the arms as he helped her slide down from the horse. "I'll try to get a blanket over here to you if I can keep it dry," he told her as he turned his horse and headed back across the river.

She watched him go back into the water to fetch Sophie. Zeb was already coming across with John and Rosemarie's little daughter, Tess, who was the same age as Sophie. Then began the arduous task of bringing over the rest of the children, then the women, except for Wanda Krueger, who insisted on riding across in her wagon. She claimed that if the wagon and more of its precious contents of handmade furniture and other items from the Old Country were going to be lost, she would just as soon go with them. She still mourned the loss of that headboard like the loss of a child.

Next came Michael's draft horses and several oxen, to which ropes would be tied that would be attached to each wagon as it came across. Clarissa did not doubt that the wagons would be the most difficult item to bring over, and she was right. Nearly every wagon started to float away with the current, so that it was amazingly difficult for the huge draft horses and the oxen to keep pulling to get each wagon up to the other side.

Things went relatively smoothly until they began pulling Eric Buettner's wagon across. Filled with supplies to open a small trading store in Montana, the wagon was heavier than the others. Buettner had refused to dump some of those supplies when climbing the lower mountains, and he'd lost two of his eight oxen to exhaustion. He'd also refused Dawson's order to take a horse across and chose instead to stay with his wagon, thinking to keep an eye on the contents to make sure something didn't come loose and float away. He'd spent last night and most of the morning securing every single item, but now the weight of the wagon made it sink lower than the others when it reached the middle of the river.

"It's not going to make it," Clarissa commented to Carolyn. She grabbed Carolyn's hand, and the two women began praying, but the current took over, and the weight of the wagon caused the tie ropes to snap. The wagon began breaking up, parts of it flowing away with the current. Buettner foolishly tried to swim after some of them, then sank from sight.

Dawson rode into the water, then dived off his horse to search. At almost the same time, Sam McCurdy rode a horse into the water from the other side. It was hard to tell if he intended to swim across or try to rescue Eric Buettner, but it appeared as if Sam panicked when his horse started swimming. In seconds he slipped off the horse and disappeared. Susan McCurdy began screaming her husband's name and running up and down the north bank, and Clarissa put a hand to her stomach when Dawson did not reappear right away.

Finally Dawson's head popped up out of the water, then he dived down again, apparently still looking for Eric Buettner. Clarissa wondered if he even knew Sam McCurdy had also gone under.

"I think they're both gone," Michael muttered. "I just hope Dawson doesn't join them."

Dawson finally reappeared several yards farther down-river, then swam for an outcropping of rocks, where he pulled himself up.

Clarissa grabbed a blanket and hurried down to where he made it to shore, dripping wet and out of breath. "Sam McCurdy rode into the water and then went under!" she told him.

Dawson ran his hands through his hair and looked out over the river, then bent over to catch his breath. "There's nothing more I can do," he panted.

Clarissa put the blanket around his shoulders. "I didn't mean that you should. I just wanted you to know."

"Go get him!" Susan McCurdy screamed, surprising them both by charging up to Dawson in a rage. "You went after Eric Buettner, but you don't care what happens to my husband, do you? Let the drunken Sam McCurdy drown! Is that it? Let him drown?" She landed into Dawson, pummeling him with her fists so that Dawson had to grasp her wrists to stop her. Then she started kicking him. Her brother-in-law ran over and shouted for her to stop, then grabbed her away kicking and screaming.

Dawson closed his eyes and turned away. "I didn't even know he'd gone in," he told Clarissa, as if having to explain. "Everyone knows that. It's all right, Dawson. He did a stupid thing, and you were already trying to save an-other man."

"You don't understand. There's something—one last thing you don't know about me." He shivered into the blanket, still watching out over the water.

Clarissa frowned. "What are you talking about?"

He rubbed the blanket over his face and hair. "Something I never told—" He closed his eyes and sighed. "Never mind." He looked at her, deep pain in his eyes. "It's not like what she said," he told her. "You know that, don't you? I would never deliberately let a man drown."

"Of course you wouldn't."

He closed his eyes and sighed deeply, as though that one gesture would rebury something. "Let's go. I have to form a search party while some of the others bring over the rest of the cattle. We should at least ride down current and see if the bodies wash up somewhere so they can be decently buried." He looked her over as though to appraise her condition. "You okay?"

"I'm more concerned about you. At least change into some dry clothes and get your boots on before you start a search." She put a hand to his arm and gave him a tug. "Come on. Get changed."

They walked back to the wagons, which all sat drying in the late-afternoon sun. Women were spreading out blankets and clothing over the canvas tops, wagon tongues, wagon gates, bushes and trees. Sue McCurdy sat near her wagon sobbing and carrying on as though someone were skinning her alive.

Chapter Twenty-Seven

❧

July 13, 1863

We suffered our worst losses crossing the North Platte. Sam McCurdy and Eric Buettner drowned, and Eric's supply wagon was lost. We must find a way to let his brother, Haans, know, as he turned back many weeks ago because of the death of his wife and daughter. Sam's brother-in-law, Ben Gobles, decided to go on to the South Pass and try to make Fort Bridger, where he hopes to find someone who can take him on to California, where it is more settled. He now has not only his own wife and children to look after, but also Sam's wife and children. He feared Montana was too wild and rugged for him to support so many there.

She added other casualties—six cattle and two calves, and several oxen, one of them hers and two Michael's, as well as, sadly, her own precious milk cow and its calf.

With those we have lost and those who have left us, we are down to only eight children, four boys and four girls, including our own; nine men, seven women, eight wagons and only fifty-three oxen. We still have all the horses and mules, and, thank goodness, Mr. Clements and Mr. Artis, without whom we could never have made this trip.

It was cold tonight, as they'd climbed foothills the past few days into ever higher elevations. She set aside her pen and rubbed her hands together for warmth, feeling a little guilty for still not entering anything in her diary about marrying Dawson Clements. How could she explain such a thing in a way that her children and grandchildren would understand why she'd done so? And because she continued to refuse a consummated marriage, in her eyes her marriage of convenience wasn't a marriage at all. Until she knew in her heart she was totally in love with Dawson Clements, and until she trusted him implicitly in every way, she could not bring herself to try to explain their marriage in a document that for all she knew could be preserved forever. And if they parted ways when they reached Montana, she'd rather the marriage was never mentioned at all.

She sat writing by lamplight next to where Sophie slept. Setting her diary aside, she moved to the front of the wagon, sat in the seat and looked up into a black sky alive with stars. She wished she could sleep, needed it desperately, but she couldn't help wondering what Dawson meant when he said she didn't know everything about him. Whatever it was, she hoped he would tell Michael about it and finish ridding himself of the ghosts from his past that made it so hard for him to enjoy the present. He'd changed so much after several talks with Michael, but the look in his eyes when Sue McCurdy lashed out at him told her he still had at least one more demon to wrestle down before he could be truly happy.

Wolves howling in the distance pulled her from her thoughts, and a chill ran down her spine when she thought she heard growling not far away. She looked into the darkness beyond the circle of wagons, then jumped when she heard a barrage of vicious growls, along with outrageous squawking that was surely loud enough to wake the dead.

Almost instantly the chickens in the crate at the side of her wagon raised a ruckus of their own, and men and women alike began pouring out from their wagons yelling, "What's that?" "It's wolves!" "Get my gun!" At almost the same time a strange screaming sound came from where the cattle were bedded down.

There came more growling followed by shouts and several gunshots and the squealing and cries of what sounded like wounded wolves.

"Mommy!" Sophie whined, sitting up.

Dawson suddenly appeared at Clarissa's wagon brandishing a rifle. "Tell Sophie everything is fine." He hurried to the center of the circle of wagons. "Everybody who has wood bundled to their wagons or a good supply of buffalo chips, build up your campfires even though you're through cooking for the night," he ordered. "There are a lot of wolves out there. We need bigger fires!"

Clarissa told Sophie to stay put and climbed down to rebuild her own campfire.

"What about the cattle and oxen?" John Clay asked.

"Stuart Clymer will help watch them the rest of the night, then ride in his folks' wagon and sleep tomorrow while Bert

Krueger takes over." Dawson walked up close to where Clarissa still sat on the wagon seat. "I need you to give up something."

She frowned. "What?"

"Your chickens."

"My *chickens!*"

"The wolves got your rooster. Wolves run in packs that can roam for up to a hundred miles, and now they've got the smell and taste of your chickens in their nostrils and on their tongues. I'm hoping that if we leave the chickens behind tomorrow morning, the wolves will become preoccupied with them and won't follow us. The smell of those chickens will be gone."

"Oh, Dawson, I can't leave those poor things behind to be helplessly slaughtered."

"They're *chickens.* If you didn't have them for laying eggs, you'd slaughter them yourself for meat. You can get more when we reach Montana. In the meantime, you could help save everybody on this wagon train from having to chase off wolves every night."

"But they attacked the cattle, too. What about them?"

"They got two of Bert's steers. We might find it was more than that come morning. A steer is a whole lot bigger than a chicken. What they killed will keep them busy for a while. With the chickens left behind to keep them busy even longer, we can put a lot of miles between them and us by tomorrow night."

Clare hated the thought of it. "There are wolves *everywhere.* It might just happen again."

"Sure it might, but we'd have a lot less bait for them with those chickens gone."

Tears filled her eyes. "They're like pets to Sophie. She helps me feed them."

"We'll tell her a story about how the chickens like it better right here and don't want to go on with us. I'll make her believe it."

Clarissa wiped at her tears. "I think I'd rather leave some of my belongings behind than those chickens."

"Think of it as for the good of everybody along. I'm sorry, but the few cattle Bert Krueger has left are worth a lot more than those chickens. Cattle will be his livelihood when he reaches Montana."

She watched his eyes by the light of growing fires. "Will gold be *your* livelihood?"

"You've got to trust me on that, Clare. You're worth more to me than all the gold in Montana."

She took a deep breath, feeling silly for crying over chickens. "Well, I suppose people have left behind things much more precious than chickens, and one knows it's better than having to leave behind a child's grave." She nodded. "All right. You can leave them for the wolves. You'll have to be the one to make up a story for Sophie, though. I can't do it."

He reached up and took her hand. "I'm sorry. So far we've had more losses than I expected. I'm just doing what I can to keep things at a minimum."

"I know that."

He started to leave, but Clarissa squeezed his hand. "Dawson, if this is going to work—between you and me, I mean—we have to be completely honest with each other." She searched his eyes for answers. "You've never told me what you meant back at the river crossing, about not understanding something about you."

He let go of her hand and turned away. "The right time will come."

Sophie called to him, then. "Hi, Dawson!"

Dawson turned to see the girl peeking around the canvas from near the wagon seat. He walked back and lifted Sophie into his arms, giving her a solid kiss on the cheek. "Guess what?"

"What?" the girl squealed.

"The chickens get to stay here."

"They do? Why?"

"Well, I had a talk with them, and they said they were tired and didn't want to go any farther."

"But who will feed them?"

"God will feed them, Sophie. He feeds everybody, even the wolves."

Clare wanted to cry—over the chickens, and with secret joy at hearing a man like Dawson Clements talk about God. If only he would feel free to tell her whatever was left that kept him from realizing God's true grace and from feeling whole again.

The danger of death was all around me;
The horrors of the grave closed in on me;
I was filled with fear and anxiety.
Then I called to the Lord,
"I beg you, Lord, save me!"

—*Psalms* 116:3-4

Chapter Twenty-Eight

❧

July 18, 1863

"Something's wrong, Clarissa. I feel so faint, and I think—" Carolyn turned away and vomited.

Clarissa leaned against a large rock. She and Carolyn had both found an area behind some boulders where they could have privacy because of diarrhea that had set in just before making noon camp. Clarissa's stomach also felt queasy, and neither woman was able to make any lunch for the girls or Michael.

"Carolyn?" Michael's voice came from the other side of the rocks.

"She's awfully sick," Clarissa called out. "So am I."

"I'm afraid I don't feel so well myself," Michael answered. "And both the girls are throwing up."

Clarissa felt as though her heart had just been put in a

vise. "No," she groaned to herself. "It can't be." Feeling faint, she walked around the rocks to see Michael looking too white. "Is anyone else sick?" she asked.

"I don't think so. Dawson is with the girls, and he told everyone else to move ahead about fifty yards and wait there away from us. He asked me if we drank any water that maybe the rest of those along didn't drink."

Clarissa closed her eyes and fought panic. "Oh, no," she moaned.

"I told him about that stream where we found those berries when we went exploring a couple of days ago. I don't think anyone else drank out of that stream, but we were so hot—"

Clarissa put up her hand. "I remember." We drank from that stream, she thought. Just us. Just us. Afterward they came upon three graves and signs that wagons had been in the same area perhaps just days earlier. There were also signs of large campfires. Now it hit Clarissa with clarity. Those burn spots were large because a great deal of things had been burned, probably clothing and blankets. Who knew what else? Dawson had probably thought about it, too.

Cholera! She'd seen only one case of it at the hospital in St. Louis, and that person had been quarantined. Still, two nurses came down with it and were also quarantined. Everything anywhere in the area was scrubbed with lye, boiled or burned. Both the nurses and the patient had died.

She vomited, then went to her knees with weakness and deep fear for poor little Sophie and Lena. She knew enough from being a nurse that the average adult was lucky to survive the dreaded disease, but children.… It took a much larger toll on children.

"Please, God, please," she begged aloud. "Don't take my Sophie! Don't take little Lena!"

Michael stepped closer. "Clare, what do you think it is?"

"I think it might be cholera," she groaned.

"Oh, no!"

The word was ugly, matching the ravages of the disease, which could kill thousands in days. Everything fit—the water, no one else sick, the symptoms. Dawson knew it, too. That's why he'd told the rest of the travelers to move ahead—away from them.

"Oh, Michael." Clarissa grasped the trunk of a pine tree to keep from passing out. "I need to be…healthy…to take care of Sophie…and Lena. Who will take care of them? What will we do?"

It came then—the stomach sickness. She could hear Carolyn behind the rocks, still vomiting.

"Jesus help us," Michael said, sitting down on a stump and resting his elbows on his knees.

When Clarissa was through being sick, she glanced toward the wagon train in the distance to see Dawson walking toward them with a little girl in each arm. Sophie was crying.

"Oh, no, oh, no," she moaned, embarrassed by her condition and devastated that little Sophie was suffering. Dawson came closer and set the girls down. He spread out a blanket and told them to lie down on it, then walked up to Clarissa. She saw such fear in his own eyes that he reminded her of a little boy.

"You know what this probably is, don't you?" he said to her. "I've seen it in the army—almost died from it myself. But I didn't, and that means I can take care of you. I've already had it."

She covered her face. "I can't let you. It's too embarrassing. Just take care of my Sophie. Don't let her die."

He grasped her arms. "*Nobody* is dying! Understand? And I'll take care of you *and* Sophie, and Lena and Michael and

Carolyn, too. I've told the rest of the group to keep going for another day, and if none of them gets sick, they're probably all right. If that's the case, they'll keep going with Zeb. When we're through this, we'll simply follow them and maybe even catch up to them."

Clarissa turned away, clinging again to the tree trunk. "I'm so sorry, Dawson. We're ruining things for everyone—and for you."

"Don't be ridiculous. I'm going back to get blankets and towels and water and other things we'll need. With everyone so sick, it's better to stay out here away from the wagons so nothing back there gets contaminated. I'll build a good fire and get my tent and keep you warm and safe and even clean you up if I have to. When this is over we'll burn everything, blankets, towels, my tent, everything." His arm came around her shoulders. "We'll get through this. And neither God nor anyone else is going to take you and Sophie from me now."

She felt his anger in the words, and her first thought was who would take care of poor, lonely Dawson if something did happen to her? What would happen to his newfound faith in God? In her sickness and depression she even regretted that she'd not allowed him to consummate their marriage.

She went to Sophie, and the dark circles that had formed under the girl's eyes in perhaps an hour terrorized her. Children suffered worse with this horrible illness, and they often died from shock and dehydration.

"Mommy," the girl whimpered, before getting to her knees and vomiting into pretty purple mountain flowers, the same kind of flowers her sweet child had picked for her just yesterday.

She wiped Sophie's mouth with the hemline of her dress and then laid down beside her, pulling her into her arms.

"We're going to be all right," she told Sophie. "And I want you to promise Mommy that no matter how bad you feel, you will drink water when Dawson tells you to, okay? It's very, very important to keep drinking water, Sophie, or you'll get even sicker. Dawson knows what to do, and sometimes he's the one who will have to take care of you because Mommy is sick, too, okay?"

"Okay," Sophie answered in a weak voice. "I like him to take cawe of me."

"Good. I'm glad."

Carolyn came over to be with Lena, who lay so still it seemed she had no life in her.

Chapter Twenty-Nine

❧

July 20, 1863

Tears ran down Dawson's cheeks as he dug like a madman. How in the world was he supposed to put a little girl in the ground? Two days! That's all it took for little Lena to die, and her mother shortly after! How could God do such a thing? How could He take away such good people?

Would he be burying Sophie next? Clare? If he had to bury them, too, he'd curse God for the rest of his life, even if he burned in hell for it!

Sweat poured off him in spite of the cool mountain air. He finished digging a hole big enough for mother and child to be buried together. He'd failed again. These people who'd been so good to him were in his care, and he'd lost them!

He threw the shovel out of the hole and climbed out, ripping off his shirt because of the sweat. Michael was kneeling beside the hole, so white, so sick from the vicious, emaciating cholera that had ravaged him and his family and Clare and Sophie over two days of vomiting and diarrhea until one would think there could not possibly be one ounce of liquid left to their bodies.

"Don't cover it completely," Michael said weakly. "I want...to be buried with them, too."

"You aren't going to be buried!" Dawson ordered.

Michael bent over. "Come closer, Dawson," he groaned.

Dawson could hardly believe this nightmare. He knelt beside the man, putting an arm around him. "Michael, I still need you to talk to, to pray with. Right now what little faith I've learned to have is fast going out the window!"

Michael shook his head. "Listen...to me." He sat back on his heels, grimacing, already looking dead. "What you've done...past couple of days...it shows me you are...good...compassionate...exactly the kind of man...Christ wants His followers...to be. Few men would...clean up these awful...messes...and take care of us...like you've done."

"I've been in the army and fought wars, Michael. I've seen just about everything, and I've had this sickness. I know how horrid it is."

"Nevertheless—" Michael hung his head again, grasping Dawson's arm with his hand. "You are...a good man...and now I know...I was just...God's instrument, Dawson...in showing you Christ's love and forgiveness. I've done my job...and now...He is taking me home."

"I don't want to hear that kind of talk."

"You have...no choice. I want you to know...in a little metal box...in my wagon...there is a piece of paper I wrote out...after you married Clare. It gives you...my land...and Carolyn's share...if we should die. It's all...adjacent to Clare's land...so you will end up with...lots of land for raising...fine horses and cattle. You can make a good life there…for you and Clare…and Sophie."

"Michael—"

"They will live. I know it…in my heart, Dawson. This is all…happening…for a reason…so that you and Clare…can have a good life together. This is God's plan…for Clare…and for you. Some day you will be…important people in Montana. I know it…I feel it…and I can see it."

Dawson wiped at his tears with a hand dirty from digging. "You're just so sick that you're seeing the worst of things for yourself. You'll be fine, Michael, and you and I will work that land together."

Michael shook his head. "My place…is with my Lena, and with Carolyn…and with the Lord. Please…go get my wife… and my baby girl. Put them where they belong now…so they can wake up to God…with new bodies…and no more sickness."

Dawson rose, kicking at rocks as he walked to where Lena and Carolyn lay under a lean-to. Clare and Sophie were in his tent sick—so sick. How would he tell Clare that Carolyn and Lena had died? Worse, what if Michael died, too? Fighting more tears that made it hard to see, he picked up the two bodies one by one and carried them to the grave, placing Carolyn in first, then Lena. He wanted to scream curses to God Himself, yet the things Michael had taught him over these past weeks and the things he'd just told him swirled in his mind in a myriad of confusion and sorrow.

"Please…pray over them," Michael asked.

"Michael, I can't—"

"Pray over them," the man pleaded again. "I'm…too weak." Feeling completely inadequate, Dawson dropped to his knees. "God, if You will—" His voice choked and he stopped to clear his throat and swallow so he could go on. "If You will accept these words from a man who denied You most of his life, and for the sake of these good, Christian people, I pray for their souls that they are already walking up to Your throne happy and well."

He didn't know what else to say. Michael began reciting the Twenty-Third Psalm, and having gone over it with Michael many times, Dawson spoke it with him from memory.

"'Surely goodness and mercy will follow me all the days of my life, and I will dwell in the House of the Lord forever,'" they finished.

Michael keeled over. Dawson got up and rushed around to his side, and when he touched Michael's shoulder, the man fell over sideways. Dawson did not have to feel for a pulse to know he was dead, but he did so anyway. Confirming his guess, he sat down beside Michael, thinking how a better man had never walked, and wondering why God took Michael instead of him. It just didn't make sense.

"Why? Why?" he muttered. "I needed his guidance, Lord." How strange that although Michael was only a couple of years older than he, Dawson had looked to the man almost as a father figure. How strange that a grown man could sit and cry over another grown man. He hardly recognized himself as the same man who'd left St. Louis so wracked with hatred and anger and with so much prejudice against preachers in general.

Sorrow so consumed him that he ached all over as he got up and retrieved a blanket to wrap around Michael. He grimaced as he picked the man up in his arms and managed to stoop down and drop him as gently as possible into the grave. He jumped down inside, feeling mad with the horror of his task. He couldn't bear for Michael to be on top of Carolyn and Lena, so he struggled in the small enclosure to rearrange the bodies so that little Lena was on top.

"God, why are You doing this to me?" he repeated as he sobbed. What would it be like if he had to do this with Clare and Sophie? He'd have to shoot himself and fall into the grave with them. What use would there be in going on?

Taking a deep breath he climbed back out of the grave, gritty and sweaty, looking up then to see Clare standing there with horror on her face—a face already looking much thinner and more gaunt after just two days of this hideous sickness that no God should allow to exist. She met his eyes.

"Which one?" she asked in a pitifully small voice.

He walked over and pulled her into his arms. "All three," he answered.

"No!" she sobbed, withering against him.

Chapter Thirty

❧

July 21, 1863

Clarissa lay on her side watching Dawson hold a sleeping Sophie. At last the vomiting and diarrhea had stopped for both of them, but poor little Sophie lay like a rag doll, and Clarissa felt the same way. After seeing the hole dug for Michael, Carolyn and Lena, she'd collapsed and Dawson had had to carry her back to the tent. With the symptoms finally diminishing, it seemed she and Sophie would live, but all her joy and excitement at going to Montana was gone.

"How will I explain to Sophie why Lena isn't here anymore?" she asked Dawson, finding barely enough strength to talk.

Dawson sighed as he leaned against his saddle. "We'll tell her God came for her and her parents because He had something important for them to do."

"She'll ask why God didn't come for her, too."

"Tell her God knew you'd be too lonely without her." Clarissa closed her eyes and rolled onto her back. "I don't know what to do. I feel so lost. Michael and Carolyn's friendship gave me such strength and joy."

"I'd like to think I can give you those things."

"Not over the past few days I haven't. I guess if I wondered if you'd still care about me after seeing me at my worst, I don't have to wonder anymore. I don't know how you made it through the horror of the last few days. I can hardly believe you didn't get sick just from seeing us so sick." She put a hand over her eyes. "It's still so embarrassing."

"A person can't help being sick. And I remember how it felt, which helped me understand what you needed."

She stared at the top of the tent, tears trickling down the sides of her face at the reality that Michael and Carolyn were gone. "I feel like I'm living a very bad dream," she said, her voice choking.

"I know." Dawson grabbed a small towel and handed it to her to wipe away her tears. She wondered at how despicable she must look by now. "I'll get back on my feet as soon as I can. I hope I haven't held things up so long that we can't make it to Montana before snow sets in."

Gently Dawson laid Sophie onto a quilt and covered her. He moved to Clarissa's side, bending his legs and wrapping his arms around his knees. "I'm glad you're still talking about going on to Montana."

Their gazes held, and it hit her that this was it. She was left with Dawson Clements to get her to Montana...and then what? "Where else would I go now? I can't turn back, and I have land in Montana."

"We have land."

She frowned. "We?" Immediately she thought of how Chad had stolen her store out from under her.

Dawson grinned and shook his head. "No, I don't intend to take over your land if you decide you don't want to share it as husband and wife. But you should know that before he died, Michael told me about a little metal box in his wagon in which he wrote down that if he didn't survive this trip, his land and Carolyn's was to go to me. So, Mrs. Clements, you and I are neighbors, if nothing more. Would you like to come over for dinner once in a while?"

She couldn't help a smile, realizing he was trying to ease the pain in her heart. "I might consider that."

"Do you promise not to put a fence up between us?"

What a good man he was. A lot of men would not have put up with what he'd gone through the past few days, certainly not Chad, who seemed so weak and cowardly compared to Dawson Clements. "I promise," she answered, "but I might keep my door locked."

He frowned. "That's not very neighborly. My door will be unlocked at all times. You can walk into my home any time you feel like it."

She reached up her hand, and he took hold of it. "I have a lot of thinking to do, Dawson. You have to admit I'm in an odd and somewhat frightening situation here. You're all I have, and you consider yourself my husband."

He rubbed the back of her hand with his thumb. "And you don't?"

She studied his big, sturdy hand. "I guess I do. I mean, nothing has been legally filed at a courthouse, and after all, we spoke vows mainly to keep others from talking. Now it doesn't much matter, I guess. It's just you and me. Who's to care?"

He lifted her hand and kissed it. "I care. I hoped you would, too."

She studied those blue eyes that moved her in strange ways. "I do care. It's just that right now I feel a little—I don't know—lost, I guess. I feel like I've been running from something this whole time, and I feel like I left a different person back in St. Louis. Sometimes it's hard to believe I ever even lived there and ran a store and went to church and got married and had a little girl and was so happy—once. When your whole life blows up in front of you, you're left wondering who you are, why on earth you were even put on the planet."

He smiled sadly. "I've asked myself those things just about every day since I was eight years old."

She squeezed his hand. "I'm sorry. When I think about how you've lived, I feel guilty complaining about anything. But a part of me still sees you as a near stranger. I need to learn to trust you in every way, especially now that it's just the two of us."

He studied her eyes. "I didn't nurse you and Sophie and clean up after you and keep you alive just so I could abuse you or abandon you when you got well. I did it because I love you, Clare. And a man doesn't hurt the one he loves. He cherishes her, in sickness and in health, I believe I vowed. I meant all of it, and if you only spoke those vows to make things look good, I understand. I knew that when I asked you to marry me. I'm just praying you'll realize you meant them all along and didn't even recognize it."

"I never said I didn't mean at least some of those vows. I guess the proud, distrusting, hurt side of me just doesn't want anyone to think I turned to you because I was a lonely woman in desperate need of a man."

He reached out and smoothed back her damp hair. "Well, put away the thought, because *I'm* the one who needs *you*, Clare. *I'm* the needy one. I'm a man who can't get along without the woman he's fallen in love with, the woman who changed his life and made him laugh and gave him purpose and whose dear friends helped me find faith in God again, although I'm not real happy with Him right now after digging that fresh grave out there. The only thing that keeps me from hating God this time is Michael himself. His words keep marching through my mind. He told me God wanted it this way, that he knew in his heart why God brought him out here and he'd done what needed doing. He said God meant for you and me to end up relying only on each other. I'm thinking maybe he was right."

"Maybe so," she said softly. "Oh, Dawson, I'll miss them so." The tears came again. "I'll miss Michael's Bible readings and the way he had of saying just the right things to people. He was truly a man of God."

He still studied her hand. "I guess we'll have to start reading the Bible to each other."

How he'd changed. God truly did work miracles. Now she needed a miracle for herself—the miracle of being able to forgive and forget and go on with life, the wisdom to decide what was truly in her heart. "You can help me learn to trust you by doing something right now, Dawson," she said, jerking in a sob.

"What's that?"

"It sure would feel good if you just…held me for a while. I'm so scared—of everything—and I really, really hate admitting that, but right now I'm just so worn-out and I miss my friends so much."

He smiled warmly, reaching over and pulling her into his arms and onto his lap, leaning against the saddle and letting her settle against his shoulder. "How's that?"

"Good. That's good. But I must smell awful."

He closed his eyes. "You smell wonderful."

The Lord saved me from death;
He stopped my tears and kept me from defeat.
And so I walked in the presence of the Lord
In the world of the living.
I kept on believing, even when I said,
"I am completely crushed."
Even when I was afraid and said,
"No one can be trusted."

—Psalms 116:8-11

Chapter Thirty-One

❧

July 26, 1863

Dawson found a small waterfall just a few yards ahead of where they'd left the wagons, and there in the pure, fresh water, Clarissa washed herself and washed Sophie, including their hair. For safety, Dawson stood not far away with his back to them, and not once did he even turn his head slightly.

Sophie screamed and laughed at how cold the water was, and the sound of her voice and laughter was music to Clarissa's ears. Her little girl, although skin and bones, was alive, and with no small thanks to Dawson.

She still found it hard to believe that her two best friends and their dear little girl were lying in the ground, that she could never talk with them again, laugh with them again. They would never realize their plans of settling together, and

Michael would never build his church. All the important people in her life were gone. Her parents, Chad, and now the only people who'd stood by her in her darkest times. Every time she thought of it, it hit her like a wave of despair and disbelief.

She rinsed her hair, allowing herself the luxury of reveling in being clean and well. She helped Sophie do the same, and the girl screamed again from the cold water. Clarissa then wrapped herself in a blanket and put one around Sophie.

"You can come and get her now," she called to Dawson.

Dawson turned and climbed up to the ledge where they stood, putting Sophie's blanket around her wet hair. "You look like a little Indian girl all wrapped up like this," he teased. She laughed as he lifted her in his arms and carried her below. He came back for the blankets the two of them had worn around themselves when coming here.

"I'll burn these with everything else," he told Clarissa, looking her over lovingly.

"Let's get back to camp. I'm freezing," she told him, clutching her blanket tighter around her.

"I can think of a few ways to warm you up, Mrs. Clements." She rolled her eyes and darted past him.

"You look beautiful that way, Clare, with your hair wet and hanging long," he called out to her.

"Flattery will get you nowhere," she yelled back.

She heard him laugh, that wonderful laugh that she'd learned to love. They'd reached the point where they could tease each other about their odd situation, and Dawson did not fail to hint that he'd like their union to be complete.

The three of them walked back to the wagons, where Clarissa and Sophie dressed while Dawson threw blankets and utensils into his tent and poured lamp oil on top of everything. When Clarissa came out of the wagon, the tent and its contents were burning, a black cloud of smoke from the oil rising into the brilliant blue sky.

"Mommy, what's he doing?"

"Dawson has to burn everything, Sophie, so people who come by after us don't get sick like we did."

Sophie watched with pursed lips. "Is Lena coming back soon?" she asked.

Clarissa closed her eyes against the pain. "No, sweetie. God wants to keep her."

"Why?"

"Well, he must have something special for her to do. Maybe she's up there in the sky watching over you."

"Why can't she come back down here and play with me?"

"It's too far to come."

She looked up at Clarissa with a pout. "I don't like God. He took Lena away, and the chickens, too, and Wuthie!"

Clarissa knelt in front of her. "He took Carolyn and Michael, too, but I still like Him, Sophie. Everything God does is for someone's good. He has a plan for all of us, and we have to trust Him to do what's best." She wasn't so sure she could do that herself, but telling Sophie helped her with her own doubts and fears. "Just remember that Lena and her mommy and daddy and Ruth are in a wonderful place where they are happy and with Jesus. Someday we'll go there, too, and we'll all be together again."

Sophie looked up the mountain beneath which they were camped. "Maybe Lena is up on top of the mountain."

Clarissa pulled her close. "Maybe."

"Maybe I could climb up thew and see hewa."

"No, Sophie. It's too high. Only God and those He comes and gets can live up there." She rose and took Sophie's hand. "Come on. Let's go see Dawson. When we come back I'll braid your hair." She ran her hands through her own still-wet hair, thinking about Dawson's remark and secretly feeling as beautiful as he'd said she was.

She walked with Sophie to the clearing where they'd spent the past several horrible days. The tent and its contents were now totally engulfed in flames, and Dawson stood over by the grave he'd worked relentlessly to dig deep enough out of the hard, rocky ground so that Carolyn and Michael and Lena could rest in peace and not be disturbed by wolves. Dawson was piling more rocks on the grave, and at the head of it was a piece of wagon wood on which Dawson had carved the names of the dead, followed by the date of their deaths and the words "Good Christian People, Now With God."

He turned to watch her walk up to him, and he picked up Sophie. "It's hard to leave them, even though they're dead," he said sadly.

Clarissa's eyes teared. "Leaving this grave behind will be just about the hardest thing I've ever done. I can only thank God that I'm not leaving my little Sophie behind."

Dawson sighed deeply, putting an arm around her shoulders and leading her away. "Let's get ourselves to Montana, Mrs. Clements. We still have a long way to go, a lot of it through mountains. It's a fact we'll not catch up to Zeb and the others, unless they've had a catastrophe of their own."

They were on their own in rugged country, yet Clarissa was unafraid. She had Dawson to protect her, and it was a good feeling.

Chapter Thirty-Two

August 2, 1863

They struggled through mountain passes and along foot-hills, heading north through Wyoming and the Bighorn Mountains, following the route of their own wagon train ahead of them. Clarissa thanked God they did not come across signs that others had come down with the dreaded cholera, something she would not wish on her worst enemy.

The first few days they did not make much progress. Clarissa was still not strong enough to put in a full day of walking, especially in the higher elevations where oxygen was thinner and where it took more strength to climb.

Since they were down to two adults, they could only take two wagons. They'd loaded every extra practical item they could from Michael's wagon and then left it behind, another painful move.

So much behind me, lost forever...

Clarissa wrote in her diary, after writing down her awful experience with cholera and the loss of Michael and Carolyn.

I'll never see St. Louis again, and I've left so many graves on the way here. God is surely watching over me and Sophie to bring us this far and get us through that dreadful disease and leave us with a man so capable of taking us the rest of the way.

Dawson is ever watchful, ever considerate, ever attentive. He is such a help with Sophie, and often he carries her on his back as we climb the passes. He understands how lonely and confused she is over Lena's absence. She gets bored and sometimes cries. Dawson picks her up and talks to her and has a way of calming her and making her laugh.

She still had not written that she and Dawson were married. She was careful to make sure whoever read her diary one day would understand they were in this situation by circumstance and that they were behaving properly, so as not to mar her reputation to her children and grandchildren. It was bad enough that they would know her as a divorced woman.

"You writing about me in there?" Dawson came to sit on a rock near where Clarissa sat writing.

Clarissa quickly closed the diary. "Maybe."

"Are you writing about how much you love me?"

She smiled, setting the diary aside. "I'm not telling."

Dawson chuckled and poured himself some coffee. They both wore jackets in spite of the summer month. High in the Bighorns, the sun did not shed the same warmth as in the valleys, and a constant wind whined and howled through rocks and canyons.

"I think we'll stay right here the rest of the night," Dawson told her. "I was only going to stop for some lunch, but you look a little pale. You need the rest."

"Dawson, look! Pwetty stones!" Sophie ran over with a handful of pink, sparkly stones. "Is it gold?"

Dawson pretended seriousness as he studied them. "Could be. You'd better save these."

"Okay! I'm gonna get mo wocks. Lena said she'd help me!" Their smiles faded. "Lena?" Clarissa asked.

"Yeah. We play all the time. She's way up high and she waves to me."

Clarissa looked at Dawson, who shrugged. "Imagination," he told her. "If it makes her happy, we might as well go along with it."

"I don't know if that's such a good idea."

"She's only three years old."

"Getting very close to four. Her birthday is in September." Sophie ran off to find more rocks, and Clarissa sighed. "Poor little thing. She and Lena were like sisters. I feel so bad for her."

"So do I." Dawson turned to look out past the ledge where their wagons sat on the mountainside, along the highest, narrowest roadway they'd followed so far. "This is the kind of country I love, Clare. Beautiful, isn't it?" He sipped his coffee.

Clarissa joined him in gazing out over a splendid scene of more mountains in the distance, beyond gaping canyons, eerie rock formations and gorgeous colors. "Yes, it's truly God's country. But I have to tell you, I'm not thrilled with these heights. I've always been afraid of high places."

"This is a solid road, and we'll be headed back down soon. We'll follow a valley then most of the way." He looked her over lovingly. "Then we'll be home."

Clarissa felt warmth move through her at what that could mean. She had to make up her mind about taking Dawson Clements as a husband in every way. "Home sounds good," she answered, blushing. "Thank you for being so patient with me, Dawson."

He smiled. "I want you to know that no matter what you decide, I'll stick around a good, long time, for Sophie's sake, and to help you get settled."

She touched his arm. "You're too good to me. I do love you, Dawson Clements. Maybe once we're completely settled, and—"

"Mommy! Look how high I am!"

Sophie's voice sounded much too far away. Both Clarissa and Dawson felt alarm as they turned to look where Sophie had been collecting rocks.

"She's not there," Dawson said, jumping up and looking around.

Clarissa felt a lurch to her heart as she, too, got up to search. "Can you see her?"

"No!"

Sophie had been told to play against the mountain wall away from the road's edge, and she'd been very good about it, but Clarissa's first thought was the worst. "Where is she?" She cupped her hands over her mouth. "Sophie!" she yelled. "Where are you?"

"Sophie!" Dawson shouted.

"Hi, Mommy."

Again the voice seemed far away, and they could not be sure at first where it was coming from. They searched the rocks above.

"Sophie, call to Mommy again!" Clarissa ordered, her heart pounding.

"Hewe I am! I'm going up to see Lena!"

Clarissa and Dawson desperately studied the shadowed mountainside. They didn't see her at first because she'd climbed much higher than they thought she could.

Dawson finally spotted her. "How did she get that high that fast?"

"Sophie! Stay there!" Clarissa screamed. "Don't go any higher! Lena's not up there!"

"Sophie! Stay put and I'll come get you!" Dawson yelled. He started toward the pathway upward, and that was when they all heard it, the chilling yowl of a mountain lion that was perched between the ledge where they stood and the place where Sophie waited.

"Help us, Lord!" Clarissa moaned.

"Don't move!" Dawson told her. He slowly made his way to his wagon, where a rifle rested in brackets on the side of it.

"Dawson, maybe he's thinking of Sophie as a meal he needs to protect!"

"I don't doubt it."

The lion screeched again, crouching and eyeing Dawson as though an enemy with whom it had to fight to keep its delectable meal for itself. Dawson grasped his rifle, and just as he raised it, the mountain lion leaped. Clarissa screamed as Dawson got off a shot a split second before the mountain lion landed on him with such force that it knocked Dawson backward…and over the edge.

Chapter Thirty-Three

✤

Clarissa ran to the edge of the narrow mountain pathway and leaned on a rock to look for Dawson. There he lay, on a ledge below, and he was either unconscious or dead. Her mind whirled with desperation as to how to get to him.

Sophie started crying and, fighting tears, Clarissa turned and ran to the mountain wall, climbing and scrambling up to where Sophie still stood, her fingers digging into rock and gravel, her feet sometimes slipping, until she finally reached her daughter.

"Sophie!" She hugged the girl tightly. "Let's go back to the wagon, Sophie. You have to stay there and wait for mommy while I try to help Dawson."

"Dawson fell down," the girl sniffled. "Did the big cat get him?"

"I don't think so, but he's hurt, Sophie. Mommy has to find a way to help him." She sat down and clung to Sophie as she mostly slid on her rear down to the roadway, then hurried to the wagon with Sophie. "You *must* stay here," she warned again. "Promise Mommy you will *not* get out of this wagon. Otherwise you could fall, too!"

"Okay." The girl pouted.

"And don't try to climb up after Lena again. Darling, Lena isn't up there. She's way, way up in the sky where you can't reach her, so please promise Mommy you won't try to climb up somewhere and find her again."

"I won't."

Clarissa grabbed hold of the back of her skirt hemline and pulled it forward and up, then brought the two ends around and tied them together, forming a kind of diaper with her dress so her legs were free. *Lord, forgive me for exposing myself this way, but how else am I going to make it down to that ledge?*

Frantically she tried to reason the best way to help Dawson. She ran and looked over the ledge again, this time noticing the mountain lion sprawled farther below, its side covered with blood. Dawson's rifle had likely tumbled even farther below.

Shaking with terror, both for Dawson and her fear of heights, she ran back to the wagon, grateful that they had not yet unyoked the oxen. With everything else she had to do, she wasn't sure she could add the work of hitching the oxen. Dawson's wagon and oxen were closer to where Dawson fell. She decided that if she could get them to move forward a few feet, the back of the wagon would be closer to where Dawson lay below. They were near a curve in the mountain road. If she could get Dawson tied to a rope at the back of the wagon and then moved the oxen forward, she might be able to use that to pull Dawson up.

"God help me," she prayed aloud, grabbing two loops of rope. Still weak from being so sick, she wasn't sure where she would find the strength to lower herself to Dawson, let alone manage to get a rope around his big frame and climb back up to the top. The drop to Dawson was straight down, a good half mile deep at the bottom. Thank goodness Dawson had landed on a ledge she might be able to reach, but how long would it hold? What moments ago she thought of as the most beautiful country God could make was now awesomely terrifying. If she fell, her precious Sophie would be left up here alone!

She checked on Sophie once more. The little girl was lying in a quilt and crying. "Please don't cry, Sophie. Everything will be all right."

"Dawson's hoot," she sobbed.

"Mommy is going to help him. You remember to stay right here in this wagon no matter what. I can't help him if I have to worry about you."

"Will you come back?"

"Of course I will. You say a little prayer for Dawson. Mommy has to go help him now."

She hurried to the lead wagon and grabbed a switch, shouting for the oxen to "Giddap!" One lead ox tossed its head, then got under way. "Whoa! Whoa!" Clarissa shouted after they moved only a few feet. One of the ox snorted and pawed, and she prayed they would not decide to take off on their own before she was ready.

Quickly she tied one end of a rope to the back of the wagon, making several knots to be sure it would hold. She moved to the edge of the road, her heart pounding with fear and dread. A mountain climber she was not, let alone having the upper-body strength for this, but she had no choice. She looked down at Dawson again and screamed his name, but he didn't move. "Don't let him be dead!"

She knew now how much she loved him, truly loved him in every way. She knew now how devastated she would be to lose him to death, which helped her realize she didn't want to lose him any other way, either. She could no more allow Dawson Clements to walk out of her life than she could stop breathing.

She removed her jacket for more freedom of her arms, then slung one loop of rope over her shoulder. She wrapped the rope that was tied to the wagon around her waist, then lay down on her belly, slowly lowering herself backward over the edge.

"God, help me," she prayed again between quick breaths of terror. Her feet slid and she screamed, but then she caught a foot on a small sprig of pine growing out of the rock. She wondered at how anything alive could come out of a rock, but she was thankful it was there.

She dared to look down again, then began sliding down using the rope. Once she slid too quickly, and rocks went tumbling. She tore skin off her hands, but terror overrode the pain. She worked her way ever downward, until finally she landed on the ledge where Dawson lay. She could only pray that whatever the both of them were perched on would hold while she knelt down beside Dawson.

She felt for a pulse, thanking God that she found one. She turned his head faceup to see a good deal of blood on the left side of his head. "Dawson!" she said aloud. "Dawson, can you hear me?"

He groaned. Clarissa began feeling around for broken bones. Miraculously his legs seemed all right, but through his jacket his left arm felt broken. She opened the jacket and felt his ribs, detecting one soft spot. He groaned when she touched it.

"I'm going to get you to the top, Dawson," she promised.

He groaned again, then opened his eyes and stared at her with a rather blank look, as though he didn't know her.

"Leave me," he muttered.

She leaned close and kissed his forehead. "Don't be silly. I can't leave you here."

"...deserve it," he said gruffly.

"You're out of your head from the fall." Clarissa tied the second rope to his ankles, yanking on a knot and then wrapping the rope around and around his legs so they were tied together. She really had no idea how to do this. She just kept wrapping, grunting and grimacing as she moved his body back and forth so she could keep winding the rope around it, tying his arms to his sides, up to his shoulders, then back down to loop what was left of the rope through the part wound around his midsection. Once she started pulling on that rope, with God's help, she could lift Dawson to the top. If only he weren't such a big man. If her knots didn't hold, Dawson would likely tumble to his death at the bottom of the canyon.

"I'm going to bring you up now, Dawson," she told him.

His eyes were open, and this time he seemed to recognize her. "Leave me," he told her again. "Too dangerous. Let me...die here."

"Don't be ridiculous!" She gently brushed some hair back from his gravel-encrusted face. "I love you, Dawson Clements. I never knew how much until now. I love you and I want to be your wife in every way. I want to go to Montana with you and settle there and spend the rest of my life with you. I don't care anymore what Chad did to me. I forgive him because it doesn't matter anymore. You are all that matters, Dawson, do you hear me?"

"You don't...understand," he answered weakly. "I...left him."

"Left who?"

He closed his eyes. "The preacher…I left the preacher…he fell from the…barn roof…hurt bad…begged me to get help…nobody home. That's when I ran away…left him there…to die in terrible…pain. This is…my punishment."

She kissed him again, realizing what he just told her must be the thing he'd been afraid to tell her until now. It explained why he was always trying to help others, explained what he told her at the river and his devastation at not being able to save Eric Buettner after nearly drowning in the effort. Most of his life had been spent trying to make up for leaving the preacher—who'd abused him—to die. He probably thought God would never forgive him for it, and that she would hate him if she knew.

There was no time to think about it now. "I'm getting you to the top no matter what it takes," she told him. She rose and looked up, her heart falling at the sight of the steep climb. Somehow she had to get herself to the top before she could help Dawson. And little Sophie was up there waiting for her.

She wrapped the rope around her hand and stepped up on another sprig. It snapped, and more small rocks tumbled, some spilling over Dawson's face. She let out a little scream of terror, then found footing in a little ledge and started up again. Her hands were bleeding badly from rope burn, but desperation brought forth the adrenaline she needed to ignore the pain and keep climbing.

A sprig of pine here, a little rock there, a crack in the earth. Surely God was giving her the strength she would never normally have to do this. She groaned and grunted with every grasp and pull, finally reaching a tiny ledge where she could place her knees and rest for a moment against the red rock wall.

She panted as she clung to the rope, sweat now pouring down her face in spite of the cool mountain air. After a few minutes she started climbing again, her entire body screaming with pain, blood from her hands running down the rope and her arms. Fear of failure brought tears to her eyes, and she was not even aware of what she was using to brace herself or of the pain in her hands or even how high she'd gone. She only knew that by some miracle she saw flat ground, a wagon wheel, oxen.

She scrambled over the edge and away from it far enough to lie down, panting and crying. She lay there a few minutes, then felt numb when she got up to realize her arms and legs were a bloody mess, her hands horribly skinned, but she still could not allow her own pain to get in the way. She stumbled to her own wagon, grunting as she climbed inside, relieved to see Sophie had cried herself to sleep.

She opened a small drawer in the top of a trunk and took out a pair of dress gloves. She had to get something over her hands so she could stand to touch things. She winced as she pulled them on, then climbed down and hurried to the lead wagon. A lone pine tree grew at the side of the roadway, and luckily the rope tied to Dawson was on this side of the tree. As the oxen moved forward and around the corner, the rope would catch on the tree so that Dawson would be pulled straight up and not sideways.

She could do this. She untied her dress and hurried to the lead wagon, again taking up the switch. She snapped it over the oxen and again ordered them to move forward. Rather reluctantly, the beasts lumbered ahead. After several feet she stopped them again and ran to make sure her idea was working. The rope was taut. That meant there was weight at the end of it. She ran to the edge and looked over. There was Dawson, hanging in the air about halfway up.

"Yes!" she cried. "Thank you, Lord!"

Back she ran to the oxen, shouting and whipping at them to keep going. As they rounded the corner to the left, she could now see the pine tree without going to the back of the wagon first. She kept the oxen going until she saw Dawson's body partway on the road.

She laughed and cried at the same time, halting the oxen again and running back to Dawson. She tugged and grunted and pulled until he was completely on the roadway, then ran for a blanket and opened it nearby. She rolled him onto the blanket and began untying the ropes, noticing her gloves were stained with blood. Hastily she got the ropes off and again felt for a pulse, finding a strong one.

She broke into exhausted tears then, lying down beside him and sobbing with happiness.

Chapter Thirty-Four

Clarissa managed to get Dawson's jacket and shirt off, and his left arm flopped. Even though he seemed only semiconscious, he yelled with pain. She felt the arm and determined the break was in the forearm and would have to be set. She ran to the lead wagon, and using strength she didn't even know she had, she yanked a thin piece of board off a crate, then climbed into the wagon and dug through supplies to find gauze.

"Thank God the skin isn't broken," she said aloud. That would mean a much greater chance of infection. She hurried back to Dawson, felt the bone again, then took a deep breath and yanked.

Dawson let out a deep moan. She placed the board on the outside of his arm and started wrapping gauze around it to hold the board against his arm to help keep the bone in place. It was all she could think to do. His left hand was swollen, but that was to be expected with a broken arm. She could only pray that was the only broken bone other than a rib, and that his head injury wasn't life threatening.

Once the arm was set she retrieved towels and a bucket of water, taking them over to wash the blood and gravel from Dawson's face and head. She noticed a bruise forming on his side, most likely from the broken rib. "Please don't let it be something worse," she prayed aloud through tears. She was a nurse, not a doctor. If he had something wrong internally, there was nothing she could do about it.

"Don't you die on me, Dawson Clements," she said as she washed him. "Not now." She finished cleaning his face and turned his head to see a cut through his thick, dark hair where blood had already dried. She decided to leave it alone rather than start it bleeding all over again.

Gently she washed his torso, rinsed the rag, then washed his neck and watched his eyes slowly open. He frowned. "Clare?"

She smiled. "Yes. I got you up here all by myself, Dawson. The mountain lion knocked you over the ledge."

He watched her a moment, noticed her torn sleeves and bleeding arms. With his good arm he lifted one wrist to see her bloody glove. "Look at you," he said weakly. "How——"

"It was God who did it. I could never have climbed down there and got you back up without His help. It's an absolute miracle I got you up here. See how much God loves you? He wants us to be together always, Dawson. When I thought you'd been killed by that fall, I knew how much I love you." She couldn't stop the tears then.

He grimaced. "Fine time…to tell me." He started to lift his left arm and cried out with pain.

"It's broken," she told him, wiping at tears. "I think you also have broken ribs. I'm not sure about your legs. You'll have to let me know what else hurts. You also have a head injury, but your eyes look clear." She laid the wet rag over his forehead. "If you want to lie inside a wagon, you'll have to get to your feet yourself. This is as far as I could get you."

"I need...water."

Clarissa got up and half stumbled on aching legs to the water barrel, dipping a ladle into it and bringing it back to Dawson. She lifted his head and helped him drink. He let out another groan and looked toward the ledge, then back at her. "I remember...falling." He closed his eyes. "I saw him lying there...screaming with pain."

She grasped his good hand. "The preacher?"

He looked at her with terrible remorse in his eyes. "How do you know?"

"You mumbled about it down there on the ledge."

"I'm sorry, Clare. I didn't want you to know...what I did. I left him there. I just...left him there to die. Maybe God meant for you...to leave me down there to die, too."

"Never." She pushed back some dark wisps of hair from his face. "Dawson, God forgave you for that a long time ago—the first time you felt terrible regret and remorse for it. You reacted as the child who for years had the feelings beat out of him. It's taken years for you to get those feelings back, and everything that has happened on this trip, meeting Michael and having those long talks with him, God bring-ing us together, you learning to forgive yourself for what happened to your parents—it's all been part of the healing. And I in turn have learned to trust again, through you. We're going to be okay, you and me. We're going to make it to Mon-tana and build a home there and have children and be the family you haven't had since you were eight years old. And my Sophie will have a real daddy."

He squeezed her hand. "You mean all that?"

She leaned closer and kissed his lips lightly. "I mean it. Why else would I have gone through all this to rescue you? I am scraped and bleeding from head to foot, and the rope tore half the skin off my hands. I don't doubt that when I wake up tomorrow I'll hardly be able to move."

He grimaced with pain again as he tried to adjust his position. "Sophie. Where's Sophie?"

"She's all right. She fell asleep in the wagon. Actually she cried herself to sleep, worried about her Dawson."

He managed a faint smile and met her gaze again. "Clare, there is something…I've already thought about doing, when we settle. I didn't tell you because…first I wanted to know for sure…we'd be together."

Everything hurt as she shifted to sit down beside him. "Tell me," she said, stroking his cheek.

"I want…to build a church."

Her eyebrows arched in surprise. "A church?"

"In Michael's memory. That's what he…wanted. At first… there won't be many people around…to come. But they will come…and until we find a preacher…we'll take turns just…reading from the Bible…things like that. I'm no preacher…that's for sure. But…I want to do something…to remember Michael…and what he taught me. And it will be a way…for me to thank God…for bringing you into my life."

Her eyes teared anew with joy at how he'd changed. "Then we'll build a church. Maybe we could call it something like Miracle Rescue Mission, for the miracle of my rescuing you from that ledge."

He watched her lovingly. "I've been rescued from more than that, Clare."

"Hello, there!" came a voice.

Clare looked up in surprise. "Zeb!" she yelled. "Dawson, it's Zeb!" She jumped up and ran to the old mountain man, who approached on foot, leading his horse. Clarissa surprised him with a firm hug. "Oh, I'm so glad to see you!"

"Whoa! Hold up there, woman!" Zeb laughed. "I'm right glad to see you, too! What's happened here? Look at you! You're covered with blood!"

"A mountain lion was threatening Sophie. Dawson shot at it, just as it leaped down on top of him. Zeb, the lion knocked Dawson over the edge! I managed to get down to him and pulled him up by tying rope to the back of the lead wagon and pulling him up that way. I don't know how I did it, other than I prayed and prayed. I never could have got him up without God's help!"

Alarmed, Zeb left her and hurried over to Dawson, kneeling beside him. "Hey, old friend, how bad is it?"

"Broken arm," Dawson told him. "I think...maybe a cracked skull and a couple broken or bruised ribs. I'm not even sure yet. I'm...afraid to move."

"Well, you're lucky to be alive. Takes a brave, smart woman to do what your wife just did."

Dawson managed a loving smile at Clarissa as she, too, knelt beside him. "How'd you...find us?" he asked Zeb then.

"Well, those on the train decided to hold up for a few days and let me come back to see what happened to you folks. They was real concerned." Zeb looked around. "Where's the Harveys?"

A lump rose in Clarissa's throat. "They died, Zeb."

"All *three* of them?"

Clarissa nodded, renewed pain gripping her heart.

"Oh, that's too bad. I'm so sorry."

"Oh, Zeb, there is so much to tell you," Clarissa said. "But for now, you have no idea how happy I am to have help! Thank goodness! You can help me get Dawson into a wagon. And you can lead the second wagon and get us down off this mountain." She leaned closer to Dawson. "We're going to make it, Dawson! We're going to make it! Thanks be to God!" She kissed his forehead. "Oh, I love you! I love you!"

"And I love you," he whispered. "Yes. Thanks be to God."

Epilogue

September 30, 1863

Already a few snowflakes were falling. Clarissa wrapped her wool cape closer around her, and Dawson stood next to her with the collar of his wool jacket turned up. He held Sophie in his right arm, his left arm still not completely healed. Sophie, her red curls popping out from under her woolen cap, hugged Dawson around the neck and put her head on her daddy's shoulder.

Settlers had come from distant settlements, most of them those who'd reached Montana on Dawson's wagon train. There were twenty-four here all together, and they stood gazing at their little log church, which over the past month men had come here to build, knowing how much Dawson wanted this, and all grieving for the Harveys. They had also built a cozy, two-room cabin for Dawson and Clarissa, promising to keep them in food and firewood until Dawson was able to hunt and chop wood on his own.

Their kindness was overwhelming, especially for Dawson, who'd never known such treatment. He and Clarissa felt blessed by God in so many ways.

Will Krueger nailed a sign to the front of the little log church. He'd cut the sign out of pine and carved out the letters that read In Memory of Michael, Carolyn and Lena Harvey.

"It's a fine church, Dawson," Otto Hensel told him. "Someday ve vill have a real preacher."

Dawson looked at Clarissa. "Yes, a real preacher."

Clarissa put her arm around him, feeling whole and loved again. Being with Dawson Clements proved to be the most fulfilling experience she'd known, for the love she shared with him was so much deeper and more meaningful than anything she'd shared with Chad.

"Let's sing a hymn." Robert Trowbridge spoke up. "How about 'Amazing Grace'?"

It was difficult for Clarissa not to cry, as she pictured Michael and Carolyn joining them. They were here. She could feel it. Their spirit came out in the form of Dawson Clements's voice as he joined in the hymn.

"'Amazing grace, how sweet the sound, that saved a wretch like me.'"

It was the first time Clarissa had heard Dawson sing. He had a fine voice. The Dawson Clements she'd met back in St. Louis would never have dreamed of praying or building a church or singing a hymn.

What miracles God could bring into peoples' lives! They were here. They were home, and their journey here had been so much more than just a physical trip. It had been a journey of the heart, a walk of faith and hope for something much more than she'd expected to find here in Montana.

"I once was lost, but now I'm found, was blind, but now I see."

They finished two stanzas of the hymn, then Dawson turned to Clarissa. "Let's go inside and have some celebration cake," he told her.

"Thank you for the church, Dawson."

He leaned down and kissed her tenderly. "Thank you for loving me." He kissed her again, more deeply. Never had she felt more loved, and never had she trusted anyone more than she trusted Dawson Clements.

They headed inside.

"Look, Mommy," Sophie called out. She pointed to the clouds. "It's Lena!"

Clarissa looked up to see brilliant golden rays where the sun was perched behind a cloud. "Yes," she answered. "I see Michael and Carolyn, too."

"Uh-huh. They like our church."

"I'm sure they do," Clarissa answered.

Dawson grinned and led them inside. In the distance sat their little cabin, where they would spend their first, long Montana winter, in deep and abiding love.

Home! They were home!

I have told you this,
So that my joy might be in you
And your joy might be complete.
This is my commandment:
Love one another as I love you.
No one has greater love than this,
To lay down one's life for one's friends.
It was not you who chose me,
But I who chose you and appointed you
To go and bear fruit that will remain,
So that whatever you ask the Father in my name,
He may give you.
This I command you: Love one another.

—*John* 15:11-13 and 16-17

* * * * *

Author's Note

All scripture used in *Walk by Faith* is taken from the *Good News Bible*, American Bible Society, New York, 1976, a version that uses slightly more modern language but still remains true to God's word.

I did not refer to any one particular book or author source in writing this story, as I have written about America's West for over twenty years and have a personal library with hundreds of books on the topic. I have a deep love for—and interest in—America's history, and especially the landscape and stories of the Old West, about which I have written over fifty books, mostly historical romance, family sagas and bigger historical fiction.

When I decided to try a slightly different genre, I still could not bring myself to leave the subject and the land I love most, and so even my inspirational stories are historicals set against the backdrop of the American West. *Where Heaven Begins* involved the Yukon gold rush, and *Walk by Faith*, my second inspirational story, involves a man and woman headed west by wagon train. My next inspirational will involve a woman whose family settled on land owned by the newly built Union Pacific Railroad.

After all my years of writing, I feel I have finally found where I truly belong in the literary world—writing stories based on one or more characters' faith in their Lord and Savior Jesus Christ. God has been calling me for years to do this. I just wasn't listening. I hope you enjoy *Walk by Faith* and will be patient with me as I learn and grow in this wonderful genre.

Thanks for your support!

JACQUELIN THOMAS
FRANCIS RAY
FELICIA MASON

HOW · SWEET · THE · SOUND

HOW SWEET THE SOUND features three beautiful and inspiring love stories born out of musical collaborations. Discover how love blooms in the most unlikely of situations.

On sale February 2005.
Visit your local bookseller.

Steeple
Hill®

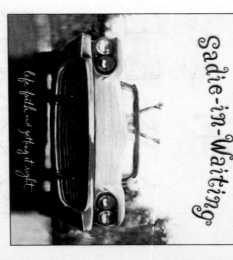

Love Inspired®

FIRST MATES

BY

CECELIA DOWDY

Cruising the Caribbean was just what Rainy Jackson needed to get over her faithless ex-fiancé…and meeting handsome fellow passenger Winston Michaels didn't hurt, either! As a new Christian, Winston was looking to reflect on his own losses. Yet as the two spent some time together both on the ship and back home in Miami, he soon realized he wanted Rainy along to share his life voyage.

Don't miss FIRST MATES
On sale February 2005

Available at your favorite retail outlet.

LIFMCDTR